A Gift for Fiona

Includes the Prequel, A Gift for Lara

Suzanne G. Rogers

Idunn Court Publishing

Contents

This book is a work of fiction. While references may be made to actual places or events, the names, characters, incidents, and locations within are from the author's imagination and are not a resemblance to actual living or dead persons, businesses, or events. Any similarity is coincidental.

Idunn Court Publishing
7 Ramshorn Court
Savannah, GA 31411

Published by Idunn Court Publishing, March 2015

ISBN: 978-1-947463-29-5

Published in the United States of America
Editor: Kathryn Riley Miller
Cover Design: Suzanne G. Rogers

Created with Vellum

A Gift for Lara

Prequel to A Gift for Fiona

Lara Robinson wrote a love letter four years ago but received no reply. Now the man to whom she gave her heart will visit Blythe Manor for Christmas. How can she enjoy the holidays knowing Miles Greystoke must despise her for revealing her feelings in such an unguarded fashion?

As an awkward youth, Miles fell in love with a kindred spirit... but his love was unrequited. Against his wishes, he's now obliged to spend the holidays at Blythe Manor. Time has wrought changes in his physique, but his devotion to Lara Robinson has never wavered. He searches for the perfect present to show her how he feels, but nothing seems quite right...until he realizes the best sort of gift will embrace the true meaning of Christmas.

Chapter 1

The Invitation

December 1875 · London

Angelica Greystoke was embroidering a screen in the drawing room after dinner while her husband sorted through the day's correspondence. When she glanced up, she noticed William had a perplexed expression on his face.

"What's wrong?"

"I've just heard from my brother Miles. He has some strange notion that he wishes to study veterinary medicine."

"Not everyone wishes to be a barrister like you."

"I can't think why not." He paused. "Perhaps if we could get him interested in marriage, he'd abandon the idea of a career."

"He's only eighteen. Besides which, *you* have a career and it's done you no harm."

"A barrister is still considered a gentleman, but a practitioner of veterinary medicine is not. Furthermore, Papa is counting on Miles to manage the family estates after he graduates from Cambridge. He can't do that if he's gallivanting all over the countryside, ministering to cows."

Angelica laughed. “I have an idea. Papa has invited us to Blythe Manor for Christmas. I’ll write back and ask if the invitation could be extended to Miles.” She slid her husband a mischievous glance. “Mistletoe can be quite inspirational to a young man if he’s in good company.”

William lifted an eyebrow. “You’re not suggesting he should consider marriage to one of the twins, are you?”

“Why not? He got along particularly well with Lara at our wedding, as I recall.”

“That was four years ago. The lad has changed a great deal since then.”

“For the better, in many ways. Miles used to be shorter than either Lara or Fiona, and a great deal thicker ’round the middle. At any rate, perhaps he and Lara will reestablish their relationship.”

“I think it’s an excellent plan,” William said. “Ordinarily, I wouldn’t interfere. In this case, however, a little intervention is warranted.”

* * *

“Our eldest daughter and her husband have accepted our invitation to visit Blythe Manor for the Christmas holiday,” Mr. Robinson announced at dinner. “I received the letter today.”

“Oh, how marvelous!” exclaimed Mrs. Robinson.

Lara exchanged an excited look with her sister. “I can’t wait to see Angelica!”

“Nor can I. It’s been far too long,” Fiona said.

“Will they bring the baby?” Mrs. Robinson asked. “I long to have little children in the house again.”

“Indeed they shall. Angelica has also asked to bring William’s brother, Miles.”

At the mention of Miles Greystoke, Lara's eyes widened. "Oh, no. Not *him*."

"He was an insufferable little lump at Angelica's wedding, wasn't he?" Fiona giggled.

"I wouldn't say that, exactly," Lara murmured.

"We'll throw a reception while they're here," Mrs. Robinson said. "I haven't hosted a Christmas party in ages."

"Let's have dancing," Fiona suggested. "I must buy a new dress for the occasion."

Lara gave her father a pleading glance. "Can't you dissuade Angelica from bringing Mr. Greystoke? Tell her we don't have room for an extra guest."

"Do no such thing, Papa!" Fiona said. "Mr. Greystoke may be an insufferable little lump, but he's of marriageable age now. Lara can afford to turn her nose up since she's prettier than I am. As for me, I'd like to have another look."

A flash of annoyance ran down Lara's spine. "If you think he's such a lump, why would you consider marrying him?"

"I've little choice," Fiona retorted. "Papa never lets us go to London."

Mr. Robinson rolled his eyes toward the ceiling. "Not this again."

Fiona pressed on without missing a beat. "Out here in the country, we never meet any eligible prospects."

"That's not entirely so," Mrs. Robinson said. "I heard a rumor Sir Harry is considering making an offer for one of you. I believe he's not yet decided which."

Fiona pulled a face. "Let it be Lara. Sir Harry is older than Papa, and he smells musty."

"Thank you for your generosity, but if my choice is between an insufferable lump and a smelly old man, I shall end a spinster," Lara said.

"I shall *not* dissuade Angelica from bringing William's

brother," Mr. Robinson said. "On the contrary, we shall show Miles every courtesy."

"I should think so," Mrs. Robinson said. "All the Greystokes are welcome here."

Mr. Robinson spread his napkin on his lap. "Let's eat before the soup grows cold."

Although Lara picked up her spoon, she took only a sip or two of the butternut squash soup. For some reason, she'd suddenly lost her appetite.

Tinsel in hand, Lara and her mother cast an appraising eye at the Christmas tree in the corner of the drawing room.

"This tree must have fewer branches than the one we had last year. I can't see where to put the rest of these decorations," Mrs. Robinson said.

"Nevertheless, it's perfectly beautiful. I love the Nuremberg angel on top."

"Thank goodness we finished decorating in time for our guests' arrival tomorrow. I was beginning to worry."

"Why didn't Fiona help?"

"She's working on Christmas presents, or so she said."

Lara sighed. "I'm not finished either and Christmas is less than a week away."

As Mrs. Robinson hastened off to finish a few last-minute mistletoe garlands, Lara wrapped the remaining blown-glass ornaments and icicles in tissue paper for storage. Thereafter, she went to her bedroom and resumed work on the muffler she was knitting. A half-hour later, Fiona danced into view, waving a handkerchief.

"I just finished Mr. Greystoke's Christmas gift. Isn't it

pretty? I hemmed a square of fine linen and embroidered it with his initials, MRG. Miles Reginald Greystoke."

"Lovely workmanship." Lara peered at the reddish letters. "Is that your *hair?*"

"Of course! It wouldn't be very personal otherwise."

"Isn't embroidering a man's handkerchief with your hair a bit...presumptuous?"

Fiona smirked at the project in Lara's lap. "No more so than knitting him a muffler in Cambridge Blue."

"There's nothing overly intimate about knitting Mr. Greystoke a muffler in his university color. You're just envious I thought of it."

Fiona shrugged. "I couldn't care less."

"If you say so."

"Lara, you're not to monopolize Mr. Greystoke like you did last time."

"I did no such thing!"

"You did so. He was here two whole weeks before Angelica's wedding, and I scarcely got a word in edgewise."

"We were little more than children, and I daresay we've grown up since then." Lara averted her eyes. "I'm sure Mr. Greystoke will show nothing more than politeness toward me." *Truth be told, he will undoubtedly avoid me altogether and I'll return the favor.*

"He'll warm up when you start talking about books and such. After I heard he was coming to visit, I started reading *War and Peace.* Mr. Greystoke and I will have a great deal to talk about during his stay."

"What with embroidering handkerchiefs and such, I can't imagine when you found the opportunity to read," Lara said dryly. "Besides which, you're wasting your time. Mr. Greystoke enjoys adventure stories best."

Fiona's eyebrows drew together in dismay. "*Now* you tell me!"

* * *

While Lara's maid was brushing her mistress's hair before bed, a gust of wind rattled the windowpanes. Lara shivered and tightened the shawl around her shoulders. "Snow began falling in earnest this afternoon. We're to have a white Christmas this year." Elsie's brush caught a snarl, and Lara winced. "Ouch!"

"Beg pardon, Miss Lara. My mind was wandering."

The young woman finished her task, painfully snagging several more snarls in the process. Each time, Elsie was very apologetic. "I'm so terribly sorry," she said finally. "I don't know what's wrong with me tonight."

"What's troubling you?"

"You're very kind to ask, but I don't wish to be a burden."

"It's no burden at all."

"Well...it's Mum. She's in the family way again and not doing well. The midwife told her to stay in bed, but she has to care for my younger brother and two sisters. Since I came to live at Blythe Manor, I can't help her."

"Where is your papa in all this turmoil?"

"Working in Barnsley to keep food on the table. After that big explosion at the Swaithe Main coal pit, there were good wages to be had repairing the damage." Elsie's smile was forced. "It'll be fine, miss. Thank you for asking."

"Tomorrow morning, I'll visit your mother and see if I can render her assistance. The least I can do is to bring food, so she won't have to cook."

"But the Greystokes are expected!"

"Not until closer to noon, and I'll be back before then."

"Your kindness does you credit."

"Nonsense. What are neighbors for, except to be useful to one another?" Lara rubbed her sore scalp. "Besides which, if you don't cheer up I may go bald before long."

Mr. Robinson was reading his paper when Lara entered the breakfast room the following morning. Mrs. Robinson was engrossed in a series of menus, and Fiona was staring out the window as if in a daydream.

"Good morning." Lara reached for a biscuit, sliced it open, and heaped a tablespoon of warm cinnamon apples on top. "Papa, may I have the carriage after breakfast? I must call on Mrs. Coogan."

"I can't spare the carriage today, my dear. Ned is picking Angelica and the Greystokes up at the train station."

"Oh, bother, that's right." At the reminder she would soon be seeing Miles again, a feeling of dread shot through her. "The carriage isn't important, I suppose. I can walk." *If only I could run far, far away from Blythe Manor and never look back!*

"There are several inches of snow on the ground already, and more expected later," Mrs. Robinson said. "Can't you postpone your outing until tomorrow?"

"Mrs. Coogan is unwell, Mama. I can wait, but she and her children cannot. Fiona, why don't you come with me? It's only half mile, and I daresay Mrs. Coogan would appreciate the extra help."

"I'm not going out of doors for anything!" Fiona exclaimed. "The cold makes my nose red and runny, and I'm not greeting Mr. Greystoke looking less than my best."

Annoyed, Lara bit her tongue. "I'll go alone, then. I've given my word."

"Be sure to bundle up," Mrs. Robinson said. "And be home

well before eleven o'clock. This will be Angelica's first visit since the wedding, and I want to receive her and her family properly."

"Yes, ma'am."

After breakfast, Lara asked Cook to pack a basket with freshly baked biscuits, a small sliced ham, a jar of preserves, and a pound cake. As she carried the basket outside, she realized it was heavier than she had anticipated. *This would have been so much easier in the carriage!* Her resolve wavered, but the vision of poor Mrs. Coogan surrounded by three hungry children swam before Lara's eyes. *Elsie no doubt sent word I would be coming. I can't let them down.*

A small handcart parked next to a stacked pile of wood gave Lara a good idea. *I can use the cart to carry the basket, and bring some firewood to the Coogans as well.* She positioned the basket in the cart, stacked a few pieces of firewood next to it, and pulled the cart down the driveway behind her. When she reached the road, she was relieved to discover the passage of carriages and wagons wheels had cleared the snow. Nevertheless, cold wind bit into her skin as she walked. Although she tugged her hat down to cover her ears and wrapped her muffler around her nose and mouth, she was chilled thoroughly by the time she arrived at her destination.

A five-year old child answered the door, bobbing up and down in a curtsy. "Morning, Miss Lara."

"Morning, Helen. I've come to see how your mama is doing."

As Lara stepped inside, she realized the tiny three-room cottage was very little warmer than outside. Two older children huddling next to the fireplace mumbled their greetings.

"Good morning, Colleen and Jack," she replied. "It's awfully cold in here. Jack, please put your coat on and fetch in the wood stacked in the cart outside. We need to get a good blaze going."

Lara glanced around, dismayed at the disheveled and dreary condition of the place. No Christmas tree brightened the corner of the room, no merry garland was draped across the rough-hewn mantle, and there was not so much as a Christmas cracker to bring holiday cheer. Blythe Manor was not nearly as grand as some estates, perhaps, but when compared to the Coogans' cottage, it was a palace. *I cannot begin to count my blessings.*

When Mrs. Coogan emerged from her bedroom, Lara was shocked at her appearance. Although the woman was swollen with child, her arms were stick-thin and she had dark circles under her eyes.

"Thank you for coming, Miss Lara."

"I'm happy to help." Lara left the basket of food on the kitchen table and helped the woman back to bed. "I'll make you tea and something to eat, Mrs. Coogan."

"Bless you, lass."

On the way from the Blythe Village train station, Miles rode in the Robinsons' brougham with his brother and sister-in-law. In a hansom cab following behind were the luggage, the baby, and the baby's nanny. When he left Cambridge at the end of term to spend the holidays with William and his family in London, he discovered he was expected to accompany them to Blythe Manor instead. His argument with his brother had been short-lived when he'd learned their father took William's view of the matter. With little other choice, he'd tried to accept the situation gracefully and had even feigned enthusiasm—for Angelica's sake. As Blythe Manor drew closer, however, Miles found it increasingly difficult to keep up the pretense. *Perhaps Lara will have forgotten what happened between us. I certainly wish I could; the memory has haunted me these past four years.*

On the outskirts of town, he noticed a well-dressed woman darting from a rude cottage with a wooden bucket in her hand. Her head was wrapped in a colorful scarf, but her slender waist and rising curves caught his eye. As she dashed toward a water pump, the wind caught the fabric of the scarf and blew it back from her face—revealing her chiseled, delicate features and honey-colored hair. Struck by her beauty, Miles leaned forward to stare. *What an exquisite creature! How odd a woman like her would live in such lowly circumstances.*

"Whose cottage did we just pass?" he asked Angelica. "The one on the end?"

"Mmm...the Coogans, I believe. Why do you ask?"

Because I just saw an angel. "Oh, no reason."

When the carriage rolled up the driveway to Blythe Manor, snow had begun to fall in earnest. Miles hastened to escort Angelica indoors while his brother made sure the baby and nanny were brought in from the cold. His stomach taut with nerves, Miles braced himself at the prospect of meeting Lara again, face to face. *If I must see her, I wish it could be without our families looking on.* Although he didn't want to admit it, a very small part of him hoped she would find some pleasure in his company. *I'm not such bumbling fool as I was before. Perhaps she will see me differently.*

Mr. and Mrs. Robinson had assembled in the entryway with one of the twins. From her auburn hair, Miles knew immediately the girl was Fiona. Although his reprieve was only temporary, he felt his shoulders relax. As the Robinsons greeted Angelica and William and met baby Billy, servants took Miles's coat, hat, and gloves.

"But where is Lara?" Angelica said, looking around. "She's not ill, is she?"

Mrs. Robinson frowned. "She went off to help Mrs. Coogan in Blythe Village. I asked her to be back in time for your arrival, and now there's a snowstorm bearing down."

A shock ran through Miles. *That beautiful woman I saw was Lara?*

"The silly thing went on foot," Fiona said. "She'll freeze on the way home."

"I'll send a servant in the carriage to fetch her," Mr. Robinson said.

"My brother will be happy to go," William said. "Won't you, Miles?"

Startled, Miles flinched. "Oh, er, yes. Of course."

Five pairs of eyes latched onto him. The Robinsons had been so engrossed with their other visitors, they'd seemingly forgotten he was there.

"You remember my brother Miles, I trust?" William asked.

Mrs. Robinson blinked at Miles. "My, but you've grown since you were here last!"

"I'm not sure if I would have known you," Mr. Robinson said. "William, your brother has become quite the gentleman."

"He's doing wonderfully well at Cambridge," Angelica said.

"And he's a valued member of the Cambridge Boat Club," William added. "We're very proud of him."

"It's lovely to see you again, Mr. Greystoke." Fiona sketched a graceful curtsy.

"The pleasure is mine." Miles bowed. "And now if I may have my coat, I'll retrieve your sister."

Fiona slid him a glance underneath her eyelashes. "How very gallant."

Chapter 2

Young Mr. Greystoke

After Lara took care of Mrs. Coogan's immediate needs, she fed the children and set them a few tasks while she cleaned and tidied the place as best she could. She'd brought a tray into Mrs. Coogan's bedroom and coaxed her into drinking a cup of hot tea and eating a biscuit with preserves. The woman's color was slightly better afterward, to Lara's relief. *There's so little food in the house, I expect she's going without so the children can eat.*

The chime of the rustic cuckoo clock hanging on the wall reminded her she was running late. She bit back a groan when she noticed heavy snowfall was pelting down outside. Worse, she'd sloshed water down the front of her dress when carrying the bucket in from the pump, and her boots were damp. *I'll be lucky not to catch my death!* As she donned her coat, she wondered if she ought not stay at the Coogans' until the storm passed. Eager to see Angelica, William, and the baby, she bit her lip with frustration. *I must admit, I'm curious to see Miles Greystoke again—despite the fact I made a complete idiot of myself with him before.*

The sound of a carriage stopping outside the cottage brought Lara running to the window. A wave of relief washed over her when she recognized her father's brougham. *Dearest Papa has come to my rescue!* She gathered up her basket, scarf, and gloves, and said good-bye to the children. The two eldest were peeling potatoes at the table, and Helen was making a mountain with the peels.

"Don't forget what I told you," Lara said. "If you put those potatoes in a pot and heat them with a bit of the ham, you'll have a nice dinner tonight. Take care of your mama, and I'll see you tomorrow."

She dashed from the house just as Ned opened the carriage door. Instead of her father, however, a tall handsome stranger emerged. Bewildered, she stopped short, skidding a short distance on a patch of ice. "Who are you?"

The young man tipped his top hat. "Hello, Miss Lara. I've come to escort you home."

His deep, masculine voice sent a delicious shiver down her spine. "I'm sorry, but are we acquainted?"

His somewhat shy smile revealed even, white teeth. "Perhaps you don't remember me, but I'm William Greystoke's younger brother, Miles."

She bit back a gasp and her mind went numb. "Of course. I remember you."

When his gaze met hers, she felt her face grow hot with embarrassment. Not only was her dress wet and dirty, but several strands of hair had come free of their pins and were drifting across her face. *Fiona didn't wish to greet Miles with a red nose, and yet here I am, looking like a charwoman!* She tucked a loose lock of hair behind one ear and glanced at the carriage driver.

"Ned, will you tie that handcart behind the carriage?"

"Yes, Miss Lara."

Miles helped her into the carriage and climbed in after, giving Lara no time to collect herself. She marveled at his transformation. Had Miles not introduced himself, she would not have known him at all...except perhaps his eyes were unchanged. His athletic physique bore no resemblance to the plump boy she remembered, and his rounded face was now angular. More familiar was his mouth...except his lower lip had grown slightly more generous—and tantalizing. Her prior innocent and tender feelings suddenly acquired a visceral quality she'd never experienced before. The unsettling sensations his physical presence aroused were unwelcome, and she tried to steel herself against their hypnotic effects. *I must wrap my shredded dignity around my heart like a coat of armor. He must never suspect my attraction to him or I will be completely undone.*

Miles took the seat facing hers. The dusting of snowflakes on his broad shoulders and the brim of his hat resembled sugar. On the short drive back to Blythe Manor, Lara attempted to fill the silence with conversation. "Mrs. Coogan needed my help today. She's to have a baby soon and she's very weak." She paused. "Nevertheless, I regret I wasn't home to receive you properly."

"Your parents and sister made me feel welcome."

"I'm terribly grateful you brought the carriage. I wasn't looking forward to walking in the snow." *Am I babbling? I cannot seem to catch my breath.*

"Fiona seemed worried you'd end up in a snowdrift."

With a sinking heart, Lara fell silent, staring out the window at nothing. *So Mr. Greystoke came for me as a favor to Fiona. He dislikes me more than ever.*

* * *

Miles drank in Lara's profile, marveling at its symmetry. *Did she always have that adorable little cleft in her chin, or am I noticing it just now?* He became acutely aware just how enticing her full lips had become—as well as the curve of her bodice. *I've cared for her the last four years, but now I find her desirable beyond all imagining. Have I changed enough to attract her notice...or does she still regard me as a dolt?* He cleared his throat. "I'm matriculating at Cambridge now."

When she turned her head toward him, he rejoiced. Her profile was beautiful, but her eyes were exquisite.

"Angelica mentioned that in her letters. Do you like it?"

"I do, yes. My classmates are congenial fellows." Several more seconds passed before Miles could think of something else to say. "H-How have you been?" He was glad the dimly lit carriage interior obscured the dull flush most assuredly creeping up from his collar. *Could I not devise anything more engaging? Why don't I just mention the weather?*

"I manage to stay busy," she replied. "There's a great deal of charity work to be done in Blythe Village, especially this time of year."

"That's very admirable."

"I hope your parents are well?"

"Tolerably, thank you. My father would like me to manage his estate when I graduate, but William wants me to be a barrister like him."

"Which way do you lean?"

"Actually, I'd like to study veterinary medicine. Many of my father's tenants raise sheep or horses, and I could make myself useful."

Did a gleam of interest set Lara's eyes dancing, or was it a trick of the light?

"That would dovetail nicely with managing your father's estate, I think," she said.

"Exactly." A pleasantly warm flame ignited within his chest. *Lara, at least, understands when my family does not.*

"You used to have a Golden Retriever, as I recall. How is she?"

"Sadly, Penelope died giving birth to a litter of puppies about three years ago."

"How terrible! I'm so sorry to hear it. You must have been devastated."

"Her loss was very difficult. I believe that's where my interest in veterinary medicine originated. I dearly wish I could have saved her—or at least the pups."

"The pups died too?"

"All but one. We named him Aladdin."

"Ah, after one of your favorite stories."

The flame inside him grew hotter. *Lara remembers our discussion of* The Book of One Thousand and One Nights. "Yes. I've had the opportunity to assist in the birth of several horses since then. It's quite a miraculous process, although it's not for the faint of heart."

"I admire your fortitude."

When the carriage stopped at Blythe Manor, Miles escorted Lara inside. They joined their families in the drawing room, and as her attention turned to Angelica, William, and the baby, he felt bereft. *It's as I feared; my attachment to Lara has only increased. I'm irrevocably in love.*

* * *

Although Lara took genuine pleasure in seeing her elder sister, brother-in-law, and nephew, she was aware of Miles's presence the entire time. Even as she cooed over the baby, she was thinking about their strangely dry conversation in the carriage. *How can I still feel so much for him and yet say so little?*

Finally, Mr. Robinson rang for servants to show the guests to their rooms. Lara retired to change her dress and fix her hair before lunch. Her reflection in the looking glass was sobering. A sooty smudge had found its way onto her jaw, her gown was filthy, and her hair was in disarray. Yet, her eyes were sparkling with excitement. *I must take care not to display my emotions so openly, lest Miles's dislike of me deepen further.*

When Elsie arrived to help her dress, Lara told her about the morning's visit.

"I don't think your mother is getting enough to eat," she said. "I'll go check on her again tomorrow."

"I'm ever so grateful for anything you could do right now, Miss Lara. As soon as my mother is on her feet again, things will get better."

"From the look of it, I believe the baby will be here any day."

Lara changed into a dress she hoped would complement her honey blond hair and gray eyes. As Elsie twisted Lara's hair into a chignon, Fiona appeared. Her gaze flickered over Lara's gown.

"Are you wearing Cambridge Blue in honor of our handsome guest?" she asked.

"It's just a blue dress," Lara replied.

"Of course it is. Mr. Greystoke is not such a little lump anymore," Fiona said. "Who could have predicted he would become so terribly good looking?"

"I'm glad you're delighted with his appearance. I daresay some ladies found him just as agreeable before."

"You needn't pretend he hasn't improved."

"Fiona, a man possessing good character, intelligence, and a kindly nature is more important than a rugged jawline, deep-set eyes, and dashing figure." *Although Mr. Greystoke possesses all those qualities.*

"Then you won't mind marriage to Sir Harry." Her sister smirked as she flounced from the room.

* * *

"We're having a party in your honor on Boxing Day," Fiona announced at lunch. "There's to be music, dancing, and games. Practically every family in the neighborhood is coming." She slid an insinuating glance toward Lara. "Including Sir Harry."

Since she was too far away to kick Fiona under the table, Lara settled for giving her a quelling glance.

William's eyebrows rose. "Does our Lara have a suitor?"

"No—" Lara began.

"Yes, she does," Fiona interrupted. "Sir Harry is madly in love with her."

Out of the corner of her eye, Lara could see Miles staring. If she'd been suddenly stripped naked, she could not have felt more embarrassed. "My sister vastly overstates the case. It's entirely possible the gentleman will make *her* an offer of marriage."

"Am I acquainted with Sir Harry?" William asked.

"He attended your wedding, but I doubt you would remember," Mr. Robinson said. "Sir Harry is a very respectable fellow, and a former military commander."

"He's a bit...mature to be contemplating marriage again, is he not?" Angelica asked. "Forgive me for saying so, but Lara would end up being his caretaker sooner rather than later."

"I've no intention of marrying Sir Harry!" Lara exclaimed. "None whatsoever."

"Lara likes taking care of people," Fiona said. "She's always doing charity work in Blythe Village, but the poor are determined to stay poor. What is your opinion, Mr. Greystoke? Do you believe ministering to the downtrodden is a worthwhile activity?"

"The human condition cannot be changed," Miles replied.

Lara peered at him, aghast. "Should those who are more fortunate than others turn a blind eye to poverty?"

"Not at all. However, I've noticed some men who inherit great fortunes fritter it all away in frivolous pastimes. Conversely, others of humble birth manage to create enormous wealth for themselves. There will always be inequality and poverty, no matter what any of us do."

"I couldn't agree more," Fiona said. "I believe the poor secretly despise us for our assistance. Let the church minister to the wretches and leave the rest of us alone."

"The church can do nothing without its congregation," Lara said. "*We* are the church."

"I'm not expressing myself particularly well," Miles said. "I simply believe that much of our efforts toward the poor are wasted."

"Exactly!" Fiona exclaimed.

A sense of disappointment made Lara's food taste like sawdust. *Mr. Greystoke used to have a far bigger heart.* As she choked down a mouthful of chicken, she realized her throat was scratchy. Her eyes stung slightly, and her head had begun to ache. With an apologetic smile, she tucked her folded napkin next to her plate and stood.

"If you'll excuse me, I'm unwell. I'm going to lie down for a while."

"It's no wonder you caught a chill, traipsing around outside in the snow," Fiona said.

"Poor dear," Mrs. Robinson said. "I'll have one of the maids bring you some tea with honey and lemon."

On the way up the stairs, Lara paused at the landing where

a white plaster bust of Queen Victoria graced a niche in the wall. After glancing over her shoulder to make sure she was unobserved, she tilted the statue and felt underneath. Nothing was there, of course, and she berated herself for a surge of disappointment. *I'm silly for hoping otherwise.*

The snowstorm abated that afternoon, and Mr. Robinson suggested the gentlemen accompany him to York for some Christmas shopping.

"Why York?" William asked. "Wouldn't Blythe Village suffice?"

Mr. Robinson leaned in, whispering so he would not be overheard. "Mrs. Robinson has mentioned several times lately that her favorite millinery shop is located in York. As a dutiful husband, I must therefore take the hint."

On the journey, Miles ceded the lion's share of the conversation to Mr. Robinson and William. As he stared out at the snowy landscape, he felt a sense of melancholy descend. Lara's wounded expression at his response to Fiona's question had cut him to the quick. Although she'd excused herself from the table, claiming she was unwell, he suspected her departure was hastened by his ill-considered remarks.

William tapped him on the shoulder. "Say, old chap, you appear to be woolgathering."

"Oh...I'm a bit worried about Miss Lara's health."

"She caught a chill this morning, no doubt," Mr. Robinson said. "I expect a good night's sleep will set her right again."

"I confess I feel somewhat oafish after our conversation at lunch. It seems I cannot please the one Miss Robinson without vexing the other."

Mr. Robinson roared with laughter. "It has always been thus from birth with those two. I think you must choose between them and behave accordingly."

Inwardly, Miles sighed. *The choice is clear, but it's the behavior that's the sticking point. It's as if I can't formulate a concise thought when Lara is near, and my tongue becomes clumsy. Oh, why do I torture myself with the hope she will ever think well of me?*

After a fitful afternoon in bed, Lara was forced to admit she had indeed caught a cold. The tea Elsie brought soothed her throat for a little while, but her rising temperature soon made her feel miserable again. Although her forehead was burning up, she could not seem to get warm. Elsie finally spread another comforter on her bed. As the maid tossed another log on the fire, Lara was reminded of the Coogans. *Perhaps if I rest quietly, I'll be well enough by morning to pay them a call.*

"Will you please tell Mama I'm ill and won't be coming down for dinner?" Her voice sounded raspy and unpleasant.

"Right away, Miss Lara."

When Lara next opened her eyes, her mother had come into the room and was draping a cold, moist compress over her forehead. "Sorry to wake you, dear. Should we call the surgeon?"

"I doubt there is anything Mr. Worth could do for me." As her mother turned away, Lara caught her hand. "Mama, if I'm not able to take food over to the Coogans tomorrow, will you go in my stead?"

"With house guests, it would be difficult for me to leave. I'll ask your sister."

Although she wanted to give Fiona the benefit of the doubt,

Lara did not believe her sister would willingly volunteer. As she drifted off to sleep, she was determined to get better as quickly as possible.

After Miles returned home from the shopping trip to York, he tucked his wrapped gifts under the Christmas tree. He'd purchased a stereoscope for the Robinson family, along with several packets of stereograph cards, a new pen for his brother, a wooden jumping jack for Billy, and a box of stationery for Angelica. As he shopped, he wished he could find something of special significance for Lara, but he didn't find anything that caught his eye. *It's just as well; she made it clear long ago my attentions are unwelcome.*

As he mounted the stairs on his way to dress for dinner, he could not stop staring at the niche at the landing. Although he felt foolish, he lifted the bust of Queen Victoria to see if anything lay underneath. He chuckled when he found nothing. *What did I anticipate?*

When he returned to the drawing room a half-hour later, Lara wasn't assembled with the others. He approached Mrs. Robinson, who was sipping a glass of sherry.

"Might I inquire after your daughter's health?"

"She's in bed with a fever, I'm sorry to say. Even in her current state, the poor dear was worried about the Coogans. Mrs. Coogan's eldest daughter Elsie is Lara's maid, and Lara's fond of her. I may have Elsie go home tomorrow morning with a hamper of provisions, to ease Lara's mind."

"I'll bring the hamper to the Coogans," Miles said. "With Miss Lara ill, it wouldn't be wise to take her maid away from her."

"That's extremely thoughtful, but you're our guest, Mr.

Greystoke," Mrs. Robinson said. "I couldn't imagine imposing on you that way."

"It's no imposition whatsoever. I'd enjoy the exercise, and it will give me a chance to see Blythe Village."

"Although I refuse to set foot in the Coogans' hovel, if it's not too cold tomorrow perhaps I'll walk into the village with you," Fiona said.

"I'd be glad for the company," Miles said, although nothing could be further from the truth.

Over breakfast the following morning, Mrs. Robinson reported Lara's fever had not improved.

"Shall I fetch a surgeon?" Miles asked.

"Lara insists not, but she isn't leaving her bed today. She was well enough, however, to badger me about the Coogans. I reassured her we'd see to their needs. After that, Lara was able to go back to sleep."

"I'll nip over with the hamper, then, as soon as it's ready," Miles said.

"It's sunny out, so I'll go too," Fiona said. "I wouldn't mind visiting a few shops in the village before returning home."

"Er...Fiona, dearest, I could use your help," Angelica said. "Nobody here draws as well as you do, and I'd love to send a drawing of Billy to his other grandparents for Christmas. Would you be a darling and oblige me this morning?"

"But I just promised Mr. Greystoke to accompany him," Fiona said. "Can't we do it this afternoon?"

"Christmas is in a few days, and if we don't put the sketch in the post right away, it might not arrive in time."

Fiona pouted. "If you insist."

Miles hoped his relief wasn't obvious. "Perhaps we'll walk together some other morning, Miss Fiona."

"I'll look forward to it."

Fiona returned to her oatmeal. Angelica caught Miles's eye and gave him a subtle wink while William snickered silently into his tea. *Do my brother and sister-in-law detect my lack of regard for Fiona, or are my feelings for Lara so obvious?*

Chapter 3

Saint Nick

In response to Miles's knock, a young boy opened the door to the Coogans' cottage and peered at him. "Can I help you, sir?"

"I'm here on behalf of Miss Lara." He tapped the hamper. "She asked me to deliver some food."

The boy's eyes grew wide, and he gave an excited wiggle. "Food? Oh, thank you! What's your name?"

Miles suddenly felt like Santa Claus. "Er...call me Nick. May I come in?"

The boy swung the door open, and Miles stepped inside. Two little girls clad in threadbare dresses were playing with rag dolls nearby. The boy pointed first to the youngest girl and then to the eldest as he introduced them.

"Nick, that's Helen. She's five. The other one is Colleen. She's eleven. My name's Jack, and I'm eight."

Miles removed his hat and gave the girls a courtly bow. "Lovely to meet you, ladies."

Colleen and Helen exchanged a surprised glance with one another, shot to their feet, and curtsied. Then all three children burst out into giggles. They flocked around Miles as he unpacked the hamper of food and put everything on the table. Inside were a crock of butter, a half-dozen scones, a roast chicken, and some fruit. While Colleen brought over plates, Miles sent Jack in to check on his mother.

In the meantime, Miles took the wooden bucket out to the pump to fetch fresh water. The pump was nearly frozen, so filling the bucket took more work than he'd anticipated. By the time he returned, Mrs. Coogan had managed to get herself to the kitchen. Right away he understood Lara's concern for the ghastly pale woman, whose face was gaunt.

"Mum, this here's Nick," Jack mumbled through a mouthful of scone.

"Good morning, Mrs. Coogan. Miss Lara is ill, but she sent me to help out," Miles said.

"She's an angel, and that's the truth."

"Yes, she is. I couldn't agree more."

While the family ate, Miles filled the tea kettle with water and swung it over the flames in the fireplace to boil for tea. As he straightened, he was struck by how little the Coogans possessed. The family was indeed in dire straits, and in need of far more than a simple hamper of food. He'd told Lara efforts on behalf of the poor were often wasted, and perhaps that was oftentimes true. In this instance, however, he couldn't turn a blind eye. *I know now what Lara's Christmas gift will be.*

He picked up his hat. "Mrs. Coogan, I'm going out to get a few things. I'll be back soon."

* * *

Three days after she first began to feel ill, Lara's fever broke, and her sore throat improved. She began to feel restless and cooped up, particularly when she realized Christmas Eve was the next day and Miles's muffler was only half finished. Elsie propped her up with extra pillows and fetched her knitting basket so she could work.

"How is your mama?" Lara asked. "Have you seen her?"

"No, Miss Lara, but she sent word that Saint Nick has been taking good care of her and the kids."

"*Saint Nick?*" Lara smiled. "How awfully strange!"

Elsie laughed and shrugged. "That's what she told Ned when I asked him to look in on her. I don't know if maybe her condition has muddled her thinking or not."

"I'll be well enough by tomorrow to pay her a call, I think. I'll get to the bottom of it then, but the important thing is she's being taken care of."

That afternoon, Lara was delighted when Angelica came for a visit. She brought a chair closer to the bed, and they chatted for a long while about the baby, London, and married life.

"I've missed talking with you so much," Lara said finally. "And now that you're home, I'm stuck in bed with a cold."

"You didn't do it on purpose," Angelica said. "I'm glad you're feeling a little better because I wanted to ask you about coming to London for a visit this spring. I've already spoken with Papa, and he's agreed to let you and Fiona stay with us for the entire Season."

Lara was filled with excitement. "You've discussed the matter with William?"

Angelica laughed. "I allowed him to think it was his idea. You girls need to find husbands, despite Papa's notions that such things grow on trees. It was a miracle I chanced to meet William, actually. If I hadn't, perhaps Sir Harry would be eying *me*."

"This is uncommonly generous, particularly since you and William have a new baby and everything."

"Nonsense. We've plenty of room, and you may even bring your maid if you like. Now there's something else you should know. I want Fiona to come with us when we return to town after the New Year. It will do her good to come out from underneath your shadow for a few months."

"My shadow?" Lara echoed. "I'm sorry, I don't understand."

"She's told me in several letters over the years that she's jealous of you."

"What?"

"She resents your pretty face and sweet temperament."

Lara averted her eyes so her elder sister wouldn't see the deep hurt her revelations had caused. "I truly had no idea Fiona felt that way."

"I believe if she can enjoy a little time in Society by herself, she just may blossom."

"Have you told her about London yet?"

"I'm planning to tell her on Christmas Eve, as a sort of present. So mum's the word."

"All right. Obviously, if Fiona wants to go to London without me, she should go." She gave Angelica a crooked smile. "In the meantime, I'll stay at Blythe Manor and stave off Sir Harry's advances as best I can."

"It won't be for long, dearest. Spring will be here before you know it."

Angelica deposited a kiss on Lara's cheek and left. Disconsolate and troubled by a sense of betrayal, Lara dropped back onto her pillow and stared at the ceiling overhead. *Fiona and I haven't always been close, but I didn't think she was jealous of me. She even wrote letters about it behind my back! Fiona hasn't even bothered to visit me once since I became ill. Perhaps Angelica is right, and we need some distance.*

* * *

Christmas Eve morning dawned bright and cheerful. Lara managed to eat most of what Elsie brought her on a breakfast tray. A long hot bath did wonders toward making her feel better. While she waited for her hair to dry, she finished knitting Miles's muffler. Afterward, she wrapped it in a square of brown paper and tied the package with a lacy ribbon.

When she was properly dressed and coiffed, she took the package down to the drawing room, where several presents were already nestled under the tree. As she placed Miles's gift alongside the others, Lara squelched the temptation to check the labels. Her mother appeared in the doorway.

"No fair peeking." Mrs. Robinson gave her a hug. "It's good to see you up and about."

"I'm glad to be on my feet again. Where is everyone?"

"I'm not entirely sure, but I believe Angelica and Fiona are in the nursery with the baby, and your father and William went riding."

"And...Mr. Greystoke?"

"He's been going out every morning for long walks. I must say, Mr. Greystoke is an ideal house guest. He seems to keep himself amused without any effort from anyone."

"Since it's such a fine day, I think I'll take a basket down to the Coogans."

"But you've been ill, Lara! You shouldn't overdo on your first day out of bed."

"I promise I won't stay long, but I must satisfy my curiosity. Rumor has it the Coogans have had Saint Nick dropping by."

"Really?" Mrs. Robinson laughed. "Well, 'tis the season for it."

* * *

Miles and Helen emerged from the cobbler's shop, hand-in-hand. The little girl could not stop staring at her new boots, which made it difficult to walk properly. She nearly barreled headlong into Fiona, who was passing by.

"Oh excuse us, Miss Fiona," Miles said, nudging Helen. "We were quite excited and weren't looking where we were going."

"Excuse me, Miss Fiona," Helen echoed.

"That's quite all right. There's so much bustling going on today, I've nearly been trod upon several times this morning."

"Look at my shoes!" Helen thrust out her foot for Fiona's benefit. "I've never had a new pair all my own before."

Fiona smiled. "Your shoes are quite lovely, Helen. No doubt your mama will love them too."

Helen pulled on Miles's hand. "Oh, yes, let's show Mum!"

Miles remained rooted to the spot. "Patience, Helen. Before we go home, I must pick up a bundle of laundry from Mrs. Fitzgerald for your mother."

Helen jumped up and down in frustration. "Can't we do it later? I want to go home *now!*"

Miles exchanged an exasperated glance with Fiona.

"Can I help?" she asked.

"That would be wonderful, actually." Miles fished money from his pocket to pay the bill. "I never realized before how squirmy children can be. Mrs. Fitzgerald is the third door down from the church. It's painted yellow."

"I'm sure I'll be able to find it by the smell of soap alone," Fiona said. "I'll be along to the Coogans directly."

"Thank you! I've been fixing up the place over the last few days."

Miles and Helen headed off down the walkway, but as he passed a sweet shop he remembered one last errand. "I'm sure you won't mind if we pop in here for a moment, do you? It's

Christmas Eve, and I promised to bring your brother and sister some hard candy."

Helen's eyes grew wide, and her rosebud mouth formed an O. "You can't break your promise then!"

"Most assuredly not."

* * *

As Lara set out with a basket of fruit, cheese, and bread, several inches of milky white snow coated the landscape on either side of the road. Sunshine sparkled off the icicles dripping from tree branches, giving the trees a bejeweled dazzle. As she approached the Coogans' cottage, the sound of boisterous laughter reached her ears. To her surprise, a cheerful holiday wreath accented with red holly berries and a colorful bow decorated the door. Colleen answered her knock, dressed in a new pinafore frock and boots. Her hair was tied back away from her face, and her usual downcast look had disappeared.

"Oh, my! Colleen, you look like a perfect little lady," Lara exclaimed.

"Christmas came early this year! Come see!"

As Lara entered the house, she was taken aback. A small Christmas tree graced the corner, a large rag rug now covered the floor in front of the hearth, and freshly laundered curtains hung from the windows. A wooden doll house, complete with furniture, was pushed up against the wall. Jack was kneeling on the rug, playing with a brightly painted set of toy soldiers. His hair had been cut, and he wore a warm jumper, a pair of corduroy breeches, woolen stockings, and new shoes. He gave her a huge grin. "Hello, Miss Lara!"

"Jack, I mistook you for a gentleman," Lara managed. "What's all this?"

"It's Saint Nick's doing," Colleen said. "He said *you* sent him."

"Did he? I can't imagine why he'd say such a thing. Where's Helen?"

"Saint Nick took her to the village. It was her turn to buy clothes and shoes today."

Stunned, Lara blinked. *Who is Nick and why is he saying I sent him?*

Mrs. Coogan waddled into the room, clad in a new gown. The woman was still too thin, but she radiated far more energy than she had before, and her cheeks had regained some of their bloom. "Good morning, Miss Lara." She lowered herself into a chair. "I hope you're feeling better. I heard you've been ill."

"Yes, but I'm fine now. Can I get you some tea?"

"Thank you, but Nick already made me eat a big breakfast. He's been spoiling all of us something dreadful the last few days. He even sent my laundry out to be done, just like I was a real lady!"

"I can't wait to thank him personally." Lara realized she was still clutching the basket. "I'll unpack this in the kitchen for later then."

As she crossed to the corner of the house where the Coogans prepared their meals, the front door burst open and Helen ran inside. The child wore a new heavy coat over a pink woolen dress, knit cap, and mittens.

"Hello, Miss Lara! Mum, look at my pretty boots! They even have tassels!"

Mrs. Coogan bade Helen turn around so she could admire her outfit. "You're absolutely splendid, Helen."

A tall man stamped snow off his feet on the mat outside and doffed his hat as he ducked through the front door. "Hello, Mrs. Coogan. We—" Miles broke off when he met Lara's gaze. "Miss Lara! You're up and about."

"Nick!" cried Jack and Colleen. "Did you bring us sweets?"

The two eldest children rushed toward the man they knew as Nick and began searching the pockets of his coat. Miles laughed and fended them off. "You won't find anything there, but let's see..." He made a big show of looking in the lining of his hat. "No, it's not here. I'm afraid I've quite forgotten where I put it."

More squeals. Finally, Miles reached into his breast pocket and produced a small bag of sweets. "Ah, here it is!" The kids jumped up and down until he dropped the bag into their waiting hands. "Be sure to share with your sister."

Completely charmed, a smile crept onto Lara's lips. *He's Saint Nick?*

"You're too good to us, lad," Mrs. Coogan said.

After a brief knock on the door, Fiona burst into the house with a large wrapped bundle in her hands. "Sorry I'm late with the laundry. Mrs. Fitzgerald was helping someone else when I arrived."

Lara gaped. "Fiona!"

"Oh, hello, Lara. I'm glad to see you're feeling better." Her sister dropped the bundle of laundry into a chair and took Miles's arm. "Mr. Greystoke and I have been fixing up the Coogans' cottage. Isn't it cozy now?"

At the sight of Fiona and Miles together, Lara's smile froze on her face. A knife to Lara's heart could not have felt more painful. "It's lovely." She lowered the basket onto the table with trembling hands. "Mrs. Coogan, your husband will be home for Christmas, I hope?"

"His last letter said he would try. That would make everything perfect."

"Well, I must be going," Lara said.

Miles disentangled himself from Fiona. "Let me escort you to Blythe Manor."

"No, thank you." Lara wouldn't meet his gaze. "I've some shopping to do first."

Feeling as stiff-necked as one of Jack's tin soldiers, she marched from the house.

* * *

Blythe Village was bustling with ebullient shoppers purchasing last minute gifts and food. Although Lara dearly wished she could share their holiday cheer, her good mood had collapsed. She ducked into the yarn shop to escape the fray, and pretended to admire the pretty skeins of wool tucked into the cubbies lining the wall. When she'd lingered long enough, she purchased several cherry red skeins, wished the merchant Merry Christmas, and left.

The sunshine had disappeared when she emerged, the temperature was dropping, and snowfall was becoming heavier by the minute. Lara trudged toward Blythe Manor, sparing only a single glance for the Coogans' cottage. Miles and Fiona had taken great pains to make sure the family was clothed and fed when she could not. Although she was happy for the Coogans, when she remembered how Fiona had taken Miles's arm, an avalanche of unhappiness welled up within her. It seemed clear the two had formed an attachment, and Lara couldn't bear it. *I'm the jealous one now, not Fiona. I should be ashamed of myself and yet all I feel is pain.*

I am in love, unrequited.

Her thoughts drifted back four years ago, when the blush of young *amour* had first captured her heart. As Angelica's wedding date had drawn near, Miles and his family had been guests at Blythe Manor. During a series of parties, receptions, and gatherings, she and Miles were thrown together. With all the seriousness fourteen-year-olds possessed, they discussed politics, music, books, and shared their hopes and dreams for the future. Although Fiona had privately sneered at Miles, Lara had looked past his burgeoning waistline and seen a young man of keen intellect and sterling character.

The bust of Queen Victoria became their secret postbox as they exchanged messages—until the day after the wedding, when the Greystokes were to return home. Her last letter to Miles expressed her regard for him openly and unreservedly, and she'd asked him if he felt anything at all for her in return. His lack of response spoke volumes, and he departed Blythe Manor without saying good-bye. Heartbroken, she'd cried her eyes out with disappointment and embarrassment at having mistaken his friendship for something more. Even now, Lara still could not think of that letter without humiliation and regret. *I pray he burned it; if he should ever show the letter to anyone, I'll die.*

Upon her return to Blythe Manor, Lara lifted her chin and forced a composed smile to her lips. *It's Christmas Eve, and I must focus on something other than my own misery.* As she passed the bust of Queen Victoria, however, she could not hold back a sob.

Chapter 4

Crisis Eve

As Lara left the Coogans' cottage, Miles's stomach twisted into a knot. He'd meant his assistance to the Coogans to be a gift for her, but Fiona had spoiled everything by taking credit. Furthermore, she'd insinuated an intimacy between them that certainly didn't—and could never—exist. Although Fiona had been openly flirting with him since he arrived, he'd given her no indication whatsoever that he wished to deepen their acquaintance. Perhaps Lara did not return his affections, but Miles didn't want to leave her with the erroneous impression that he'd formed a design on her sister!

Reminding himself he was a gentleman, he held his irritation in check as he escorted Fiona up the road to Blythe Manor. At first, she prattled on about little Billy and his attempts to roll over. Even though Miles adored his nephew, a steady narrative of his babyish antics quickly became tiresome. Apparently, Fiona sensed his waning attention because she changed the subject abruptly. "I've recently begun to read *War and Peace.*"

"You have?" He tried to keep the note of disbelief from his voice.

"Yes." Fiona seemed defensive. "What is your opinion of it?"

"I confess I've not had the pleasure of reading that work. My tastes run to adventure and science fiction."

Fiona made a sound of disgust. "Lara told me you'd say that."

"She did?" A burst of pleasure lifted Miles's step. *Lara remembered my taste in literature.*

"You'll be leaving Blythe Manor in a few days," Fiona said. "You may write to me from Cambridge if you wish."

Astonishment at her presumptuousness slowed his steps. "Miss Fiona, if I've given you the impression I feel anything more than familial regard for you, I apologize."

A frown of annoyance rippled across Fiona's brow. "I wasn't suggesting anything of the sort, but then *secret* correspondence is more to your liking, isn't it? Good day."

She hastened off, leaving a bewildered Miles standing in the middle of the road.

* * *

Inside her bedroom, Lara splashed cold water on her face to soothe the ravages of her recent bout of self-pity. *Hopefully the redness and swelling will subside before I join the others for church tonight.*

Fiona entered her room without knocking. "There you are! I thought you'd never come home." Almost crackling with resentment, she began to pace. "Mr. Greystoke is an insufferable idiot who thinks far too highly of himself. I want nothing to do with him anymore, so I'll have to think of something else as a Christmas gift other than that handkerchief." She peered at Lara. "What are you bawling about? I thought you'd be pleased about all the money Mr. Greystoke spent on the Coogans. It's as if he adopted them as pets."

Lara was taken aback. "It was all Mr. Greystoke's doing? You said earlier it was both of you."

"Perhaps I did, but I take it back. All I did was fetch Mrs. Coogan's wretched parcel from the laundress." She shuddered. "Thank goodness I was wearing gloves."

Anger at her sister boiled over. "You deliberately misled me!"

"It was a harmless fib. Why are you so cross?"

"Perhaps it's because I also found out about the letters!"

With a gasp, Fiona looked almost panic-stricken. "How—?"

"I confess I feel betrayed," Lara continued. "You and I are sisters. What would make you do such a thing?"

She wilted. "It was only meant to be a silly prank."

"A *prank?*" Lara was taken aback. "If I'd written such things about you, you wouldn't be so dismissive."

Confusion creased Fiona's brow. "What are you talking of?"

"Your letters about me to Angelica, of course."

"Oh *those!* Yes, well, you know I'm a wicked little thing." Fiona edged toward the door. "I'll pray to be a better person in church tonight, all right?"

As her sister spun around and fled from the room, Lara was perplexed. Fiona had often been flighty, but her behavior just now bordered on peculiar. *She acted guilty about the letters, yet didn't bother to offer so much as an apology.*

Heavy snowfall was pelting her window, and Lara moved over to look out at the view. The garden below was completely covered with white drifts, and she couldn't see past the tall hedges separating the garden from the field beyond. *It will be difficult for anyone traveling anywhere tonight. I hope Mr. Coogan stays safe.*

* * *

The Christmas Eve church service was canceled due to the inclement weather. The Robinson and Greystoke families assembled in the drawing room before dinner, where Mr. Robinson brought out the family Bible. He read the Nativity Story from Luke, after which came a time for silent prayer. As everyone else closed their eyes and bowed their heads, Lara chanced to meet Miles's gaze across the room. A flurry of emotional turmoil ensued. *Oh why did he have to come back into my life and stir up feelings which had lain fallow?* She tore her eyes away from him and stared at the patterned oriental rug instead.

After the prayer, Mrs. Robinson sat down at the piano in the corner and played "O Holy Night." William gave the Christmas carol voice first, but then baritone Miles joined with his brother's clear tenor for a beautiful duet. A hush fell over the room as they sang, and Lara felt her troubles lift for a short while.

A footman handed around glasses of mulled wine while they waited for the dinner gong. Angelica cleared her throat. "Perhaps now would be a good time to announce the first gift of the evening. Fiona, Papa has given his permission for you to come with us to town after the New Year. You'll be staying until the Season."

Fiona squealed in excitement, spilling wine from her glass onto the carpet. As the footman hastened to blot the stain, she ran to give her father and Angelica a kiss. Even though Lara was still angry with Fiona, she smiled at the look of pure joy on her sister's face. During the animated conversation following Angelica's announcement, Lara crossed the room to speak with Miles.

"Fiona confessed to me earlier today she had nothing to do

with helping the Coogans. So it is to you I offer my sincere thanks. I was very moved by everything you did."

His cheekbones took on a rosy hue. "When I saw their need, I couldn't stand by and do nothing." He swallowed. "N-Nevertheless, what I did was out of regard for our former friendship."

His words reminded her of the love letter she wished she'd never written. Blood rushed to her face. "Perhaps the less said about that, the better. It was long ago, and I would prefer to forget it."

To her surprise, Miles almost recoiled. "Forgive me. I didn't mean to remind you of anything unpleasant." He bowed, excused himself, and strode over to join his brother near the fireplace. His posture was stiff, and his expression was strained. Lara was left with the uncomfortable feeling she'd said something horribly wrong.

Although William was speaking to him, Miles scarcely heard a word. When the footman passed by with a tray, Miles drained the remainder of his wine and exchanged his empty glass for a full one. His mind was reeling, and he suddenly felt as if he were fourteen again, with a thick waistline and spots on his face. It was foolish; for some time now he'd been aware of the sidelong glances ladies cast his way. All the admiration in the world was empty, however, unless it came from the woman he loved. *How could I have been so stupid as to pour my heart out in that letter! I poisoned my relationship with Lara forever by confessing my unguarded feelings too soon. Now she can never think of me as a man, but only as a clumsy, besotted boy.*

"Woolgathering again?" William asked.

Miles came to his senses. "I-I was just thinking of our

parents, actually. It seems rather hard they must spend the holidays without either of their sons. If you don't mind, I'm going to take the morning train home on Boxing Day."

William steered him to one side. "It's abominably rude to the Robinsons to cut your visit short, particularly when they've planned a party in our honor."

"They won't care a jot. You, Angelica, and Billy are the main attraction. I'm just a hanger-on at this point."

"But—"

The dinner gong sounded.

"I'm leaving," Miles said evenly. "I don't want to hear another word about it." He walked over to Fiona and offered her his arm. "May I escort you in to dinner?"

For Lara, the evening was a ghastly affair. Confusion and bewilderment were her dinner partners, and they were exceedingly poor company. Miles had turned into a granite statue, and she knew she was the cause. *I merely said I wished to forget our prior relationship. Is he offended I no longer wish to be seen as a lovesick child?*

Although Cook had outdone herself, Lara merely picked at her food, counting on her recent illness to explain her lack of appetite. *Perhaps I was not effusive enough in my praise for his help to the Coogans...or maybe I was too lavish? Was it bad manners to have mentioned it at all?* Fortunately, Fiona's nonstop vivacity regarding her upcoming Season negated any need for Lara to add to the conversation.

"Lara's scarcely eaten any dinner," Fiona said finally. "I believe my good news has upset her."

"On the contrary, I'm quite happy for you," Lara said.

"You're to join me in the spring. Until then, we can correspond by post," Fiona said.

Miles suddenly thawed. "Letters are overrated. Once you've written your silly thoughts down on paper, you're at the complete mercy of whomever reads them."

Stabbing pains lanced Lara's temples. *My thoughts were silly, were they?* "One would hope the recipient of the letter would be more gracious than to sneer at heartfelt sentiments."

"Sadly, that's not always the case, it is?" he shot back. "Unguarded sentimentality always lends itself to mockery by the undeserved."

Lara lifted her chin. "I think persons of good character ought to return unwanted love letters to the sender, so as to spare their feelings."

"I agree, even if a lengthy period of time has passed. There is truly no excuse for behaving in a cavalier fashion in cases of unrequited affection."

A chuckle escaped William's lips. "You sound a trifle jaded, Miles. Don't tell me you've already had your heart broken at the tender age of eighteen?"

Miles lanced Lara with his eyes. "Not recently."

His remark, which Lara interpreted as flippant, filled her with hurt and anger. *Why would he mock me so?* She opened her mouth to reply, but a sudden commotion in the entryway checked her rebuke. Shortly thereafter, the butler hastened into the dining room.

"Forgive the interruption, Mr. Robinson, but Mrs. Coogan's little boy has come to the door. He's asking for Miss Lara."

Jack! Tossing her napkin to the table, Lara rushed from the room. She was followed closely by her father, mother, and Miles. Jack stood shivering in the entryway, his clothes encrusted with snow. His frantic expression twisted something inside her chest.

"What's wrong, Jack?"

"It's Mum. The baby's coming, she's alone with my sisters, and I'm scared. She sent me to fetch the midwife, but Mrs. Murphy's gone off to visit her sister in Leeds for Christmas." His face crumpled. "Papa isn't home yet and I don't know what to do!"

"You did the right thing by coming here." Lara beckoned to a footman. "Please take Jack downstairs to the kitchen, get his wet things off, and give him a blanket and hot chocolate. Find Elsie and let her know her brother is here. Maybe she can find some dry clothes for him."

"I'll take the carriage to fetch Mr. Worth for Mrs. Coogan," Mr. Robinson said.

"But it's still snowing!" Mrs. Robinson exclaimed. "The roads aren't safe!"

"I can't stand by and let the poor woman suffer," Mr. Robinson replied.

"Nor can I," Miles said. "Let me get my hat and coat. I'll stay with Mrs. Coogan until the surgeon arrives."

"Helen and Colleen are probably scared out of their wits," Lara said. "I'm going too."

* * *

Helen was curled up on the rug near the fireplace when the door opened. When she saw Miles and Lara, she ran into Lara's arms and began to cry. Colleen appeared in the doorway to Mrs. Coogan's bedroom. When she realized her brother hadn't brought the midwife, she began to sob too. "Where's Jack! Isn't Mrs. Murphy coming to help?"

Lara gave both girls a hug. "Jack is safe and sound at Blythe

Manor, the midwife has gone off to Leeds and Mr. Robinson has gone to fetch the surgeon. You've been very brave, but I need to see to your mother now. Colleen, be a big girl and take care of your sister, all right?"

The girls settled into the chairs closest to the warmth of the fire. Lara covered Helen with her coat, and Miles draped his own over Colleen. Whimpering noises were coming from the bedroom, and Lara exchanged a worried glance with Miles. "Wait here." She hastened into the room, which was dimly lit by a sputtering oil lantern. Mrs. Coogan was lying on her side on the straw-stuffed mattress. Her loose-fitting gown, soaked through with perspiration, was bunched up around her knees. "Miss Lara, the baby's coming."

A spasm of pain contorted the woman's features as she gritted her teeth. Lara used her handkerchief to blot the woman's face. "Don't worry, Mrs. Coogan. My father is bringing the surgeon as quick as he can."

The woman writhed in pain and grabbed the bedclothes. "Baby's not waiting for the surgeon," she gasped. "No offense."

Miles appeared in the doorway in his shirtsleeves. "Forgive me, but I couldn't help overhearing we seem to have a crisis."

"This is no place for a man, Mr. Greystoke," Lara said.

"Have you ever brought a baby into the world, Miss Lara?"

"Well no, but—"

"Help Mrs. Coogan to lie on her back and bring me another lantern. We're going to need more light." As he spoke, Miles unbuttoned his cuffs and rolled his sleeves up over his elbows.

Lara crossed to him. "Horses are vastly different than human beings, Mr. Greystoke. Do you know what you're doing?" she whispered.

"Not completely, but I'm all she's got."

Although the whole situation was unseemly, Lara

conceded his point. She was virtually useless when it came to childbirth, and despite the strain of concentration on his face, Miles exuded an air of quiet competence.

"All right. Just tell me what you need," she said.

"Find some clean rags or towels, some twine, and a pair of shears."

Glad for a task, Lara hastened to comply. Whatever Miles asked her to do thereafter, she did it without hesitation. In between, she held Mrs. Coogan's hand and blotted the perspiration from her brow. After drops of sweat began rolling into Miles's eyes, Lara wiped them away with a clean rag too.

When the baby boy emerged at last, he was blue. Mrs. Coogan lost consciousness, and Miles muttered a curse word under his breath.

"What's wrong?" Lara asked.

"Umbilical cord is wrapped around the baby's neck."

His hands moved rapidly to lift the slippery cord from around the baby's slender neck. Lara never heard any knock on the door, but suddenly Mr. Worth was there. As he slid his overcoat and cutaway jacket off, the surgeon gave the baby a cursory glance.

"Stillborn."

Miles gave no verbal response but continued clearing out the baby's nose and mouth with a finger. "Get me a towel, Lara."

Lara stepped around Mr. Worth to bring Miles the towel. He rubbed the baby's blue skin gently with the towel, patted his tiny bottom, and blew on his face.

"Come on, little one. I know you want to join us," he murmured. "Just breathe."

As Miles continued to work, Lara felt tears spring to her eyes. Seconds passed, but it felt like eternity.

"Lad, it's a lost cause," Mr. Worth said.

Suddenly Lara heard a tiny little gasping sound, and then the baby began to cry. It was a weak mewling cry at first, but then the cry grew stronger.

"I can't believe it," Lara said.

"Neither can I," Mr. Worth said, clearly taken aback. "I've never seen a baby that blue take a breath."

When Miles gently touched the baby's hand, its tiny little fingers closed around his index finger. He gave Lara a crooked smile. "I think we need that twine and shears now."

With deft precision, Mr. Worth tied off the baby's umbilical cord, cut it, and handed the towel-wrapped baby to Lara. Miles inhaled sharply. "Mrs. Coogan's bleeding!"

The surgeon's expression became sober. "I need your help, lad. If we can't stop the bleeding, she'll die."

Mrs. Coogan had still not regained consciousness, and to Lara's horror, bright red blood was staining the sheets. Miles and Mr. Worth worked to stanch the flow, but their efforts seemed to be for naught. Helpless to do anything for the woman except pray, Lara backed off into a corner with the infant in her arms. To her relief, his skin color was improving and had more pink to it now. She was amazed at how very small and wrinkled he was, and so terribly vulnerable.

"I'm afraid we're losing her," Mr. Worth murmured to Miles. "Press down here as hard as you can."

A chill ran down Lara's spine at the surgeon's words. She moved out into the front room, where the two girls were fast asleep. Mr. Robinson, who was waiting next to the fireplace, looked up as she tiptoed over. A relieved smile crept onto his lips when he saw the bundle in her arms, but Lara gave him a sober look.

"Please fetch Elsie. And ask the staff if they know anyone who has recently given birth. We're going to need a wet nurse."

Chapter 5

Cordially Yours

Lara and Miles took turns holding the baby while the other one replenished the oil in the lanterns, cleared away blood-soaked rags from Mrs. Coogan's bedroom, and brought in fresh ones. After Miles carried the two sleeping girls into the tiny second bedroom, Lara removed their shoes and tucked them into bed. When they were settled, Miles handed the baby off to Lara once more so he could assist Mr. Worth.

As the minutes passed, however, it was becoming increasingly more difficult for Lara to soothe the baby. The snow had stopped falling and it was after midnight when the carriage returned. Almost before the horses came to a halt, Elsie burst from the carriage and rushed into the house. Her face was taut with fear. "Is Mama all right?"

"Go see her, Elsie," Lara said.

A few moments after the young woman disappeared into the bedroom, Lara was surprised to see Mr. Robinson escort Angelica through the front door. As Angelica shrugged off her coat and hat, her unbound hair tumbled over her shoulder. *Papa must have woken her to accompany him.* Lara brought her sister the fretful baby.

"He's crying, and I don't know what to do."

Angelica took the bundle and cradled him. "Poor little thing is hungry, and he needs a fresh diaper. Is there a place we can be alone so I can feed him?"

Lara gasped. "You'd do that?"

"I'm not heartless, Lara. I feel certain Mrs. Coogan would do the same for me if the situation were reversed."

Miles appeared. Exhaustion showed in his eyes, and he almost staggered when he moved into the front room. His dress shirt was bloodstained, and red smears were visible on his hands and forearms. He crossed into the kitchen to wash his hands in the basin.

"Is she—?" Lara could not finish her sentence.

"Mr. Worth stopped the bleeding, but Mrs. Coogan's pulse is very weak." He dried his hands on a dishrag and leaned against the counter. "I don't know if she'll live until morning."

* * *

Lara showed Angelica into the children's bedroom where she could nurse the baby in private. Miles sank into a straight-backed chair at the table and stared at a knothole in the wood. Mr. Robinson sat across from him, produced a slender metal flask from his inner coat pocket, and slid it in his direction.

"Have some brandy, lad. You look as if you need it."

With a nod of gratitude, Miles took a long swallow...and then he took a second one. With a shudder, he gritted his teeth as the brandy warmed his stomach and sent burning tendrils through his limbs. "Thanks." He returned the flask to Mr. Robinson.

Elsie emerged from Mrs. Coogan's bedroom and crossed into the kitchen.

"Any news?" Miles asked.

"Mum's awake. She's asked to see the baby and for something to drink. Mr. Worth says that's a good sign." Elsie poured a glass of water from a pitcher. "I understand you delivered the baby, Mr. Greystoke. We're ever so grateful to you."

She left with the water, and Miles realized Mr. Robinson was gaping at him.

"Great Scott, man. *You* delivered the child?"

Miles gave him a crooked smile. "I had little choice."

Mr. Robinson shoved the flask into his hand. "Have the rest of that brandy. You deserve it."

The last few sips of brandy went down more smoothly, but Miles began to feel the accumulated effects of the evening. He put his head down on his folded arms to rest his eyes for a little while. The sound of voices woke him from a deep sleep, and Mr. Robinson was patting him on the back. "It's time to go home, lad."

He sat up in a panic and wiped the drool from his mouth. "Mrs. Coogan—?"

"She's doing fine so far, but Mr. Coogan just arrived. He caught a ride from Barnsley with a local farmer. Mr. Worth will stay at Mrs. Coogan's bedside until morning."

"And the baby?"

"He's coming home with us for now."

Upon waking late Christmas morning, Lara dressed herself and headed into the nursery to make sure the Coogan baby was all right. Angelica was sitting in a rocking chair near the window, nursing the little infant. A sigh of relief escaped Lara's lips.

"Oh, thank Heaven he's still alive. Merry Christmas, Angelica."

"Merry Christmas, Lara." Angelica glanced at the nearby crib, where Billy was napping. "One never stops worrying about babies. William and I still check Billy's breathing while he's asleep."

Lara sank into a chair.

"Mr. Greystoke was magnificent last night. I wish you could have seen it. Mr. Worth assumed the baby was stillborn at first, but Mr. Greystoke wouldn't give up trying to get him to breathe. Then he worked with Mr. Worth to save Mrs. Coogan." She paused. "Is there any word on her condition?"

"Papa left a little while ago to take Jack home. He'll bring news when he returns."

"Have you spoken with Mr. Greystoke yet this morning?"

"Miles is still abed, I believe. None of us had the heart to wake him."

Lara's gaze shifted to the sunshine streaming through the window. Following the tumultuous crisis the night before, Christmas Day had dawned bright and serene. Deep within her, however, a confusing maelstrom of emotions threatened to pull her into an abyss. Her sigh attracted her sister's notice.

"I don't wish to force a confidence, Lara, but I hate to see you unhappy," Angelica said. "Can you tell me what has you so sad?"

"I'm desperately in love with Mr. Greystoke, but he despises me."

"Despises you? What on Earth makes you think that?"

"The day after your wedding, I foolishly confessed my feelings for him in a letter. We'd secretly been exchanging messages by leaving them underneath Queen Victoria's bust on the staircase, you see. Mr. Greystoke was so horrified by my sentiments that he avoided me after that and left without saying good-bye. I blame myself for the whole affair, but I've never stopped loving him. After last night, I don't think I could ever think of another man the same way."

A tap on the open doorway made Lara jump. Fiona appeared, looking unusually subdued.

"Merry Christmas, Lara. You weren't in your room, so I hoped I would find you here. Papa has returned from the Coogans'."

* * *

The Robinsons and the Greystokes assembled in the drawing room to hear the news. With his hair slightly tousled and his cravat somewhat askew, Miles looked as if he'd dressed quickly. He exchanged a brief smile with Lara when he entered the room, but then he seemingly turned to granite once more. The easy intimacy they'd established at the Coogans had vanished, and with it Lara's hope for a new beginning. She swallowed hard and focused her eyes on her father.

"Mrs. Coogan has survived," Mr. Robinson announced. A collective sigh of relief broke the tension in the room. "Mr. Worth believes she'll live, but it may be weeks before she can leave her bed. Mr. Coogan is sending for his sister, Mrs. Pooler, in Harrogate, whose own child is about Billy's age. Mrs. Pooler will take care of Nicholas and Mrs. Coogan while Mr. Coogan returns to work."

"Nicholas?" Lara echoed.

"Mrs. Coogan woke long enough to insist the baby be named Nicholas."

Lara's glance slid to Miles. His color had risen, and he wore an embarrassed grin.

"Until Mrs. Pooler arrives, Mrs. Coogan needs peace and quiet," Mr. Robinson said. "I propose the three children should stay at Blythe Manor along with Nicholas—assuming Mrs. Robinson has no objection?"

Mrs. Robinson's lips curved into a smile. "What a perfectly delightful idea!"

"I'm so glad I'm leaving soon," Fiona whispered to Lara. "I can't bear screaming children."

"I'll send word for Elsie to bring the children for Christmas dinner this afternoon." Mr. Robinson rubbed his hands together. "Now, let's ring for a late tray so our sleepy hero and heroine can eat breakfast."

"And I'll hand out their presents," Fiona said. "Everyone else has already opened theirs."

* * *

The three-dimensional photograph of a London street scene made Lara gasp. "It's almost like I could reach out my hand and touch the people!"

She sat next to Fiona on the settee, surrounded by discarded wrapping papers and ribbons. Everyone else except for Miles had disappeared. He was perched in the window seat, glancing through *The Mysterious Island* by Jules Verne—a gift from his brother.

Fiona pulled the card out of the stereoscope and replaced it with one of a lake. "When I saw this one, I could have sword I saw a fish jump out of the water."

Miles closed his book and crossed the room carrying Lara's blue muffler.

"I wanted to thank you for this." He looped it around his neck in a jaunty fashion. "My classmates will be quite envious. And since I left my other muffler at the Coogans, this will come in very handy."

"We can walk over tomorrow to retrieve your muffler," Lara said. "I'm certain Mr. and Mrs. Coogan won't mind."

He averted his eyes. "Actually, I'm leaving first thing tomorrow morning. I want to spend some time with my parents before the start of next term."

Lara's heart sank, but she forced a smile to her lips. "I see. Yes, of course you should visit your parents. I'm sure they will consider it a blessing."

Fiona made a sound of disgust as she stood. "I haven't given either of you my gift yet. Wait here a moment."

She strode over to the Christmas tree and reached into its branches. Miles exchanged a grimace with Lara. "I'm almost afraid to ask," he murmured.

"Before I forget, I want to tell you how brilliant you were last night," Lara said.

"Me? *You* were the one who was brilliant. If you hadn't had faith in me, I'm not sure I could have kept on. Truthfully, I nearly lost my nerve."

"If that's so, you kept it to yourself admirably."

Fiona returned with her hands hidden behind her back. "My gift is in two parts, actually. The first part is where I take responsibility for something thoughtless and childish I did four years ago. I hope you can forgive me."

"What are you talking about?" Lara asked.

"I knew both of you were secretly exchanging letters using the bust of Queen Victoria. I was jealous, so I took Lara's last letter."

A rushing sound filled Lara's ears. "What?"

"And I took Mr. Greystoke's last letter too. I never read them, I promise, and I didn't realize until this morning how important they were. So here."

Fiona held out the two letters, but then crossed her arms as she realized she'd handed them to the wrong recipient. Miles took the one Lara had written to him, and Lara took the one Miles had written to her. Blinking back tears, Fiona edged toward the door.

"I'll leave you to it. Merry Christmas."

She fled. As Lara stared down at the slightly yellowed envelope in her hands, she saw her name written in Miles's handwriting. The wax seal on the back was cracked, but unbroken. Her throat swelled up with emotion, and her hands began to tremble. When she glanced up at Miles, he seemed similarly affected. He thrust her letter toward her. "I won't read it if you don't want me to."

Albeit reluctantly, she offered his back as well. "Neither will I then."

They exchanged envelopes.

"Of course, I don't mind if you read mine," Miles said. "I stand by what I wrote." He pressed his letter back into her hand and stepped back.

"You can read mine if you promise me one thing," she said. "No matter what's in the letters, we will remain friends."

"Cordial friends."

"The best of friends who respect one another."

"Agreed."

Miles took Lara's proffered letter and retreated to the far side of the room. With her heart pounding, Lara broke the seal on the envelope and unfolded the letter inside. She was obliged to blink several times before she could read the spidery words Miles had written four years ago. The note was short, and when she finished, tears were streaming from her eyes. Across the room, Miles looked up from his letter and stared at her as if she were the Nuremberg angel come to life. Moments later, she was wrapped in his warm, strong arms.

"Friends," she whispered.

"Cordial friends."

"The best of friends."
"Who love each other."
"Always."
"Always and forever."
They kissed.

The End

Keep reading for *A Gift for Fiona*...

A Gift for Fiona

With one sister married and another soon to be engaged, Fiona Robinson worries she'll be on the shelf. She pins her hopes on a handsome viscount, but his unexpected proposal to another girl hands her a stinging and demoralizing defeat. A new acquaintance awakens all her senses—until she realizes he's related to the girl who stole her beau. On the heels of her public humiliation, should Fiona instead consider marriage to a much older man whom she could never love?

Chapter 6

Challenges

June 1876 • London

Was tonight the night Fiona Robinson would get engaged to a viscount? She could almost taste triumph on the tip of her tongue. As she arrived at Bowerhaven Hall with her sister, Lara, and Lara's escort, Miles Greystoke, the very atmosphere was filled with expectation. In the imposingly large foyer, matrons had donned the latest Parisian fashions along with their finest jewels, and gentlemen wore meticulously tailored evening clothes and scrupulously polished shoes. The younger ladies were displaying their physical charms as advantageously as possible; sometimes scandalously so, since a revealing décolletage was always in demand. Cheeks bloomed with rosy hues brought about by surreptitious pinches, and eyes sparkled with hope. The delicate fragrance of expensive perfumes competed with the many floral arrangements set out here and there, and a string quartet was seated in an alcove, producing unobtrusive music to set the mood.

Fiona and Lara passed through the receiving line, followed by Miles. After they'd exchanged greetings and pleasantries with their hostess, Lady Quarterbury, the trio moved to the far end of the foyer to make way for newcomers. Miles craned his neck as he scanned the crowd.

"Are you looking for someone in particular?" Fiona asked.

"Actually, yes. I talked my good friend Rory into coming tonight, but I don't think I'll find him if I'm standing in a corner. If you'll forgive me, I'm going to leave you ladies for a short while to search."

"We'll endeavor to stay out of trouble," Lara said.

As Miles strode off, Fiona gave her sister a teasing glance. "I'm glad *you're* the one who promised to stay out of trouble because I could never manage it."

"You haven't fallen into the punchbowl even once this Season."

"Let tonight not be the first."

When Fiona glanced at her sister, she was struck by how truly stunning she looked. Her fair complexion, paired with dainty features and dazzling golden tresses, gave her the appearance of an exquisite porcelain figurine. Fiona's heart swelled with pride.

"You're so beautiful tonight, Lara, just like an angel. And your gown suits you so well. I do wish I could wear pink, but it clashes dreadfully with my hair."

"Thank you, but I've never see *you* look better," Lara said. "In fact, standing by your side, I feel washed out."

Fiona was grateful for her sister's kindness, but she couldn't have disagreed more. Although the two girls were twins, the differences between them were striking.

"Now you're being silly, but you're sweet to say that."

"I mean it, too. And as to our gowns, mint is definitely more fashionable than pink this year."

"Possibly...but I wore it because Lord Moordale mentioned green was his favorite color."

"Aha! Most certainly he won't fail to notice."

A feminine voice lanced through the air like an arrow. "If it isn't the Misses Robinson."

Iris Braithwaite, clad in an off-the-shoulder gown, joined them. She was a tall, handsome woman with dark honey blond hair and blue eyes, but her somewhat self-satisfied and superior expression detracted greatly from her beauty. Fiona's gaze was drawn to Iris's ostentatious diamond necklace sparkling under the light of the chandelier. In her opinion, such jewels would be more appropriate on a far older woman.

"Good evening, Miss Braithwaite." Fiona and Lara spoke at the same time.

"Good evening. Your gown is very plucky, Miss Fiona. Although mint *is* all the rage in Paris, I've not yet seen a woman in London sufficiently fashionable to pull it off."

Fiona bristled, but Lara's face became a polite mask. "Have you recently been to Paris, Miss Braithwaite? Your gown is lovely."

"Thank you, yes. It's a Worth original."

"Oh, my!" Fiona exclaimed. "A Worth original, did you say? I wonder that you chose to pair a couture gown with heavy diamonds. It seems to me flamboyant jewelry competes with the dress for attention, but then I'm not sufficiently fashionable to comment, I suppose."

The woman's eyes narrowed, but before she could reply, a glossy dark-haired gentleman appeared at Fiona's elbow. Although his clothes were largely the same as every other gentleman at the ball, he seemed to wear them with extra panache.

"Good evening, ladies." He sketched an exaggerated bow.

Lara and Iris murmured greetings and curtsied, but Fiona

dipped into a deep curtsy—the better to show her décolleté. As she rose, she held the man's gaze.

"Good evening, Lord Moordale."

He smiled. "Before I'm outdone by another fortunate fellow, may I have the pleasure of escorting you in to dinner later this evening, Miss Fiona?"

Iris made an angry noise deep in her throat and hastened off with a swish of her lavishly trimmed silk skirts. If Lord Moordale noticed her reaction, his expression didn't reveal it. Fiona gave the handsome viscount a dimpled smile.

"I'm happy to accept, sir, and look forward to it with anticipation."

He beamed. "Good. Excellent."

A newly arrived gentleman called out Lord Moordale's name just then, and the viscount excused himself. After he was out of earshot, Fiona permitted herself a giggle.

"I'm to dine with Lord Moordale...yet again!"

"What a coup. I'm thrilled for you!"

"Did you see how his invitation put Miss Braithwaite's nose out of joint?"

"Indeed, I did. She certainly made no secret of her feelings on the matter."

"I'm sorry, but if anyone deserves comeuppance, it's her. Every time she crosses my path these days, she thinks of something increasingly evil to say. I'm not easily intimidated, but her campaign of insults is beginning to take its toll."

"I don't wish to take pleasure in anyone's unhappiness, but I admit she *has* always been extremely uncivil to you. I've heard whispers that she'd had her hopes pinned on Lord Moordale until you came along."

"I've heard the same thing, but it's not my fault he prefers me. I only hope I'll be the one to secure him before long. Perhaps a walk in the moonlight after dinner will do the trick?"

"He seems quite smitten with you, but I'll keep my fingers crossed anyway." Lara leaned closer and lowered her voice. "Don't look now, but our neighbor, Sir Harry, has just arrived."

Fiona moaned. "Not *him* again! He's been following me around all Season like a puppy. You're lucky the old fellow decided you were a lost cause." She took her sister by the arm and propelled her down the hallway. "Let's slip inside the ballroom before he sees us."

The twins stepped into the ballroom, which resembled the inside of a jewelry box. Overhead, crystal gaslit chandeliers provided sparkling illumination flattering to every complexion. The gleaming inlaid wood floor spread out in dazzling splendor, as if in invitation to dance. Although the dancing had not yet commenced, guests were already filtering into the room and settling into the chairs pushed against the walls. Gentlemen were crossing over to ladies and scribbling their names on their dance cards, and musicians were tuning their instruments in the corner, awaiting the signal to begin from the manager of the ball.

Over Lara's shoulder, Fiona noticed Miles appear in the doorway along with a fair-haired gentleman in tow. Her jaw dropped open slightly, which caused her sister to follow her glance.

"That must be Miles's friend?" Lara murmured.

Unable to respond, Fiona could only nod. She'd met many handsome and debonair gentlemen during her time in London, but she'd never seen one quite so...*manly*. He moved with athletic grace, his gaze scanning young women like a lion on the prowl. When his eyes found hers, the resulting shock made her jump. Her pulse began to race, and as he and Miles approached, she prayed she could speak without mangling her words. The man's eyes rested on Lara momentarily, but returned almost immediately to Fiona. She was so flustered by his frank admiration, she barely listened to Miles's introduction.

"Miss Lara Robinson, and Miss Fiona Robinson, I'm pleased to introduce Rory Braithwaite," Miles said. "Rory, these are the Misses Robinson I've been telling you about. My brother William is married to their elder sister, Angelica."

"It's a pleasure to meet you, sir," Fiona managed.

"Likewise." His voice had a deep, purring quality that weakened her knees.

Lara gave the man a warm smile. "Are you any relation to Miss Iris Braithwaite, perchance?"

"Iris is my twin sister."

"Another pair of twins, then," Lara said. "We're in good company."

As if the man had cracked a whip next to her ear, Fiona snapped out of whatever momentary emotional stupor she'd fallen into. Indeed, she could see the family resemblance now, although the strong nose, square jaw and chiseled cheekbones found more favor on Rory's face than his sister's. Nevertheless, the man might as well have sprouted hair from his ears and clusters of warts from his chin for all the appeal he held for her now.

"Miss Fiona, may I reserve the first dance this evening?" he asked.

"I'm afraid it's already taken." Her tone was as cool as she could muster without being overtly rude.

"The second, then."

"That's taken, too."

Iris appeared, sliding her hand around her brother's arm in a possessive manner. "I see you've met Rory."

"Yes, indeed. Mr. Braithwaite, how have we never managed to see you in town before now?" Lara asked.

"I've spent the last year in India, working with missionaries."

"Are you pursuing the church as a profession, then?" Lara asked.

Iris laughed. "Heaven's no! Rory studied engineering at Cambridge."

"That's where he and I met," Miles said. "He was very kind to an underclassman."

"You've graduated then, Mr. Braithwaite?" Lara asked.

"Yes, and thereafter accompanied missionaries to India to help with the construction of wells," Rory said. "You can't imagine how a simple thing like clean drinking water can improve the quality of life in one village."

"What an admirable and worthy occupation," Lara said. "Although your presence in London has surely been missed, your work in India has been a blessing."

Fiona kept her mouth firmly closed. Any admiration she may have felt for Rory's charitable impulses was blunted by the toxic presence of his wretched sister, who was openly sneering at Fiona's coiffeur. Her gaze was so critical, Fiona had to stifle the impulse to reach up a hand to see if some strands had come loose.

"Rory visited me in the country after my end of term, and I convinced him to come to town," Miles said. "Good dance partners are always needed during the Season."

Rory chuckled. "I believe your exact words were 'You must do your part for England!'"

Everyone laughed except for Fiona, and Iris took the opportunity to pounce.

"Are you feeling quite well, Miss Fiona? I do believe your pallor is somewhat sickly."

Rory's eyebrows drew together, and he gave his sister a

sharp glance. "You're mistaken, Iris. Miss Fiona looks in perfect health."

Despite the man's unsolicited defense, Fiona's dander rose at the woman's barb.

"I've never felt better, Miss Braithwaite."

"I'm so relieved. You must take every opportunity to secure a husband as soon as possible. With one sister wed and Miss Lara soon to be engaged, you'll be the last Robinson girl on the shelf. People might think there was something amiss." Iris snickered. "Too bad there aren't any spare Greystokes for you to marry."

Although Fiona tried to keep her temper under control, anger shot down her spine.

"Thank you for your concern, Miss Braithwaite. I'm not quite as desperate as you might imagine, but I do intend to enjoy myself thoroughly tonight. In fact, I've just promised the first two dances to your brother." She curtsied. "If you'll excuse me."

Fiona walked toward the open doors of the nearest balcony in as stately a manner as she could manage, considering she was trembling with fury. Furthermore, she was annoyed with her response just now. Why couldn't she have thought of some other way to irritate Iris than by sacrificing her first two dances to Rory?

As Fiona left, Iris's lips thinned and her eyes flashed. "If you've asked Miss Fiona to dance, I'm afraid you're off to an inauspicious beginning this evening, brother." She flounced off.

Puzzled, Rory gave Miles and Lara a quizzical glance. "I must have missed something?"

Lara sighed. "There's ill will between my sister and yours, I'm afraid." She cast a worried glance toward the balcony. "I should go talk to Fiona."

She hastened away, leaving Miles and Rory perplexed.

"I see my sister is in rare form this evening," Rory said. "I'm awfully sorry to hear she's failed to endear herself to Miss Fiona, although I can't say I'm surprised."

"I'll be happy to take your two dances with Fiona if you like."

Rory chuckled. "I wouldn't dream of it."

"Why would you want to follow through? It's obvious to me that Fiona's dislike for Miss Braithwaite extends to you as well."

"I won't back away from a challenge. In fact, I look forward to changing Miss Fiona's opinion of me."

"She's not the sort of girl to be easily persuaded. You'll never win her over."

"We'll see about that."

Miles gave him a pointed look. "See here, Rory. I intend to marry Lara, which makes her sister's welfare my concern. Despite my regard for you, I won't have you trifling with Fiona's affections just to prove a point."

Rory waved off his concerns. "No need for fisticuffs! As it happens, she intrigues me to no end. I've never met a girl with such fire in her eyes before, and despite my shrew of a sister, I intend to know Miss Fiona better." He held out his hand. "You have my word as a gentleman, I'll do her no harm."

Although he shook Rory's hand, Miles had one eyebrow raised. "See that you don't. Now, we have a few minutes before the dancing begins. What would you say to a drink?"

"Not punch." Rory shuddered. "Too sticky sweet for my taste."

"No, I think we can find ourselves something stronger."

"Excellent. I could use a bracing beverage before I throw myself into the fray tonight. In gatherings such as these, there are always skirmishes and conflicts to navigate—as we've just had proof."

Miles laughed. "The smoking room down the hall is equipped with a full bar. I suggest we avail ourselves of it."

* * *

In the cool of the night air, Fiona gripped the stone balustrade and tried to control her emotions. Moments later, Lara joined her.

"Are you all right?"

"I will be, eventually." Fiona made a sound of exasperation. "I shouldn't let that woman get under my skin, but she has a talent for it! Because of her, I hate this dress now and I feel like everyone's laughing at me behind my back. And she's not wrong about my being the last Robinson sister on the shelf. As soon as you're engaged, everyone will assume I'm a hopeless case.

"Oh, Fiona, your dress is splendid, and you've been receiving only the most admiring glances. Also, consider that this is only our first Season! Angelica didn't get engaged until her third, and the only reason Miles and I will become engaged soon is because we've known each other for so long."

"No thanks to the trouble I caused between you."

"That's all forgotten now."

Fiona gave her twin a crooked smile. "You and Miles are decent to have forgiven me for my interference, but I'm having a difficult time forgiving myself. To be perfectly honest, I recognize my bad behavior in Miss Braithwaite. I suspect we're both cut from the same cloth."

"Ridiculous!"

"You know it's true. I *am* trying to be a better person, truly. But deep down, I'm not sure I deserve to be happy."

"Of course you do. Never think otherwise."

Fiona tried to shake off her doldrums, realizing if she continued to feel sorry for herself she'd burst into tears and spoil the entire evening for her sister. She forced a smile to her lips.

"You're right. I've every reason to be of good cheer. When Lord Moordale escorts me in to dinner, everyone will be impressed!" She embraced Lara. "Thank you for being so wonderful. I suppose we should return to the ballroom, or our dance cards will remain empty."

Lara giggled. "Not *yours*. You've already promised the first two dances to Mr. Braithwaite."

"Don't remind me!"

Although he didn't wish to admit it to Miles, Rory was grateful for the stiff drink that warmed his blood and took the edge off his nerves. Despite his earlier bravado, it had been a long time since Rory had mixed with society, and he felt out of practice. His sojourn to India had served many purposes, not the least of which was to avoid the London Season. He'd allowed Miles to coax him to town only out of his deep regard for the man. Nevertheless, Rory had been—and still was—dubious about the prospect of finding a bride. He'd already attended a few dull dinners and tedious soirées, but he hadn't met a woman who'd excited his imagination. When he saw Fiona tonight, however, he'd felt a magnetic attraction for her. From her expression, he thought she might have felt the same...until she realized his relationship to Iris and turned cold. He was used to solving problematic engineering predicaments, but women were far more complicated. Could he reignite the connection between him and Fiona, despite her animosity toward his sister? Whatever the cost, he suspected she was worth it.

Chapter 7

Intermission

Rory and Miles returned to the ballroom just as the dancing was about to begin. Miles chuckled and gave him an irrepressible grin.

"Good luck with Fiona. You're going to need it."

"You're not boosting my confidence, Miles."

"I confess, I think you should be more realistic. Although I have the utmost respect for my future sister-in-law, I'll admit Fiona can be tempestuous."

"Nothing you say will dissuade me."

"Fine. After you finish licking your wounds from the injuries you're bound to suffer, there are plenty of other ladies here who will be happy to boost your confidence. I suggest you choose one of them."

"I'll take that under advisement."

They parted company to claim their respective partners for the first dance. In a sea of rather ordinary girls, Fiona's mass of dark auburn hair made her easy to spot. In addition, the soothing light green color of her gown was distinctive against the yards of safe pink or bland white satin favored by the other debutantes. She was chatting with friends when he approached, and he paused to admire her profile. Fiona was not a classic beauty by any stretch of the imagination, but he liked her appearance very much indeed. Was it her mischievous spark that drew him, or the temperamental way she tossed her head? Even her figure stood out, especially compared to the straight-laced and underfed girls moving about the room like ethereal butterflies. No, Fiona was definitely earthy, and he found her all the more intriguing for it.

As if he'd called her by name, Fiona suddenly turned her head toward him. She flinched when she met his gaze...as did he, if truth be told. To cover the sudden increase in his pulse, he gave her a cocky smile. Instinctively, he knew the way to appeal to this untamed spirit was to eschew careful politeness for a bold and decisive manner. He covered the last few yards between them with long strides, and presented her with his arm.

"The orchestra is about to play. Shall we take our place on the floor?"

"Thank you, yes."

The surrounding females were either gaping at him or smiling in a simpering fashion he found unattractive. By contrast, Fiona met his gaze with a direct one of her own, placing her hand so lightly on his sleeve, it barely touched the fabric.

He slid her a reproachful glance. "I don't bite."

"I do. If I were you, I'd keep my distance."

"And if I don't wish to?"

"Be prepared to suffer the consequences."

"You're quite severe toward a complete stranger."

"You're not a complete stranger, Mr. Braithwaite. I can't look at you without seeing your sister."

"Iris and I may be twins, but I'm nothing like her."

"You have similar features, your hair is the same color, and even your eyes are the same shade of blue."

"I'm flattered you noticed."

A pink flush crept across her cheekbones, and she averted her gaze.

"I'm determined to make you like me," he said.

She met his gaze. "You're wasting your time."

"Perhaps, but it's my time to waste."

As Rory led her toward the dance floor, a tall, older man with crisp gray hair and a neatly trimmed beard approached.

"There you are, Miss Fiona! I hope you will spare me a dance or two?"

"Good evening, Sir Harry. Allow me to introduce Mr. Rory Braithwaite. Mr. Braithwaite, this is my neighbor from Blythe Village, Sir Harry Wren."

Although the fellow returned his bow, Rory was taken aback—and slightly amused—to see a hard glint in the gentleman's eye. If he was not greatly mistaken, Sir Harry was intent on courting Miss Fiona and didn't relish competition for her hand. Talk about impossible dreams! Rory's suspicions were confirmed when Sir Harry signed Fiona's dance card not once, but three times, the maximum number etiquette would permit.

She curtsied. "You do me great honor, sir."

"Not at all." Sir Harry paused. "May I escort you into dinner this evening?"

Blazes! Rory could have kicked himself for not asking Miss Fiona first. He really was out of practice.

"Thank you, but Lord Moordale has already asked me," she replied.

Lord Moordale? Rory fought to keep his countenance. Iris had written a letter about a month ago, mentioning the viscount as one of her suitors. If he'd since transferred his affections to Fiona, it was no wonder Iris disliked her so much!

A small tic pulled at the side of Sir Harry's mouth. "Ah. I look forward to dancing with you, at least." He flashed Rory a terse smile, bowed, and disappeared into the crowd.

"I believe you have an ardent admirer, Miss Fiona," Rory murmured.

She sighed. "Indeed."

Although she seemed to take little pleasure in the attentions of Sir Harry, the pride in her voice when she'd mentioned Lord Moordale had been obvious. Why did women find that preening, ridiculous man attractive? His features were regular, admittedly, but rumors said his morals were not. Yes, he was a viscount, but Rory had also heard the Moordale estate was in rapid decline. Any woman who agreed to marry him had best have an enormous income and a limitless tolerance for gambling and his other vices.

The music began, and Rory devoted himself to partnering Fiona in a showy style that made her laugh. If nothing else, at least he was capable of amusing her. She was a graceful and skilled dancer, but he truly wouldn't have cared if she'd lumbered to and fro like a drunken sailor as long as she continued to smile at him.

At the end of their second dance, Rory bowed. "Do you like me a little better now, Miss Fiona?"

She glanced at him through her lashes. "Perhaps a little, but it's a hopeless case."

His cocksure attitude slipped. "I'm sorry to hear that."

A flicker of emotion crossed her face. "Forgive me for being so blunt about my feelings, but I wish to be forthright with you."

"Fair enough. Thank you for your honesty."

Somewhat crestfallen, he relinquished Fiona to her next partner and went in search of Iris. He found her on the side-lines, and asked her to dance...the better to talk in private. As they waltzed together, Rory spoke his mind.

"You've been uncivil to Miss Fiona, and I won't have it."

"Why do you care? She's nothing to you."

"Not at present, but I'd like to pursue her."

"Ha! Lord Moordale has shown marked interest in the girl. Compared to a viscount, you haven't a prayer of success."

"I'm not impressed. The man has a propensity to be fickle, evidently. Didn't you expect him to propose to you?"

Iris's lips pressed together in annoyance. "He *would* have... until Miss Fiona lured him away."

"I can assure you, no man can be lured where he doesn't wish to go. What do you see in a preening dandy like Moordale, anyway?"

"Keep your judgment to yourself, brother. I'm nearly twenty-four, and can't afford to be terribly choosy. Lord Moordale's family is respectable and he possesses an older title. Besides which, he's handsome and I like him a great deal."

"Be that as it may, you're to leave Miss Fiona alone. If I hear about you taunting her even once more, I'll be forced to tell Father about it."

"You wouldn't!"

"I never make threats, Iris, only promises."

They finished the dance in cold silence, after which Rory found himself in need of another stiff beverage. He left the ball-room and made his way back to the smoking room. Several gentlemen had already taken up residence inside, either relaxing with a drink, or playing pool at the billiards table. Rory noticed Lord Moordale and Sir Harry conducting a seemingly terse conversation with one another at the far end of the bar.

Their body language didn't invite company, so he ordered a double scotch from the bartender and brought his drink with him to the patio in the back of the house. As he leaned against the railing and gazed out at the garden, he wondered how to make his next move with Fiona. If the opportunity presented itself, he might mention he'd taken Iris in hand. Perhaps if she felt his sister had dropped her hostility, she might feel more kindly toward him. In the meantime, after he'd finished his drink, he'd return to the ballroom and dance with any and all ladies who would have him—the better to distract him from the one lady who wouldn't.

* * *

During a break in the dancing, Fiona and Lara hastened to the ladies' sitting room to check their coiffeurs and gowns.

"How did your dances go with Mr. Braithwaite?" Lara asked.

Fiona shrugged. "I believe I managed to frighten him off."

"All the ladies are talking about how good-looking he is. He's caused quite a stir."

"I don't care if he just climbed down off Mount Olympus, he's Miss Braithwaite's brother. I've no interest in him whatsoever."

"Since you were stuck dumb at his appearance, I could have sworn otherwise."

"You're mistaken! I was merely shocked with his resemblance to his sister, that's all."

"Miles told me just now how much he respects Mr. Braithwaite. He's says they're great friends."

"Really?" Fiona was dismayed. "I wish I'd known as much before we danced!"

"Would it have changed your opinion of him?"

"No, but I mightn't have been so impertinent. He'll most certainly give a bad report of me to Miles, I'm afraid." She sighed. "There I go again, giving offense when it isn't strictly necessary. Perhaps I should apologize."

Iris entered the sitting room and swept past Lara and Fiona without saying a word. The sisters exchanged a puzzled glance as they left.

"I was expecting her to say something nasty to me," Fiona murmured as they returned to the ballroom. "I wonder how she managed to resist?"

"I'm surprised she didn't, either," Lara said. "I noticed her dancing with her brother earlier, and she looked quite cross. I wonder if he took her to task for her insulting behavior?"

Lady Quarterbury sailed over, a vision of mature beauty in a gown of crimson satin. Her mink-colored hair was touched by only a hint of gray, and her defined eyebrows framed sparkling eyes. "Why aren't you two girls dancing? I don't know what's wrong with men these days!"

"Well...there's no music at present," Lara said.

"The musicians have taken a short recess," Fiona added.

"A *jeune homme* in love needs no *musique* to woo the woman of his dreams!" The countess giggled and set off down the hall toward a trio of debutantes. "Ladies, why aren't you dancing?"

Lara and Fiona exchanged an amused glance.

"Too much champagne?" Lara wondered.

"I can't rule it out, but Lady Quarterbury has always been a little flighty."

"Why does she persist in sprinkling French into her speech?"

"Perhaps the countess thinks it gives her a sophisticated air." Fiona lowered her voice. "Before she married her late husband, Lady Quarterbury was a governess, they say."

"I heard she was a shop girl." Lara shrugged. "I feel a little sorry for her, actually. She has no children of her own, and I daresay she's lonely."

"You're probably right. She was widowed quite young when her husband was killed on an African safari, and before that, he was always traveling. I don't think it was a love match."

"How sad! I can't imagine being married to a man who was never at home."

Just as the musicians filed back into the ballroom, Sir Harry approached. "Good evening, Miss Lara. I've come to claim a dance with your sister."

Lara curtsied. "Good evening, Sir Harry. I leave her in your capable hands."

Fiona took the older man's arm and allowed him to lead her onto the floor. While they danced, she tried to make small talk.

"I believe gentlemen outnumber the ladies this Season," she said.

"Yes, and the competition amongst us is fierce. Oh, to be young and dashing again."

Politeness compelled her to dissent. "Perhaps you're not as youthful as some, Sir Harry, but you cut quite a swath nevertheless."

He pulled her in a little closer. "You flatter me."

The sudden heat in his expression shocked Fiona—and embarrassed her. Sir Harry was older than her father, and a widower. She'd been aware of his interest in remarrying for some time, but she'd assumed it was for companionship only. Obviously, she was quite wrong. Although she smiled at him, she was relieved when their dance ended and she was able to move on to her next partner.

Only a few more dances remained before the intermission for dinner, and she could hardly wait. If she managed to secure Lord Moordale tonight, all her problems would be solved. Sir

Harry's unwelcome passion would be extinguished, she'd triumph over the despicable Miss Braithwaite, *and* the highest levels of society would be forced to welcome her into their hallowed ranks. Most importantly, nobody would laugh at her for being the last Robinson sister on the shelf. A shaft of excitement traveled through her body at the prospect of her imminent engagement. It was entirely possible tonight could be the best night of her life.

After Rory returned to the ballroom, he made a special point to dance only with those ladies, young and old, who wouldn't otherwise be dancing. The look of pleasure on their faces when he asked them to dance was extremely satisfying. By that measure, he had a grand time—despite the fact Fiona ignored him whenever they happened to pass one another on the dance floor. His sister ignored him, too, but her coolness was to be expected. Whenever they'd quarreled as children, she'd refuse to speak with him for days afterward.

Nevertheless, Rory realized it was his duty to escort his sister into dinner if she hadn't received another invitation. Although he looked for Iris during the last set of dances before the intermission, she was nowhere to be found. Had she gone off somewhere to pout? He decided to wait for her near the double doors to the banquet room. If she didn't appear, he'd be obliged to enlist the servants to search the premises.

To his surprise, Fiona was also waiting by the doors when he arrived. She looked disconcerted at his arrival, and he sought to put her mind at ease.

"Hello. Please let me know if Iris says anything untoward to you from now on. I've asked her to leave off, in no uncertain terms."

"Thank you." She paused. "I-I believe I was rude to you earlier, and I apologize."

"Considering what you've endured at the hands of my sister, I completely understand. Speaking of Iris, have you happened to see her pass this way?"

"No, I haven't."

Guests were flowing from the ballroom and into the banquet hall in earnest by then, but still there was no sign of Iris. Rory began to feel the awkward silence between him and Fiona, and he ventured to make conversation.

"Er...Miles tells me you're an excellent artist."

"He flatters me, but I do enjoy it. Have you an interest in art?"

"I like to sketch, actually. I spent a great deal of time in India, doing just that." He chuckled. "I never got close enough to a rhinoceros to draw it—lest the beast skewer me—but I have many drawings of elephants and monkeys."

Her eyebrows lifted. "I'm quite envious! I'm afraid my drawings of wildlife are limited to ordinary creatures, such as butterflies, birds, and horses."

He leaned closer to whisper, "I confess, society often reminds me of a monkey colony."

Fiona's spirited laugh was music to his ears.

"What a dreadful thing to say, Mr. Braithwaite! I believe you may be as wicked as I am!"

"Wicked is the last word I'd use to describe you."

Miles and Lara appeared just then, and Rory raised his hand in greeting. Miles's puzzled gaze flickered from him to Fiona and back again.

Rory gave him a wry grin and a slight shake of his head. "I'm waiting for Iris."

Understanding dawned. "Oh."

"And I'm waiting for Lord Moordale," Fiona said. "Lara,

would you save us two seats at your table? He should be along directly."

"Yes, of course," Lara said. "Gladly."

"How about you, Rory? Will you and your sister be dining with us?" Miles asked.

Fiona visibly stiffened at the suggestion, and Rory picked up on the hint.

"As much as I would enjoy that, I expect Iris has made arrangements for us to dine with her friends."

"All right." Miles nodded. "See you later, then."

He and Lara disappeared into the banquet room, and Rory was left alone with Fiona once more. She seemed to have relaxed her guard somewhat, and was actually smiling again.

"I've never been to India," she said.

"I've never been to Blythe Village, so we're even."

She laughed. "What's it like in India?"

"Hot. What's it like in Blythe Village?"

"It's a small, quaint little town..."

Her voice trailed off and her eyes widened. Rory followed her glance and was shocked to discover Lord Moordale and Iris approaching, arm in arm. His sister's features had been transformed from sulky to beatific, but Moordale's expression seemed strained.

"Oh, Rory, you'll never guess what's transpired!" Iris gushed. "Lord Moordale has just asked me to marry him, and I've accepted!"

Fiona gasped, and the bloom left her cheeks. Iris's announcement caused a ripple of excitement to spread through the guests passing by, and a few of them cast amused glances Fiona's way. As Lord Moordale quickly ushered Iris into the banquet room, Rory gave Fiona a concerned look. Before he could speak, however, Sir Harry brushed past.

"My dear, you look as if you've taken a turn. Would you like to sit down?"

"Yes. Thank you, Sir Harry."

Although Rory was stunned at his sister's unexpected engagement, his main concern was for Fiona. He followed Sir Harry as he led her toward the entryway down the hall. When she sank onto a chaise, the older man sat next to her—too close for propriety, in Rory's opinion. In addition, he kept Fiona's hand in his, as if she would run off if he didn't keep her on a tether.

Sir Harry all but glared at him. "Mr. Braithwaite, why don't you fetch Miss Lara?"

Fiona shook her head. "No. I don't wish to disturb my sister, but I've developed a headache and I'd like to leave."

"I'll see you home," Rory said. "I've no reason to stay."

Her hazel eyes lanced him, as sharp as pins, but she directed her remark to the gentleman at her side. "Will *you* summon my carriage, Sir Harry?"

"I'll do better than that. I'll escort you home myself." Sir Harry rose to his feet. "Wait here and I'll return directly."

As he strode off, Fiona stared off into space with a stony expression. Rory knew nothing he could say would help the situation, but he felt compelled to try.

"Miss Fiona, please believe me when I tell you I'm aghast at what has happened. I can't explain what may have prompted Lord Moordale's sudden declaration to Iris."

She rose. "You may render me two services, Mr. Braithwaite."

"Anything."

"After I depart, please inform Lara that Sir Harry has seen me home. I wish her to stay and enjoy herself at the ball."

"Yes, of course. And how else may I be of service?"

"Never, *ever* speak to me again."

Rory took a half-step back, almost as if she'd struck him. Although he wished to remonstrate with her, as a gentleman he was obliged to abide by her wishes. Moments later, Sir Harry returned with Fiona's cloak and draped it over her shoulders. Rory was forced to watch as the man escorted Fiona from the house. Only after Sir Harry and Fiona disappeared through the front door did Rory realize his fists were clenched at his side.

Chapter 8

Very Truly Yours

Fiona couldn't remember ever having been so dispirited. She rode in Sir Harry's carriage dry-eyed, but she knew the tears wouldn't be long in coming once she returned to the Greystoke townhouse. Sir Harry rode on the facing seat in comforting silence, making no attempt to engage her in conversation. Although she was too numb to feel much of anything, she realized she owed the man a great debt. He'd been there right after she heard about Lord Moordale's engagement, and he'd managed everything so she could leave the Quarterbury ball without delay.

When the carriage finally came to a stop, Sir Harry climbed out and helped her step down to the pavement personally.

"I'm very grateful to you, Sir Harry," she said. "I'm not sure what I would have done without you tonight."

"I was glad to be of some small service, Miss Fiona."

When she stood on her tiptoes to kiss his cheek, his beard brushed up against her face like fuzzy caterpillars. He gave her a kindly smile afterward, and a wink.

"At the moment, it may seem as if the world has stopped

turning, but take heart. You're worth so much more than to be discarded by a ridiculous popinjay like Moordale. Only a fool wouldn't recognize you're a brilliant jewel to be treasured."

Her throat swelled with emotion. "Thank you for that."

"In you go, my dear. I'll call on you tomorrow to see how you're getting along."

One of the maids let Fiona inside the house. Due to her delicate condition, Angelica had already turned in for the night, but William came out from his study to greet her.

"I didn't expect you for hours yet. Where are Miles and Lara?"

Although Fiona had a great deal of affection for her brother-in-law, she simply couldn't put into words what had occurred. She forced herself to smile.

"They're still at the ball. I developed a headache, so Sir Harry kindly brought me home."

William's eyebrows drew together. "Shall I summon a physician?"

"Please don't concern yourself. I'll use a headache powder and then go straight to bed. Good night."

In her bedchamber, Fiona let Moira undress her and thereafter she slipped under the covers. As soon as the light was doused and she was alone, the tears began to flow. Her heart was a throbbing wound which no amount of salve could comfort. She found Lord Moordale's proposal to Miss Braithwaite to be absolutely galling, and she burned with fury in between crying jags. Why had he acted in such a caddish fashion and rejected her in public? Furthermore, she'd contributed to her own downfall by prattling to everyone all night long about his invitation to dine.

Lara came home in the wee hours of the morning, and opened her door, but Fiona pretended to be asleep. Eventually, the pretense became reality and she drifted into a troubled dream of slipping on a patch of ice in front of Buckingham Palace. As she lay flat on her back, she was horrified to discover she was stark naked and the object of mocking scorn to all who passed. Children laughed as they pelted her with rotten vegetables and horse muck, and Fiona finally woke, trembling and crying once more.

As dawn broke, she stared at the murky light creeping around the edges of the drapery and tried to decide what to do. If the point of the Season was to find a husband, she'd utterly failed. Until the memory of Lord Moordale's rejection faded, it was unlikely any eligible men would attempt to court her. Lara was all but officially engaged, and when she made it official, Fiona would be considered on the shelf. She was doomed.

When her maid came in to dress her, Fiona claimed illness, and not even Lara could persuade her to come downstairs for breakfast. When Angelica came to speak with her, however, Fiona finally sat up out of guilt. Her elder sister had dark circles under her eyes, and was shuffling around with a handkerchief pressed against her lips from pregnancy-induced nausea.

"You should keep to your bed, Angelica! Truly, you look dreadful."

"I can't rest while you're suffering." Her sister lowered herself into a chair. "Lara told me what happened with Lord Moordale last night. I could scarcely believe my ears."

Fiona hung her head. "I've brought it on myself for my past wickedness."

"Don't be silly."

"You know it's true. I was always envious of Lara's looks and sweetness when we were children."

"Envy is indeed a failing, but you've made great strides to overcome it. And consider that your beauty is simply different than Lara's, no better and no worse. The right man will love your looks exactly as they are, above any other woman."

"But envy isn't my only sin, Angelica. I was jealous of Lara's relationship with Miles and interfered abominably, even as recently as last Christmas. Such ugliness never goes unanswered in the grand scheme of things."

"You've apologized for your interference and improved since then."

"I *have* changed, I think. Truly, I'd never do anything to hurt Lara again...or Miles either, for that matter."

"Of course you wouldn't. Miles and Lara have forgiven you, but I don't think you've forgiven yourself. If you continue to hold on to your guilt, you'll never move forward."

Fiona nodded. "I can hear the wisdom in what you say, but I still want to go home."

"Why? You'll just feel even sorrier for yourself, knowing you're missing all the fun here in town."

"I don't know if I can hold my head up! Everyone's laughing at me!"

"Surely not everybody." Angelica's smile was teasing. "I expect there are some gentlemen who are relieved Lord Moordale will no longer be a rival for your affections."

Fiona plucked at the bedcover. "I can't think who...unless you mean Sir Harry."

"Perish the thought! No, you won't know for sure until you get up and throw yourself 'once more unto the breach,' as the Bard would say."

Angelica was so adamant, Fiona allowed herself to be persuaded. "I'll stay in town a little while longer, but only because I don't want to be seen as a coward."

"That's the spirit. I know it seems hopeless at the moment, but these things often work out for the best." Angelica paused. "I've met Lord Moordale, and I confess I wouldn't have been happy to call him my brother-in-law. His manners are charming enough, but he comes off as quite pleased with himself."

Fiona was astonished. "Why didn't you say so before now?"

"You were delighted with his attentions, and I didn't want to spoil it for you. To be perfectly honest, I feel somewhat sorry for Miss Braithwaite. I hope she realizes her mistake before it's too late."

Something like a smile found its way onto Fiona's lips, and a sense of relief began to crack open the weight on her chest.

"I've always trusted your judgment, Angelica. Perhaps you're right."

"At the risk of sounding pompous, I'm most certainly right about Lord Moordale. Tell me, were you really in love with him?"

"Not especially. I mean, I liked him well enough, but I thought my feelings were unimportant compared to other considerations. He's a viscount, after all, and marriage to him would have been impressive."

"Ah. My advice is to listen to your heart next time and put those other considerations aside."

Fiona rose and gave her sister a kiss on the forehead. "Thank you, I shall. Now let me don my wrapper and I'll help you back to your room."

* * *

Rory could feel his sister's gaze upon him as they ate breakfast with their father, Peyton Braithwaite. Due to his throbbing hangover, Rory had no wish to converse with anyone, much less nibble on food.

Peyton finally seemed to take notice of his condition. "You're awfully quiet this morning, Rory."

"Yes, he's as silent as a monk and twice as jolly," Iris said. "In fact, he disappeared after dinner last night and I didn't see him until it was time to leave the ball."

"I was drinking in the bar during the second half of the ball and socializing with the other gentlemen."

Peyton chuckled. "Best thing to do at a ball."

Iris's eyes flashed. "Not *once* have I heard Rory say he's happy about my engagement."

Rory bit back a retort he knew would hurt his sister's feelings and make him look boorish in the bargain. Instead, he murmured, "You have my best wishes."

"That's all I'm to expect after my engagement to a viscount?"

"Leave it alone, Iris," Peyton said. "As far as I'm concerned, you're not engaged until Moordale asks my permission to marry you."

"He's to come around today. This afternoon, in fact."

Iris was so smug, Rory couldn't let it pass. "Speaking of which, how did you manage to extract his proposal?"

"I didn't *extract* anything! Iggy asked to speak to me in private and thereafter confessed his love."

"Iggy?" The word tasted foul in Rory's mouth.

"His given name is Ignacio Wallace Montague, the Viscount of Moordale." She giggled. "I'm to be Lady Moordale. Isn't that wonderful?"

Rory's response was as flat as possible. "I can scarcely contain my enthusiasm."

His father gave him a warning glance. "Rory."

Iris tossed her head. "Never mind, Papa. Rory's just in a foul temper because the object of his affection is the laughingstock of London."

Peyton peered at him, quizzically. "What's Iris talking about?"

Rory was so annoyed at his sister, he barely heard his father's question.

"We've vastly different notions of what constitutes a laughingstock," Rory retorted. "And she's not the object of my affection any longer. I rather think she wishes I would drop dead."

Iris's eyebrows rose. "Oh, her dislike for me has extended to you, has it? A thousand pardons."

"Insincerity oozes from your every pore."

"Wait just a moment." Peyton held up his hands. "I insist on knowing of whom you're speaking?"

Rory and Iris answered at the same time. "Miss Fiona Robinson."

The elder Mr. Braithwaite thought a moment. "Isn't she William Greystoke's sister-in-law? One of a pair of twins, as I recall."

"The very same, but Miss Lara is the pretty one," Iris said.

Rory bristled. "You wouldn't know a true beauty if the queen pointed her out." He turned to Peyton. "If you wish to hear the sordid details, sir, Lord Moordale was courting Miss Fiona before his sudden and ill-timed proposal to Iris last night."

"No, Iggy was courting *me* before he was courting *her*," Iris replied. "If you really like Miss Fiona, I've done you a favor, actually. She's now free of any entanglements."

"Yes, now that you've taken Moordale off Miss Fiona's hands, the lady detests all the Braithwaites rather thoroughly. You have my eternal gratitude, Iris, but please keep any future benefaction to yourself."

"Enough bickering!" Peyton exclaimed. "Iris, your conceited manner this morning is intolerable, I must say."

"Thank you, Father," Rory said. "I couldn't agree more."

"And as for you, Rory, however much you may dislike Lord Moordale, if he's to marry your sister, you must welcome him to the family. I suggest you get to know him better."

"Thank you for that, Papa," Iris said. "It's the least he can do."

Rory's eyes narrowed. Despite what his sister might believe, he was convinced the man's change of heart wasn't as it seemed. He'd spent the latter part of the evening on a fact-gathering mission, and Moordale's intentions hadn't passed muster.

"Might I have a word with you after breakfast, Father? There are some things we must discuss."

Once Angelica was settled comfortably in her bedchamber, Fiona dressed quickly and went downstairs. As she gazed into the mirror, her blotchy, wan reflection made her groan, but there was little she could do to improve her appearance at present.

When she entered the dining room at long last, the conversation came to a halt. The guilty way Lara's eyes dropped to her plate told Fiona she'd been the topic of discourse.

"I'm sorry I'm late," she said. "I had a difficult night."

She went to the sideboard buffet to fill her plate with stewed figs, eggs, bacon, toast, and sliced tomatoes. Even though her back was turned, she suspected her family was exchanging glances with one another.

Fiona sighed. "It's all right; I know full well how dreadful I look." She sat down at the table. "William, I assume you've heard about Lord Moordale's engagement from Lara and Miles?"

"Yes, and I consider Moordale's actions to be ungentlemanly in the extreme."

She gave William an apologetic smile. "I'm sorry I didn't tell you myself when I came in last night, but I was too dispirited." A pause. "Angelica just informed me that she never liked him."

From the uncomfortable expressions around the table, Fiona concluded everyone agreed with her elder sister.

"If that's the general sentiment toward the man, I suppose I'm better off."

"I didn't dislike him...necessarily," Lara said. "He just didn't seem to be a man of substance."

"All of us want to see you happy, Fiona," William said.

"Thank you. After last night I *was* considering going home, but Angelica convinced me otherwise."

"Good for her." Miles nodded. "Retreat is not the solution to your troubles."

"I don't think you should let one disappointment ruin your Season," Lara said.

"I agree," William said. "In fact, I'm relieved Moordale's engaged to someone else. It's not generally known, but he's fallen on hard times financially and I've heard he's a spendthrift."

Fiona stared at him, wide-eyed. "I'd no idea! Perhaps I should have asked your opinion before now."

"Rory has my condolences," Miles said. "It sounds as if Moordale will be an unfortunate addition to the family. I can't imagine anything more unpleasant than disliking an in-law."

"Speaking of Mr. Braithwaite, when he told us what had happened last night, he was exceedingly crestfallen," Lara said.

"I agree, now that you mention it," Miles said. "His dark mood was very out of character."

William shrugged. "Perhaps he disapproves of Moordale as much as we do and doesn't wish to see the man wed to his sister?"

Miles shook his head. "It was more than that. No, there's something else bothering him." He shrugged. "I'll get it out of him, sooner or later."

Consumed with guilt, Fiona could only pick at her food.

Had she been responsible for Rory's bad mood? She'd spoken to him very harshly, and the memory of his wounded expression haunted her. Although she'd been sent reeling by Lord Moordale's defection, she'd had no right to take it out on Rory. In addition, he'd protected her in a gentlemanly fashion by not mentioning her tongue-lashing to Miles. Despite what she'd said to Angelica, clearly she hadn't reformed enough. She was still a wicked person and would have to find a way to apologize to Rory without anyone else finding out how she'd behaved.

"Is something troubling you, Fiona? You're frowning," Lara said.

"No, I..." She trailed off and cast about for another subject. "I was just feeling rather regretful for any uncomplimentary remarks I've made in the past regarding Sir Harry. He was terribly kind to me last night."

"I wish I'd been there to help, but I'm glad he took care of you at least," Lara said. "He's been a good neighbor in more ways than one."

"Sir Harry's fortunes have risen. Apparently he's made several astute business investments which have paid off handsomely." William chuckled. "Perhaps Miss Braithwaite should have solicited *his* proposal instead."

* * *

Shortly after breakfast was over, Fiona went to the drawing room and sat down to write the most difficult letter she'd ever managed. Her fingers were trembling slightly as she wrote, so her penmanship wasn't up to snuff. Nevertheless, she didn't think Rory's forgiveness or lack thereof would hinge on the beauty of her hand. Instead, she tried to concentrate on sincerity and lack of guile. She'd spoken in a rude, ill-mannered, and altogether intemperate way to him, and must beg his pardon. Although she'd no right to expect anything, she had to try.

Dear Mr. Braithwaite,

I write to you this morning heartily ashamed about the harsh manner in which I addressed you last night. You aren't to blame for my misfortunes, nor did you contribute to them in any way. Indeed, at no time did you behave in anything other than a most gentlemanly fashion, and better than I deserve. I freely admit I've fallen short of the mark, and it grieves me deeply to think I've caused you any pain. I owe you my most sincere apology, Mr. Braithwaite. I take back what I said, but I'll understand if you can't excuse me. I'm having difficulty forgiving myself, if truth be told. Should your offer of friendship still stand, please tell me so. Absent any affirmative action on your part, I'll assume you've no wish to continue our acquaintance. I can assure you, however, I'll hold you blameless either way.

Very Truly Yours,

Fiona Robinson

Miles's address book was at hand, so Fiona looked up the Braithwaite's London address, copied it onto an envelope and gave the letter to a footman to deliver. Although she prayed her sentiments would find a receptive audience, she was resigned to estrangement. Feeling guilty and wretched, she went into the garden to get some fresh air. As she contemplated the beautiful rose bushes, she marveled at how soft blooms and sharp thorns could grow on the same plant. Of course, the same juxtaposition could be found amongst the Robinson sisters. Angelica and Lara were like lovely, perfect rose petals, and she was a thorn. Would she ever learn to curb her temper, or was she destined to prick everyone who tried to get close?

* * *

Moordale stared at his attorney, Mr. Whitehead, uncomprehending. What he'd just been told could not be true. It had to be some sort of hideous nightmare. As he sat in the man's staid, book-lined office, he felt as if he were in the eye of a tornado.

"What if I partitioned off part of the property? Surely I can sell enough outlying parcels to settle the tax bill."

"The problem is one of time. If you don't settle the bill within thirty days, the authorities intend to seize the property in its entirely and auction it to the highest bidder."

"Can I lease out Bramble Hall? It's a beautiful house with a rich history. There must be families who long to live in the country."

"I've already made inquiries on your behalf, and have had no interest. If you'd offered it for lease when the property was in its prime, you might have had better success. As it is, the house has fallen into disrepair and the gardens are a shambles." The attorney gave him a look of sympathy. "This isn't entirely your fault, Lord Moordale. Your father made poor investments and left you Bramble Hall without enough principal to maintain it. There's no shame in selling the property and getting on with your life."

Moordale gritted his teeth to stave off his emotions. "You're wrong, Mr. Whitehead. There's quite a bit of shame in being the first Viscount of Moordale to preside over the loss of the family estate. I'm a failure."

"Take heart, lad. After the property is sold and the taxes paid, there should be enough money for you to live comfortably...provided your outlays are modest." He paused. "By the way, what are you living on these days?"

"Every so often, I get lucky at cards. Last year, however, I did quite well for myself in another line of work." His chuckle held no mirth. "I proposed to two young ladies whose dowries would have paid my tax bill. Once their fathers learned of my financial woes, however, they paid me to go away." His face burned with the memory. "God help me, but I took the money. I couldn't afford to do otherwise."

Mr. Whitehead opened a drawer and retrieved a bottle of spirits and a glass. He poured Moordale a stiff drink and pushed it across the desk toward him.

"My advice to you is to accept the inevitable. Once Bramble Hall is gone, marry a lass with a bit of money, buy a more modest property, and learn something about making proper investments. It's not the end of the world—however it may seem to you right now."

Moordale downed the drink in one gulp. "Thank you, Mr. Whitehead, but it's the end of *my* world—as pathetic as that sounds."

* * *

Iris was exhilarated. Her fiancé was due to arrive at the Braithwaite residence any moment, and she couldn't wait. In the drawing room, she paced while Rory worked on a sketch from his perch in the window seat. Eventually, he sighed and shot her a level look.

"Can't you embroider a screen or read a book? You're as nervous as a cat and I can't concentrate."

"I'm not nervous, I'm happy. In a very little while, my engagement will be official and I'll be the envy of every woman in London."

"I'm sure there are a few ladies who don't give a fig."

"Must you always be unpleasant?"

"That depends on the company I'm with."

"I liked you far better when you were in India."

"Likewise."

Her gaze fell to the drawing board in Rory's hands. "What are you working on?"

"It's nothing to do with you. Would you prefer I play the piano? *Music has charms to sooth a savage breast*, as the saying goes."

"Don't quote Congreve to me, and if you try to play the piano, I'll sit on the keyboard. I'm listening for the doorbell."

Her curiosity piqued, she moved toward her brother. Before she could see his drawing, however, he quickly covered it with a piece of paper.

"If you don't mind, Iris, I'd prefer a little privacy—"

The door chime rang and she jumped. "That's him!"

Rory put down his work, stretched, and brushed past her.

"Where are you going?" she asked.

"Papa has left instructions for Moordale to be shown into his study. I intend to be there."

"Why?"

He paused. "You wanted me to take an interest, didn't you? Really, Iris, you should make up your mind."

Iris heard her brother greet Moordale, and accompany him down the hall. A few moments later, and to her frustration, the study door was firmly shut. When the doorbell rang again, Iris wondered if she had another caller, but it was only a messenger. She emerged from the drawing room to see the butler with an envelope in his hand.

"What's that, Glade?"

"A message for Master Rory."

"Oh. I'll give it to him."

"Very good, Miss Iris."

The butler resumed his duties, and she returned to the

drawing room with the letter in hand. When she saw it was from Fiona Robinson, she curled her lip. Was the stupid girl corresponding with Rory in a desperate attempt to spoil her engagement with a falsehood? Without thinking too long about it, she used the tip of a letter opener to pop off the wax seal. She could always claim the letter had arrived that way...or better yet, she could replace the seal with a fresh blob of sealing wax. Depending on what the letter said, perhaps she wouldn't give it to Rory at all.

Iris slid the stationery out of the envelope and brought it over to the window seat to read. The contents disgusted her. So Fiona had said something *untoward* the night before—probably as a result of her humiliation—and now she wanted Rory to forgive her? What a simpering little idiot! A niggling suspicion prompted Iris to look at her brother's sketch. As she feared, the woman he'd been drawing bore more than a passing resemblance to Fiona. How extraordinarily nauseating to think of the two of them together!

Iris stuffed the letter back in its envelope and dribbled sealing wax over the broken spot. Her besotted brother would be so eager to read the letter he wouldn't know the difference.

Chapter 9

Poison Pen

Rory ushered Moordale into the study and introduced him to the senior Mr. Braithwaite. Peyton came around his desk and shook his hand.

"I've heard much about you."

Moordale appeared not to notice the grim note in Peyton's voice. "I'm so glad." He beamed as he settled himself into a chair. "I suppose Iris has told you I've proposed?"

Rory and his father exchanged a glance.

"She has, but quite frankly, your proposal is troublesome," Peyton replied.

The man's smile slipped. "In what way?"

"Rory informs me you'd been pursuing Miss Fiona Robinson. What made you change your mind in favor of Iris?"

Moordale's complexion reddened noticeably and he shifted in his seat. "Er...surely I needn't remind you of your daughter's considerable charms."

"But Miss Fiona is charming as well," Rory said.

"Certainly, she is. In the end, however, she doesn't hold a candle to Iris."

Although Rory felt like snorting in derision, as a gentleman he held it in. "No, of course not."

"Forgive me, but I've heard your financial situation leaves something to be desired," Peyton said. "Your debts, for example, far exceed your income."

The viscount was the very picture of confusion. "I've no idea to what you must be referring."

Rory folded his arms across his chest. "Don't you? Furthermore, I'm given to understand you attempted to elope with two different ladies last year, and were compensated to go away."

"That's the basest sort of gossip, and beneath you, sir!"

"Perhaps so, but that doesn't mean it isn't true," Rory said.

Moordale's spine straightened. "I'm not a horse to be bought off!"

Peyton withdrew a bank book from a drawer and dropped in onto his desk. "If I write you a bank draft for ten thousand pounds, will you agree to leave Iris alone?"

The man averted his eyes. "I suppose if you feel that strongly against having me for a son-in-law, I wouldn't press my suit."

"Father, write him a draft for fifty pounds," Rory said. "That should do it."

"Done." Peyton dipped pen in ink and bent over the bank book.

At that, Moordale became incensed. "Hang on...what do you take me for?"

Rory shook his head in disappointment. He'd expected a better game, but the man had made it entirely too easy. "Everyone knows what you are, sir. We're just haggling over the price, as they say."

Although Moordale sputtered in outrage, he waited until Peyton gave him the bank draft before storming from the house.

"Well, that's done," Rory said.

"I hope we've done the proper thing for Iris," Peyton said.

"Having met Moordale, do you really have any doubts? What sort of man would take money for withdrawing a legitimate offer of marriage?"

Peyton sighed. "You're right, but I regret having to deal with your sister. I suppose you'd best call her in."

But Iris was already pushing her way into the study. "Why did Iggy leave without speaking to me? What's happened?"

Rory winced. "I'll leave you to it, Father."

He backed from the office, shut the door, and returned to the drawing room. Just as he reached for his sketch, he heard a shriek. Moments later, Iris stormed into the room and pointed her finger at him. "This is *your* doing, I just know it!"

As she strode toward him with blood in her eyes, Rory held up his hands.

"Listen to me, Iris! He's a fortune-hunting scoundrel with a mountain of debt!"

"You don't know *anything* of the sort!"

Her voice raised in volume until the last word was a scream. The picture of fury, she shoved him so hard with both hands that he staggered backward into the piano, knocking the instrument several inches from its original position. As Peyton appeared in the doorway, Iris darted past him and up the stairs. Rory and his father stood in awkward silence until the sound of a slamming door overhead reached their ears.

Peyton cleared his throat. "She didn't take the news as well as I'd hoped."

* * *

Trembling with emotion, Iris threw herself on her bed and pounded the pillows with her fists. She knew without a doubt her father would have consented to the match if Rory hadn't interfered. Her father had told her Moordale had accepted fifty pounds to withdraw his proposal, but what of it? The man should walk away with something for his trouble, shouldn't he? His feelings had motivated his choice of her over Fiona, and that was all the proof she needed of his genuine affection.

Oh, what was she to do? The viscount had been her absolute last chance to marry, and now she'd be considered a spinster. After the first wave of grief passed, icy anger took its place...along with a thirst for revenge. All society would be laughing at her heartache and despair—especially Fiona Robinson—and it was all Rory's fault! Her brother had always been an annoyance ever since she could remember. He'd always commanded attention with his looks, talents, and manners, and she'd never disliked him more passionately than now. He wanted to see her end an old maid, and he'd likely get his wish.

There wasn't much she could do to her brother and get away with it, but she wasn't without other options. Rory might be out of reach, but the object of his affection was not. Iris pulled Fiona's letter from her pocket, slit it open, and read the missive again for clues on how best to proceed. It was clear the girl was ridden with guilt for some reason, and her guilt left her extremely vulnerable. Rarely had a person ever delivered themselves so completely into the hands of an enemy, and Iris giggled with delight. She'd answer the letter—as Rory—in as hurtful a manner as possible. Since Fiona's acquaintance with him was of short duration, she wouldn't be familiar with his handwriting.

With a smile on her lips, Iris sat at her writing desk and composed the letter, relishing each word.

Dear Miss Fiona,

There's no need to ask my forgiveness. Were you in possession of your sister's looks or manners, I might have felt dismay at your actions, but the lion's share of virtues fell into Miss Lara's lap at birth. It must be difficult for you to live up to her example, especially since you are twins.

Miles Greystoke has related to me in private his distaste for your company. If not for you, he would have proposed to Miss Lara by now. I've encouraged him to ask your sister for her hand, but he continues to balk. I believe if you were absent, he might finally bend his knee. Knowing this, I'm sure you'll do what's right.

Sincerely,

Rory Braithwaite

As Iris sealed the envelope, she imagined how it would be when Fiona read the letter. Oh, how she wished she could be there to see the expression on the girl's face! Fiona would never forgive Rory for his sentiments, and would cut him socially. He'd never know the reason behind Fiona's hatred, and it would eat him up from the inside. Everything had always come easily to her wretched brother—until now. Iris was looking forward to watching him suffer.

Sir Harry entered the Greystoke drawing room with a spring in his step. Fiona noticed his waistcoat was more splendid than usual, his neatly cropped hair and beard seemed to have been freshly trimmed, and his walking stick sported a fashionable blue glass knob.

"I'm afraid you find me alone this afternoon, Sir Harry. Miles is off riding, and Lara has gone to tea at a friend's house."

What she didn't mention was that she'd been invited to the tea as well, but had been too tired from her difficult night to attend. She asked Sir Harry to sit on the sofa with her, but he preferred to pose next to the mantle. Had he been a younger man, she might have imagined he stayed standing out of vanity, to show off his fine figure. No softness had settled around his middle, like so many older men, and she recalled Sir Harry had once been a distinguished officer in the army.

"How are you feeling?" he asked.

"As well as might be expected, thank you. Although I received a bit of a shock last night, I'll be all right in a day or two."

"I wish to ease your mind regarding Lord Moordale. After his father died, Moordale has been unable to keep up his estate. He's seeking to marry an heiress."

Fiona frowned. "Why are you telling me this?"

"His regard for you might have been genuine, my dear, but he can't afford to marry where his inclination leads him. Nevertheless, I cannot excuse his lack of manners toward you. It was badly done on his part."

"He made me look ridiculous in front of everyone."

"Not so." Sir Harry cleared his throat. "Miss Fiona, you're aware, I think, how much I admire you. If you'd agree to marry me, you'd make me the happiest of men. I'm not young, but I have other virtues. My home in Blythe Village is the finest in the county, and you'd want for nothing. As my wife, you'd be able to travel to London whenever you like. Several carriages would be at your disposal, along with a lady's maid and a houseful of servants. I'm not a peer, but I have friends at the highest level of society, and few doors would be closed to you. You needn't answer right away, but please say you'll consider my offer?"

Her tongue was stilled by astonishment—not at Sir Harry's proposal, but at the fact she was not immediately rejecting it. She'd mocked him behind his back last year for being old and musty, but that had been childish, uncharitable, and untrue. In fact, whenever she'd been near him, he'd smelled pleasantly of expensive cologne. In addition, she couldn't deny he'd been especially kind to her last night, just when she'd needed it most. Was she...could she...seriously consider accepting him?

"I-I need some time to think about what you've said, Sir Harry. Much has happened recently to cloud my judgment, and I wish to do your proposal justice."

Sir Harry crossed to the sofa and lifted her hand to his lips. "Miss Fiona, just to know you'll consider me is enough for now. I'm returning to Blythe Village for a few days to deal with some business, and I'll see you when I return."

After sketching a bow, he took his leave. Slightly confused and bewildered, she stared at the empty fireplace. Considering her somewhat precarious situation socially, she'd be a fool to simply dismiss his proposal. Girls often married far older men for a variety of very good reasons, so the match wouldn't even be particularly unusual. Although she felt little attraction for Sir Harry, she wasn't repelled by him, either. The notion of becoming Lady Wren wasn't as glamorous as Lady Moordale, perhaps, but it sounded grand nevertheless.

And yet, as soon as she'd almost persuaded herself to accept Sir Harry's offer, Rory's handsome face flashed into her mind. Blast it all...despite his shrewish sister, she suddenly yearned to know him better. He wasn't a viscount like Lord Moordale, or quite as rich as Sir Harry, but Rory Braithwaite had a certain something in his manner that appealed to her. Although she hadn't wanted to admit it until now, dancing and talking with him at the ball had been wonderful fun. He was a more polished dancer than Lord Moordale, if truth be told, and she enjoyed Rory's sense of humor far better. Had she poisoned the well with her sharp tongue, or had her letter of apology paved the way for a cordial relationship? If there was even the slightest possibility of a future with Rory, she'd put Sir Harry off.

Already woozy from lack of sleep, she lay back on the sofa, closed her eyes, and drifted off into a dream about a tall, handsome young man whose lips made her knees grow weak. Seemingly moments later, she was roused by the sound of the doorbell. Although she sat up, she was still groggy when the butler entered the room with a silver salver.

"A message was just delivered for you, Miss Fiona."

Fiona glanced at the envelope long enough to confirm the message was from Rory. As she took the letter from the tray, her stomach fluttered with excitement.

"Thank you, Kendrick."

Although she hadn't expected a reply quite so soon, perhaps her letter had struck a responsive chord. It was fortuitous that she happened to be alone when his message arrived! Certainly if Lara or Miles knew about their correspondence, she'd be obliged to answer awkward questions. She'd be forced to confess her rudeness and subsequent apology. If at all possible, she'd prefer to leave them in the dark about the entire mess forever, and deal with her shame in private.

Her fingers trembled as she retrieved a letter opener and slit open the top of the envelope. She swallowed hard as she unfolded the stationery and began to read. *There's no need to ask my forgiveness.*

"Oh, thank goodness!"

A broad smile of relief lifted the corners of her mouth, but it soon faded. Blood hammered in her ears and the breath caught in her throat as she continued to read the missive. When she was finished, she sank to the floor, boneless. Her head bowed, agony wracked her body, and she buried her face in her hands. Deep down she'd always known Lara was prettier and kinder than she was, but it hurt to realize it was so obvious to everyone else. Rory's dismissive words were not written on paper so much as they were now etched in her soul. And the notion that Miles secretly disliked her was so unbearable, she wasn't sure she could stand it. How could she ever look at him again, knowing he wished her elsewhere? Even worse, Lara would be engaged by now if it weren't for her. Oh, why had she ever been born?

A band of steel squeezed her throat, a hot poker lanced her temples, and suddenly she couldn't breathe. With both palms flat on the floor, Fiona forced herself to inhale and exhale until the dizziness retreated. A noise somewhere in the house reminded her that a servant or Angelica might walk in on her distress at any moment, so she got to her feet. With the horrible letter crushed into her pocket, Fiona ascended the stairs and rang for her lady's maid.

"Moira, I'm unwell."

"Shall I send for a doctor?"

"That's not necessary, but I shan't be leaving my room tonight. Please let Mrs. Greystoke know I won't be down for tea or dinner, and tell her I've asked not to be disturbed. If I'm coming down with a cold, I don't want anyone else to be exposed—especially not her."

"Shall I bring you tea?"

"I'll ring if I want anything, thank you."

After Moira left, Fiona curled up on her bed with her knees hugged to her chest and sobbed. Her life as she'd known it was destroyed, and she desperately wished to go home. Her absence from the Greystoke residence would undoubtedly give pleasure to everyone except perhaps Angelica and her little nephew, Billy. Since Sir Harry's offer was likely the only one she'd ever receive, she'd accept him and be grateful. If truth be told, he was probably better than she deserved.

* * *

Moordale's emotions weighed down on him and made it difficult to mount the stairs in his boarding house residence. He tried not to notice the scratched wallpaper in the stairwell, or the unvarnished handrail which had taken on a blackened appearance from dirt. The place also had its own smell, which he'd come to realize was the odor of deprivation. Still, the boarding house was at least located in Pimlico, and not the East End. If he couldn't bring his rent up to date, his next residence would smell like utter destitution. As depressing as it was, the sale of Bramble Hall would keep the wolf at bay. The only challenge would be in surviving long enough to see the money.

As soon as he reached the stop of the stairs, a squeak in the floorboards announced his presence. His landlord all but burst from his own residence to confront him.

"You're behind in the rent, Moordale. I've got a family to feed, you know."

Moordale winced. The fifty pounds he'd received from Peyton Braithwaite had largely been spent earlier that day when he'd paid other outstanding debts. Although prudence dictated he pay his rent first, he'd been forced to pay those creditors who might reveal his financial strain to those gentlemen who frequented the same establishments. Any additional funds in his wallet must be kept in reserve for his next game of cards.

"Yes, I appreciate your forbearance, Mr. Smith." He felt in his pocket for some coins and handed them over with an apologetic smile. "Let me give you something on account, and I'll try to get caught up by the end of the week."

The landlord examined the few coins and all but growled. "You're testing my patience, Your Lordship."

The last two words had a mocking tone to them, which Moordale ignored. The time had long since passed he could afford to take offense.

"Quite so, but I need just a few more days."

With another grunting growl, the landlord returned to his residence. Moordale let himself into his small, shabby apartment, shut the door, and sank into the rickety chair next to the desk. Tears burned the back of his eyes, but he refused to let them fall. Giving in to his humiliation would only make things worse.

* * *

After a ride in Hyde Park, Rory and Miles arranged to meet at their club on St. James for drinks and dinner. As they were seated at a table, Rory gave Miles a rueful smile.

"I'm glad we're dining out tonight. Iris is in high dudgeon."

"Really? I should have thought otherwise, considering her engagement."

"There's no engagement after all. Father and I sent Moordale packing, and Iris is furious at my interference."

"Why did you do that? You've been wishing her married for ages!"

Rory related what he'd learned about the viscount's aborted elopements. Miles peered at him, obviously aghast.

"I knew he had financial difficulties, but I hadn't thought him so morally bankrupt. It seems both Fiona and your sister have had a narrow escape!"

"Yes, but I'm not certain either of them see the situation that way." Rory paused. "How is Miss Fiona?"

"She looked dreadful when I saw her this morning, and she's keeping to her room tonight. Her lady's maid said she's feeling ill."

"I'm sorry to hear it."

"What are you going to do about your sister?"

"Iris has demanded to go to our aunt in Paris, and Father has asked me to accompany her. She's vexed about that, too, but we can't have her running off to Moordale on the sly. If he manages to ruin her, we'd have to pay him a huge amount of money to marry her."

Miles shuddered. "What a dreadful notion."

"At any rate, Iris and I will be leaving tomorrow, and I'll return as soon as she's settled."

"I hope this entire incident with Moordale will have blown over and we'll be back to normal by then. I don't like to see Fiona distressed."

"Nor do I."

Rory took a sip of wine to cover his own unhappiness. Would his absence from London for a week or ten days be long enough for Fiona's anger toward him to cool? Surely once she realized she was better off without the slimy viscount, she might feel more kindly toward Rory. If not, it was going to be a very long Season indeed.

Chapter 10

Wilting Iris

Fiona entered the dining room for breakfast the following morning, clad in a traveling suit. She was pleased to see Angelica at the table for the first time in a long while...as much as she could be pleased at anything. In fact, she felt rather dead inside, even as she plastered a vapid smile on her face.

"Good morning. I'm glad you're well enough to be downstairs, Angelica."

"Yes, I'm feeling much more myself this morning. How about you?"

"Tolerably well, thank you."

Although she wasn't hungry, Fiona helped herself to toast and tea. She sat down at the table on the same side as Miles, so she wouldn't have to look at him directly.

"Why are you dressed that way?" Lara asked.

"I've had a change of plans. Moira and I are taking the train to Blythe Village today," Fiona said.

Lara gasped. "Why?"

"We talked about this, Fiona," Angelica said. "I thought you'd agreed to stay."

"Yes I did, but Sir Harry paid me a call yesterday afternoon. He proposed marriage, and I mean to accept."

A cacophony of protests ensued, but Fiona was unmoved. She'd resolved upon a course of action, and staying focused was the only way she could get through the morning without an emotional meltdown.

"Please don't try to change my mind," she said. "It's a very good match for me, and certainly a step up the social ladder."

Another round of remonstrations ensued. Finally, Miles held up his hands for quiet.

"I don't think you should accept Sir Harry's proposal until you're feeling better about Lord Moordale. Rory discovered some things about Moordale that might help put him in perspective. His finances are in shambles."

"Yes, Sir Harry mentioned as much."

"That's not all. Apparently, Rory learned that Moordale was paid to abandon his pursuit of certain young ladies last year."

William's eyebrows shot upward. "That's a rather spectacular accusation. Does Mr. Braithwaite have any proof?"

"He talked to several gentlemen at Lady Quarterbury's ball who claimed to have intimate knowledge of the situation."

"I'm afraid that sort of testimony would never hold up in court, Miles," William said.

"Perhaps not, but we're in court of public opinion, so the same rules don't apply."

Fiona stirred sugar into her tea with feigned calmness. "I'm dismayed Mr. Braithwaite would stoop to gossip."

"It *is* a rather thin evidence, Miles," Lara said. "You know how cruel society can be."

"In fact, Mr. Braithwaite's assertion is somewhat unflattering to his own sister, if truth be told," Angelica said.

Miles reddened. "Ordinarily, I wouldn't have repeated what Rory told me, but I never imagined Fiona might consider accepting Sir Harry. I just don't think she should make any decisions while in an emotional state." He paused. "One other thing; Moordale isn't to marry Miss Braithwaite after all. Her father also paid him a small sum of money to withdraw."

Fiona's hurt stemmed not from Lord Moordale's defection, but from another source entirely. Unfortunately, she couldn't reveal the truth without divulging Rory's letter.

"I'm sorry for Miss Braithwaite, I suppose, but her broken engagement is of little consequence to me." Fiona put down her teacup and stood. "Excuse me, but I must see how my maid is getting along. I'd like to catch the nine o'clock."

Moira was in Fiona's room when she returned, frantically filling trunks and suitcases with gowns, shoes, hats, and accessories.

"Oh, don't bother packing everything, Moira. I just need a small trunk with essentials for now. Mrs. Greystoke will make sure the rest of my clothes are sent along directly. Are your things packed?"

"Yes, Miss Fiona."

"Good. Run downstairs and ask Kendrick to summon a cab, please."

* * *

Nobody said a word after Fiona left the dining room...until they were sure she was out of earshot.

"This is all exceedingly strange," Angelica said finally. "I've never seen Fiona like this before."

"She seems very preoccupied, to say the least," Miles said. "Perhaps it's my imagination, but I felt as if she was avoiding my gaze."

Lara sighed as she tucked her napkin by her plate. "I'll go talk to her. Maybe she'll tell me what's really going on."

Angelica shook her head. "No, she needs to be alone for a little while, I think. Maybe the loss of Lord Moordale was more of a blow than we'd imagined and she needs time to sort it out."

"Miles is right about one thing; I hope Fiona sorts through her feelings before she agrees to marry Sir Harry," Lara said. "He's respectable and wealthy to be sure, but I don't think he's suited to her temperament."

"I couldn't agree more, but I'm reluctant to press the point with her at the moment," Angelica said. "In a day or two, she'll see things differently and come to her senses."

"Forgive me for saying so, but I find Rory Braithwaite's interference in this matter quite odd, particularly when any evidence of wrong-doing is so thin," William said. "If he's mistaken, he's slandered Lord Moordale rather dreadfully."

"From what I understand, it would be difficult to slander Lord Moordale," Angelica said. "He did accept money from the senior Mr. Braithwaite to withdraw his offer of marriage. That fact, at least, isn't open to debate."

"Although I've always trusted Rory's judgment implicitly, I confess you've managed to poke holes in his story," Miles said. "Now I wish I hadn't said anything. I seem to have worsened matters."

"No, your concern for Fiona's welfare does you credit, and she's entitled to know all the facts before she makes up her mind," Lara said. "Is it possible Mr. Braithwaite has some further evidence to buttress his argument?"

"Unfortunately, I can't inquire. He's to escort his sister to Paris today and won't be back for a week or so. Nevertheless,

I'll probe a bit deeper upon his return." Miles's eyebrows drew together. "I don't mean to betray a confidence, but he's expressed his regard for Fiona in no uncertain terms. I can't imagine he'd do anything to hurt her."

"If he's formed a design on her, his judgment may be flawed," William said.

"Indeed," Angelica said. "Perhaps he's guilty of casting aspersions in order to clear the field for himself?"

"I simply can't believe that," Miles said. "I'd sooner accuse you of mischief, William, than I'd accuse Rory Braithwaite."

* * *

Lara, Miles, and Angelica were assembled in the entryway, along with the nanny and little Billy, when Fiona and Moira descended the stairs,

"Oh, dear," Fiona said. "I didn't mean to discommode you all."

"William was obliged to leave for work, but the rest of us want to say good-bye," Angelica said. "William sends his best wishes for a safe journey."

The butler stood by the doorway. "Your trunk has been loaded, Miss Fiona."

"Thank you, Kendrick."

Fiona gave her elder sister a hug. "Angelica, I can't thank you and William enough for letting me stay with you these past few months. I've imposed far too long on your hospitality."

"Not at all. Take whatever time you need, and then hasten your return."

"You're very kind. I hope it isn't too much trouble to send my things along? Moira and I are traveling light today."

"I'll take care of it, I promise."

Fiona moved over to embrace Lara. "Write and tell me all your news."

"Nothing will be quite so much fun without you. Please don't rush into anything as far as Sir Harry is concerned."

Again, Fiona merely smiled. Miles was next, and she extended her hand. "I hope you find the rest of the Season to be enjoyable."

He shook her hand. "Thank you, Fiona. Don't stay gone too long."

Angelica gestured to her son. "Come along, Billy, and give your aunt a hug."

The nanny had the toddler by the hand, but as soon as Fiona knelt and held out her arms, he broke away and ran to her. When she buried her face in his chubby neck, she was almost undone. The little boy smelled of Castile soap and some other mysterious, wonderful fragrance of his own. Her throat began to burn with suppressed tears, and she wished there were some way to deaden her emotions.

"I'm going to miss you," she murmured. "Be a good boy while I'm gone and take care of your mama."

He nodded with solemnity. "I will."

Fiona stood. "Come along, Moira. We've a train to catch."

She strode through the door without looking back, unwilling to let anyone see the tears coursing down her cheeks. Although her departure was difficult for her, at least her family would feel relief at her absence. Miles would propose to Lara at last, and life at the Greystoke townhouse would be happy once more.

* * *

Billy burst into tears when the front door closed. Although

Angelica tried to comfort him, the little boy seemed inconsolable. Finally, the nanny clucked her tongue.

"Come along, luv, and let's see if we can find you a biscuit." As the nanny led Billy toward the kitchen, his wails softened into the occasional snuffle.

Lara touched Miles's arm. "You look troubled."

"There's definitely something wrong. Fiona was awfully formal with me, did you notice?"

"I did, rather," Lara admitted.

"I can't imagine what I've done to offend her."

"Perhaps nothing," Angelica said. "I daresay we'll understand a little more as time goes on. Let's not worry about it at present."

Miles and Lara disappeared into the drawing room, and Angelica made her way upstairs. Despite her advice to Lara and Miles, she was dreadfully concerned about Fiona. Of the two twins, Fiona had always had the more difficult time coping with disappointments. Although she'd occasionally made some bad choices, she'd always managed to make things right in the end. Angelica had almost always been taken into Fiona's confidence before now, and the girl's reticence worried her more than anything else. Whatever her troubles, why hadn't she asked for help?

As Angelica approached Fiona's room, one of the maids appeared with a wrinkled blue and white striped gown draped over her arm. "Mrs. Greystoke, this was in the laundry room. I think Moira must have forgotten about it."

Angelica recognized the dress as one Fiona had worn the day before.

"It's in a dreadful condition, I'm afraid. Would you sponge and press it, please? I don't want to send along a dirty gown."

"Yes, ma'am, but I found this letter in the pocket." The

maid produced a crushed envelope. "I didn't know if Miss Fiona meant to throw it away or not."

"Thank you, Emma."

After the maid left with the dress, Angelica smoothed out the crushed letter. She was taken aback to discover it was from Rory Braithwaite. Fiona hadn't said a word about receiving a letter from the man, and she'd had every opportunity to say so at breakfast. Something must be amiss, or her sister wouldn't have taken such pains to conceal it. Had he written something to upset Fiona so badly she'd decided to flee London as a result? Angelica bit her lip, struggling against the temptation to read the letter. To do so was not only a breach of etiquette, but it might even be considered unforgivable. Oh, *blazes*, she should just take responsibility and read it. It wasn't as if she didn't have her sister's best interests at heart.

Halfway through reading the missive, she sat down in a nearby rocking chair with her hand over her mouth in dismay. Afterward, she rang for a servant to fetch Miles immediately. He came at a run, with Lara hard on his heels.

"Are you unwell, Angelica?"

She shook her head. "There's nothing wrong with me, but you've been greatly mistaken in your friendship with Rory Braithwaite." Tears sprang to her eyes as she gestured toward the letter. "He wrote a letter to Fiona, and I've never read anything so horrible in my life."

Miles exchanged a bewildered glance with Lara. "I can't believe it."

"Just listen."

Although she nearly choked on the words, Angelica read the letter aloud. Miles audibly gasped when she read the part about his distaste for Fiona's company, and Lara dissolved into tears.

He held his tongue until she reached the end. "That's

complete and utter tripe from beginning to end!" he exclaimed finally. "May I see that letter?"

Angelica relinquished it to him.

Blotting moisture from her eyes with a handkerchief, Lara sank onto the footstool next to Angelica's chair. "Poor Fiona! Even though it's all lies, I can't bear to think what she must be going through!"

"I wish she'd shown the letter to me," Angelica said. "I only happened upon it when she left it behind in her haste to depart."

"I imagine she was too mortified to confide in anyone," Lara said. "I told her that Mr. Braithwaite and Miles are as close as brothers, so she would have taken what he wrote to heart."

Miles peered at the letter. "He didn't write it. This doesn't sound like Rory, and I don't recognize the handwriting." He glanced up, stricken. "How could Fiona ever imagine I have less than the warmest regard for her?"

"Because of Lord Moordale's shabby treatment, she was demoralized when she read the letter," Angelica said. "Sometimes when you're at your lowest, you'll believe anything."

"This cannot be allowed to stand." He folded the letter into his pocket. "I'll call on Rory immediately and get things cleared up."

"What if Mr. Braithwaite and his sister have already left for Paris?" Angelica asked.

"I'd follow Rory to Paris if I must, to settle this on Fiona's behalf."

Lara stood and gave him a hug and a kiss. "Do hurry!"

In the library, Rory perused the shelves as he searched for books to bring with him on his journey. Although he wished he could just escort Iris to Aunt Naomi's house in the Faubourg Saint-Germain district and leave right away, his aunt would consider an abrupt departure ill-mannered. So he planned to spend his time wisely by enlisting Aunt Naomi's help with her favorite niece. The woman was well-connected and wealthy and surely could make a match for Iris with some hapless Frenchman who wouldn't mind being hen-pecked for the rest of his life. Certainly if Iris took up residence in France, Rory wouldn't complain.

Just as he selected Hardy's *Far From the Madding Crowd* from the bookshelf, the sound of a row in the entryway gave him pause. The butler appeared with a harassed expression on his normally placid face. "Excuse me, Master Rory, but—"

Miles brushed past, looking more upset than Rory had ever seen him. "I must speak with you on an urgent matter that can't wait!"

The poor butler turned pink and sputtered in protest, but Rory held up a quelling hand.

"It's all right, Glade. If Mr. Greystoke says it's important, I'll make the time."

"Very good, sir." The butler shot Miles a deadly glance and left.

Rory peered at his friend with concern. "What's happened?"

Miles thrust a creased envelope toward him. "Did you send this letter to Fiona?"

"I've not sent her any correspondence at all, why?"

"Read it."

Although he was bewildered, Rory slid the stationery from the envelope and read what was written thereon. A sense of horror came over him. "No, I didn't write this, and nothing would have induced me to do so!"

"I didn't think you had, but we must get to the bottom of it for Fiona's sake. She left London for Blythe Village this morning, thinking you and I both dislike her."

A wave of emotional pain tore through Rory's heart, but he forced himself to examine the letter again. It didn't take long for him to realize who'd written the letter, and why. He tugged on the bell pull, and Glade appeared almost instantly.

"Yes, sir?"

"Summon my sister and father, please," Rory said.

The man hesitated. "And if Miss Iris declines to come?"

"Inform her I'll be up directly to yank her downstairs by the collar, if necessary."

A whisper of a smile lifted the corners of the butler's mouth. "Yes, sir."

After Glade disappeared, Rory gave Miles a grim glance.

"This poisonous letter is my sister's handiwork."

"What?"

"I've no doubt Iris meant to punish me in the worst possible way by hurting Miss Fiona, and she succeeded."

"I'm appalled, Rory."

"As am I."

"Did you have an argument with Fiona? That letter seemed to suggest she'd sent some sort of apology to you."

"If so, Iris intercepted it."

"You never mentioned having had a disagreement."

"It was between me and Miss Fiona. You see, she was a little put out after Moordale's betrayal, and didn't want to have anything to do with the Braithwaites. Although it grieved me, I can't say that I blamed her."

Peyton strode into the library. "What the devil is going on? Your sister's in an uproar, and neither of you is ready to leave for—" He broke off when he spotted Miles. "Hello, Mr. Greystoke. I was unaware you'd come to call."

"It's not a social visit, sir."

"Paris will have to be postponed, Father," Rory said. "We've a grave situation to sort out involving Iris. I believe—"

Iris stormed into the room. She was fully dressed for travel, but her hair was hanging down around her shoulders in hanks, as if she'd been interrupted mid-coiffeur. "This had better be worthwhile, brother! Glade related your primitive, brutish sentiments, and I consider them to be extraordinarily rude!"

Her gaze fell onto Miles, and her expression turned wary. "Oh...good morning."

"Good morning, Miss Braithwaite." Miles's tone was icy.

The butler reached for the door handle, to pull the door closed.

"Pardon me, Glade, one more thing. Did I receive a letter yesterday?" Rory asked.

"Er...yes, sir. A letter came by messenger and I gave it to Miss Iris for safekeeping. I hope I didn't do anything wrong?"

"No, of course not. Thank you, Glade."

As the door closed, Iris's gaze dropped to the oriental rug underneath her feet.

Rory cleared his throat. "Father, Miss Fiona Robinson sent me a letter which Iris intercepted. Thereafter, she took it upon herself to answer it in my name and in doing so has caused untold havoc and injury!" He held up the offensive missive. "Fortunately, Miles has just brought this entire debacle to my attention."

"Let me see that." Peyton took the letter and perused the contents.

A flicker of apprehension crossed Iris's face. "It was a silly joke. Nobody sensible could ever have taken it seriously."

"Where's the letter Miss Fiona sent me?" Rory demanded.

Her voice became child-like. "I'm not certain."

"If you don't find it, I'll search your room myself. Trust me when I say I'll think nothing of ripping up all your hats and gowns in the process."

Her eyes flashed with anger. "You're a horrible bully!"

Fortunately for Iris, the rude response bubbling up onto Rory's lips was quelled by the presence of Miles. Peyton muttered an oath under his breath as he read the letter, and thereafter he lanced Iris with his gaze. "You wrote this?"

A tiny nod.

"And you intercepted Miss Fiona's letter to your brother?"

Another tiny nod.

"I'm glad your mother isn't alive to see what you've become."

Her face crumpled and she began to cry. Peyton pointed to the writing desk in the corner.

"Write an apology to Miss Fiona immediately. Afterward, you will return her purloined letter to your brother."

Without protest, Iris hastened over to the desk, sat, and began to write. Her pen made scratching noises on the stationery as she scrawled out the apology. While she worked, Peyton paced back and forth, deep in thought. Rory and Miles exchanged a glance, but nobody spoke until Iris set down her pen. "I'm done."

Rory crossed over to his sister, picked up the letter, and read it. Although perfunctorily, Iris had explained what she'd done, taken responsibility for her actions, and offered her apology.

He handed the letter to Miles. "If that will do, I'll make plans to depart for Blythe Village immediately. I intend to deliver the letter personally to Miss Fiona and explain this entire mess from beginning to end."

Miles read the letter, nodded, and gave it back to him. "The personal approach would be best."

"I just wish there was some way to make amends," Rory said.

"Perhaps Miss Fiona will take some solace in Iris's exile," Peyton said.

She hung her head. "I'm to go to Paris permanently, then?"

"Paris would be too much of a treat, I wager," Peyton said. "No, I have cousins living abroad who might be willing to take you in, given the proper financial inducement. You'll do very well in Philadelphia, I imagine."

"*America?*" Iris shrieked. "Why, that's too cruel! Papa, how *could* you?"

Chapter 11

Blythe Manor

"It will take some weeks to arrange the journey," Peyton said. "First, I must write to James and Katrina to make sure they're amenable to having company. Then, I'll book passage for both of us on a steamship from Liverpool. I'll escort you myself, of course, to make sure you're well supervised. Until then, Iris, you're to decline all invitations and be confined to the house, except for church on Sundays."

With a long, drawn-out wail, she fled from the room.

Peyton glanced at Miles. "I apologize for my daughter's appalling behavior. Do you suppose her punishment will bring Miss Fiona some comfort?"

"Yes, sir," Miles replied. "Thank you, Mr. Braithwaite. You've behaved in a very gentlemanly fashion, and nobody could ask anything more."

"It's the least I can do, all things considered." He shook his head. "My daughter is a very unhappy woman. Perhaps a new start in America is what she needs to improve herself."

Rory was unconcerned with his sister's improvement. "Father, I'm going to Blythe Village this afternoon."

"You're getting such a late start, I daresay you'll have to spend the night at an inn."

"Probably so, but I'm already packed." He tucked the letter of apology into his coat pocket. "I hope Miss Fiona will agree to see me."

"I'll go with you, just to make sure she does," Miles said. "Let me go back to the townhouse to pack a few things and then I'll meet you at the station. If we hurry, we can catch the one o'clock and arrive well before nightfall."

Miles took his leave. Before Rory went upstairs to speak with his valet, Peyton gave him a sorrowful smile.

"I'm sorry, Rory."

"What for? You didn't have anything to do with Iris's mischief."

"Not directly perhaps, but it's as much my fault as anyone's. Iris's character took a dark turn after your mother died, and I should have used a firmer hand with her." He paused. "You've an abundance of regard for Miss Fiona, I take it?"

"She's the most intriguing girl I've ever met."

"Don't let her get away, then. Your mother was the most intriguing women I ever met and I never regretted marrying her."

"I'll do my best, Father, but I fear the task is truly impossible."

"Perhaps not. I daresay Miss Fiona wouldn't have been quite so hurt by your sister's ridiculous letter if she hadn't cared a great deal about your opinion."

A sudden surge of hope made Rory smile. "I hadn't thought of it that way. Thank you, Father."

Peyton chuckled. "Carry on, then. Perhaps you should plan to stay a few days, to conduct a campaign, as it were."

"Why not?"

Rory grabbed the Thomas Hardy book, hastened from the library, and loped up the stairs. When he made his way to his sister's room to demand the return of Fiona's letter, he discovered it torn into quarters in the hallway outside her closed door. With a sigh, he picked up the pieces and continued on to his own room, where his valet had not yet finished packing his trunk.

"We've a change of plans, Garrison. Instead of traveling to Paris, we're taking the train north to Blythe Village."

His valet gave a sigh of relief. "Oh, thank heavens. The crossing always makes me exceedingly ill."

"I'm not certain how long we'll be staying, but be sure to pack evening and riding clothes, just to prepare for all eventualities." Rory checked his timepiece. "And since we're to catch the one o'clock, you'll have to be quick about it."

While his valet worked, Rory went to his desk and pieced together Fiona's letter. As he read her sweet sentiments, his eyes grew slightly moist with emotion. It was little wonder Iris had reacted so badly, since she didn't seem capable of such honesty herself. Poor Fiona had laid herself bare, and Iris had answered her letter with such vicious spitefulness as took his breath away. No doubt, Fiona now thought him a foul fiend from the pits of the underworld. Even when he told her the truth, would she ever be able to look at him again without abhorrence?

* * *

As they welcomed Fiona into the drawing room at Blythe Manor, her parents had an air of bewilderment.

"Why did you give us no notice of your arrival, child?" Mr. Robinson asked.

"And where is Lara?" Mrs. Robinson added. "Has something dreadful happened?"

Fiona forced a laugh. "No, no, nothing at all. It's just that yesterday I received a proposal of marriage, and I wished to have a few days of solitude to consider the matter before I accept."

Mrs. Robinson's face lit up with excitement. "Are we to have a viscount in the family, then? You mentioned a Lord Moordale in your letters."

"No, that's over with." Fiona sank onto a chair. "Is it too early for tea?"

Her mother rang for a servant, and then settled herself next to her husband on the sofa.

"Are we to learn the name of your suitor, or must we play charades?" Mr. Robinson asked.

"It's Sir Harry, actually."

Her parents' shocked reaction was almost comical.

"Are you mad?" Mr. Robinson exclaimed.

"You must be joking," Mrs. Robinson said at the same time.

"I'm perfectly serious," Fiona replied. "As it turns out, Sir Harry has been very kind and attentive to me all Season long, and I find my opinion of him has changed."

"Why did I send you all the way to London if you were just going to accept the neighbor?" Mr. Robinson sputtered. "I could have saved myself a fortune!"

A maid appeared, and the conversation was interrupted long enough for Mrs. Robinson to order tea.

"And bring a bottle of port," Mr. Robinson added as the maid turned to leave.

"Yes, sir."

Inwardly, Fiona sighed. It seemed as if her parents would require more convincing than she'd anticipated. "If nothing else, my time in London has shown me what sort of qualities I value in a husband. Sir Harry possesses those in abundance."

"But do you care for him?" Mr. Robinson asked.

Fiona couldn't bring herself to lie. "No, but love is a luxury few girls can afford."

Her mother, at least, was nodding. "As a practical matter, I suppose you could do far worse."

"I don't see how. If you've some notion of being a young widow, you should understand Sir Harry is as healthy as a horse," Mr. Robinson said. "His father reached the age of ninety before he passed on, and his mother is still as vigorous as ever. Sir Harry will likely outlast us all."

"I'm glad to hear he'll live long enough to be a good father to our children."

Her father shuddered. "Well, you're old enough to know your own mind."

"Indeed, I am."

"I noticed you brought very few trunks with you," Mrs. Robinson said. "Will you be returning to town soon?"

"No, Angelica will send along my things directly."

Her father peered at her. "You're quitting the Season entirely?"

"I'm inclined to accept Sir Harry's proposal, so to continue is pointless." To her horror, Fiona felt a lump forming in her throat. She rose. "If you'll excuse me, I'm going to freshen up before tea."

As she hastened from the room, she hoped her parents hadn't noticed the quaver in her voice. Truly, the only thing she wished to do was to crawl into bed and have another cry, but she could ill afford to do so. If her parents felt there was anything amiss, they'd attempt to pry her secrets out of her and she'd be undone. No matter what, she could never confess

Miles's dislike for her, lest his feelings sow seeds of resentment on the part of her family.

On her way up the stairs, she passed the small niche where a bust of Queen Elizabeth was displayed. When Angelica was to be married to William five years ago, the Greystoke family had come for a long visit beforehand. Lara and Miles had corresponded with one another by hiding secret letters underneath the statue. The hiding place suddenly reminded her of Rory's letter, which she'd stuffed in the pocket of the dress she'd been wearing the day before. Oh, no, had she left it behind? She took the remainder of the steps two at a time.

Her lady's maid was in Fiona's room, hanging up the few gowns she'd brought with her.

"Moira, did you pack my blue and white striped afternoon dress?"

The maid's eyes grew wide. "The gown was so wrinkled, I meant to sponge and press it, but I left it in the laundry room downstairs at the Greystoke's residence."

Fiona bit her lip. "Don't be concerned. Mrs. Greystoke will send it with the rest of my things soon enough."

The chances of anyone discovering the letter were slim, of course, but Fiona wished she'd taken care to tuck it in her reticule. Reading it over every so often would stiffen her resolve regarding Sir Harry—much like smelling salts for her courage.

When Fiona returned to the drawing room, she was glad the tea cart had arrived. Her father had eschewed the refreshments, however, and was drinking a glass of port instead.

"This looks delicious." Fiona helped herself from a platter of small sandwiches and one of thinly sliced cake. "I've had nothing to eat all day."

"Perhaps that explains how you could contemplate marriage to Sir Harry," her father said. "You're light-headed."

"Now, Charles," Mrs. Robinson murmured.

Her father's statement, albeit somewhat insulting, provided Fiona with an opening to hasten the inevitable.

"I have a wonderful idea," she said. "It's rather last minute, but may I send a message to Sir Harry, inviting him to dine with us tonight?"

Her mother's eyebrows rose. "He's not in London?"

"No, he returned to Blythe Village yesterday, or so he said."

Her father had seemingly resolved himself to the inevitable. "Might as well have him over to dinner and get this messy engagement business behind us. I don't relish a lovesick silver-haired gentleman springing out at me from the bushes when I least expect it, begging for my daughter's hand."

The notion of Sir Harry doing anything of the sort made Fiona giggle. In between deviled ham and sips of tea, she scrawled out the invitation and gave it to one of the footman to deliver. If all went well tonight, she'd be officially affianced.

* * *

Although the Hardy novel rested on top of his coat on the seat next to him, Rory ignored it. He stared out the window instead, willing the train to go faster.

"You haven't relaxed since we boarded," Miles said. "Truth be told, I'm wound up too. I wish I'd brought a bottle of spirits."

"Now that's an idea." Rory reached into his inside coat pocket for a thin silver flask and offered it to his friend. "My valet thinks of these things."

Miles took a sip and returned it to Rory. "A rather invaluable valet."

"Indeed." Rory took a long pull before capping the flask and slipping it back into his coat pocket. "Can you recommend some decent accommodations in Blythe Village? I need a place to stay while I work on my redemption with Miss Fiona. Considering my handicap, it may take a while."

"There are several in town, but it will be late afternoon when we arrive. Let's take a cab to Blythe Manor first, and after we've had a word with Fiona, we'll borrow the carriage to ferry you and your valet to an inn."

"I don't want to embarrass Miss Fiona in front of her parents. What reason shall we give for having come?"

"Ugh...I hadn't thought of that." Miles tapped his chin. "It's a bit far-fetched, but in Mrs. Robinson's last letter to Lara, she mentioned a summer storm had flooded part of the church rather extensively. We can say you wish to volunteer your services as an engineer, and I'm going to assist you."

"That's quite clever, actually, and I *would* like to do some good if I can." He paused. "I can't help feeling apprehensive about speaking with Miss Fiona. She might be inclined to slap my face and have Mr. Robinson horsewhip me before I can explain myself properly."

"She won't. She's hurt, not angry."

"What brings you to that conclusion?"

"She kept your letter secret. Angelica only found it by happenstance after she left. If Fiona had wished to retaliate, she would have shown it to us and blackened your name."

Rory nodded, and his gaze became fixed on the window once more. Each mile that passed brought him closer to stanching her pain...and that of his own heart.

* * *

The footman brought Sir Harry's reply to Fiona within an hour after she'd sent her invitation to dinner. She promptly informed the cook to expect an extra guest that evening and sought out her mother to let her know Sir Harry would be in attendance. Mrs. Robinson was in the pantry, arranging a vase of flowers.

"Mama, Sir Harry has accepted our invitation for tonight."

"You'd best tell your father so he can prepare himself."

"I'm not sure why he's being so difficult. I thought he enjoyed Sir Harry's company."

"As friends, they get along quite well. I just don't think he wanted either of you girls to marry the man." Mrs. Robinson patted Fiona's hand. "Don't worry, he'll come around."

"Where is Papa?"

"Your father is having a stroll in the garden. Be sure and put on a broad-brimmed hat if you go outside. Buttermilk and lemon can only do so much for freckles."

After donning the requisite hat, Fiona made her way to the garden, where her father was enjoying the afternoon breeze next to an arbor of fragrant honeysuckle.

"Are you checking the bushes for silver-haired gentlemen?" she teased.

"At every opportunity."

"Sir Harry will be dining with us."

"I feared as much." Her father rested his hands on her shoulders. "I confess, I find this match less than ideal, and I don't believe you've thought it through. Even if I give my consent, I'd like you to have a lengthy engagement. Perhaps in time you'll come to your senses."

"I see no reason for haste."

"No doubt Sir Harry wishes to rush you to the altar before you change your mind. He may be nearly three times your age, but I can assure you he's still very much a goat."

A painful blush stung Fiona's cheeks. "You needn't be so vulgar, Papa."

"I speak the truth. Your mother and I only want the best for you, my dear."

"I understand and love you for it."

As Fiona walked arm in arm with her father, she wondered if she'd ever be truly cheerful again. Angelica was fond of the phrase *time heals all wounds*, but Fiona wasn't convinced. Since he was family, avoiding Miles forever was impossible. Because Rory Braithwaite was great friends with Miles, she probably couldn't avoid him forever either. Perhaps once she was Lady Wren, the added poise of being a matron would help her deal with them both. Fortunately, Blythe Village was far enough away from London that she wouldn't see either of them for a good long while.

Her father gave her a sidelong glance. "Why are you sighing, child?"

"Oh, am I? I-I'm just happy to be here. The hustle and bustle of town can be so very trying on my nerves."

The butler hastened toward them. "Forgive me, but company has just arrived. Mrs. Robinson begs you to come to the drawing room at your earliest possible convenience."

"Thank you, Truman," Mr. Robinson said. "We'll be along directly."

Since it was only five thirty or so, Fiona was confused. "Truman, has Sir Harry arrived so soon?"

"No, Miss Fiona. It's Mr. Miles Greystoke and a Mr. Rory Braithwaite." He bowed and strode off.

Fiona squeaked and took a half-step backward.

Her father peered at her. "Is anything amiss?"

"I should have worn a bigger hat. The sun has given me a horrendous headache. Please give Miles and his friend my regards. Perhaps I'll see them later."

"Don't be silly, Fiona! You can take a headache powder later, but I insist you come along and greet Miles." He gave her a gentle tug toward the house. "Did you know he was arriving today?"

She gulped. "No, I had absolutely no idea whatsoever. Miles said nothing to me about it when I left town this morning."

"Well, I haven't seen the lad since Christmas." He beamed. "And any friend of Miles's is welcome at Blythe Manor."

"Yes." Fiona felt like a rabbit in the shadow of a hawk. Why had Miles come, and what had possessed him to bring a man who despised her so? *Stay calm*, she told herself...as if staying calm was even in the realm of possibilities.

* * *

Rory tried hard to maintain a pleasant and relaxed demeanor as he chatted with Mrs. Robinson, but his eyes kept flickering toward the drawing room doors in anticipation of Fiona's entrance. Would she appear, or would she send in some excuse for her absence with one of the servants?

Suddenly he realized Mrs. Robinson had asked him a question.

"What? Forgive me, but I'm afraid I'm a bit distracted this afternoon."

"Perfectly understandable. Any time I travel, I leave a bit of my mind behind for a day or two."

Miles cleared his throat. "I was just telling Mrs. Robinson that we met at Cambridge, and that you've come about the flooding at St. James."

Rory was grateful for the prompt. "Oh, *yes*. I studied engineering, you see, and when Miles mentioned you'd had damage to your local church, I was hoping to volunteer my services."

"That's so very kind! All the girls were baptized in St. James, and—"

A male voice rang out. "Hello!" Mr. Robinson strolled in with Fiona by his side.

Miles and Rory both lurched to their feet. A slight smile was etched on Fiona's lips while Miles introduced him to Mr. Robinson, but her face was otherwise an impenetrable mask. After Rory shook Mr. Robinson's hand, he turned to Fiona.

"It's lovely to see you again, Miss Fiona."

"Good afternoon, sir."

She looked right through him and his heart sank.

"I take it you two are acquainted?" Mrs. Robinson asked.

"A little, Mama," Fiona said.

Everyone was seated.

"Miss Fiona, before I forget, I wanted to tell you my sister played a silly prank on you the other day, and she sends along her apologies." Rory forced himself to chuckle as he gave Mr. and Mrs. Robinson a sheepish glance. "It seems Iris sent Miss Fiona a letter which she signed with my name. Although my sister has confessed everything and said she meant it as a bit of a joke, I think things like that can be misunderstood."

He retrieved the letter of apology from his pocket and passed it to Fiona, who'd grown very pale. Although she murmured her thanks, she made no attempt to open the envelope or read the letter. As she sat on the sofa with her eyes lowered and her hands in her lap, she resembled a wax doll.

"Is your sister frequently given to playing pranks, Mr. Braithwaite?" Mrs. Robinson asked.

"Indeed she is, and my father has taken it upon himself to remedy the situation. Iris is to go to America to reside with cousins as soon as it can be arranged," Rory said.

Mr. Robinson grimaced. "Isn't that a somewhat harsh punishment for a little prank?"

Miles came to Rory's rescue. "Actually, I believe Miss Braithwaite is looking forward to the change. I'm given to understand she recently suffered a romantic setback."

"Yes, we're all hopeful Iris will find a suitable husband overseas," Rory said.

The conversation shifted to the damaged church again, and although Rory paid more heed to what was said, he kept one eye on Fiona the entire time. Had she understood what he was trying to say, and would she ever be able to absolve him of blame for her heartbreak?

Chapter 12

Across the Bow

As the conversation in the drawing room continued, Fiona tried to make sense of what she'd just been told. Could Iris truly have intercepted her apology to Rory and thereafter written a letter of malicious lies to hurt her? What a nasty trick! The woman had always had the uncanny ability to find and attack her most vulnerable spots. Her gaze fell to the unopened envelope on the table. The small, neat handwriting was the same as on the letter that had almost destroyed her. Now that Fiona thought about it, the letter *had* sounded like Iris's voice. The band around Fiona's heart eased as she realized the evidence fit together. Better still, Iris was being sent far away, never to bedevil her again! Miles didn't hate her after all, and Rory didn't think her less worthy than Lara. It was almost too good to be true.

"Mr. and Mrs. Robinson, I've trespassed too long on your kindness," Rory said finally. "Might I trouble you for the use of your carriage? My valet and I will be staying in town at an inn."

"Nonsense!" Mr. Robinson exclaimed. "You're more than

welcome here, and we've plenty of room. You're welcome to stay as long as you like."

"That's a very generous offer, but I couldn't possibly intrude," Rory said.

"Yes, you must stay," Fiona said. "We've much to discuss, I think. Besides which, Sir Harry is coming to dine this evening, and two more will round out the party nicely."

Rory exchanged a glance with Miles, who gave him a tiny nod.

"In that case, I'd be very happy to accept," Rory said.

"Wonderful!" Mrs. Robinson smiled with genuine pleasure. "I do so love a full house. With the girls being gone these past few months, it's been terribly lonely. Excuse me while I speak to the servants about making up your rooms."

She bustled out.

Mr. Robinson rubbed his hands together, seemingly no less delighted to have company.

"I confess, I'm looking forward to having a little masculine conversation. I'll leave you young people to visit a while. Dinner is at seven, but do come down at six thirty or so for drinks and conversation."

After her father left, Fiona tore open Iris's letter and read it. Her eyes moist, she glanced up at Miles and Rory afterward. "I'm not sure what to say."

Rory leaned forward, an earnest, almost pleading expression on his face. "Never doubt I have anything but the highest regard for you, Miss Fiona, and I'm mortified you would have believed otherwise. Iris confessed her crime this morning and returned your letter to me. I've read it, and can assure you my offer of friendship still stands, if you'll have it."

"I'm horrified you thought I could harbor any dislike for you whatsoever," Miles said. "I think of you like my sister. And although Lara and I have an understanding, I'm waiting until my graduation to formally propose. The delay has nothing to do with you at all."

"I must admit, Iris's letter knocked me flat."

"Angelica discovered it," Miles said. "She was very concerned about you this morning, as were we all."

"After Miles brought it to my attention, I couldn't rest until you knew the truth," Rory said. "My father also extends his apology for any injury Iris has inflicted. He's to escort her to America personally."

"I'm quite grateful. I've no wish to ever see her again."

"Now that we've cleared up the matter, will you allow us to escort you back to London tomorrow?" Miles asked. "Angelica had your things packed, but she won't ship them until you send the word."

"Thank you, but no. I'm considering Sir Harry's marriage proposal, and I need time to mull it over."

"What?" Rory exclaimed. "Sir Harry has proposed?"

"He's really a very nice man," Fiona said. "You'll have the opportunity to visit with him tonight and you can form your own opinion."

"I meant no disrespect," Rory said. "If you like him, I look forward to getting to know him better."

"So you've come to volunteer engineering services to St. James?"

When Rory nodded, she gave him a wry smile.

"If you should happen to receive an urgent message from your father, I think no one would look askance at your departure." She winked. "I certainly would understand completely."

Fiona stood, and the two gentlemen did the same.

"I'm going to my room to rest until dinner. Servants will be along directly to show you upstairs, but Miles knows his way around." She paused. "Thank you for coming all this way to speak with me. I'm touched."

* * *

With conflicting emotions, Rory watched Fiona disappear from the drawing room. Although he was glad he'd managed to settle her mind about the stupid letter, he was more than disappointed to hear about her impending engagement. Why did it seem as if he was always one step behind?

"I'm sorry I didn't say anything about Sir Harry's proposal," Miles said.

"You knew?"

"Believe it or not, it slipped my mind."

"Don't worry about it, Miles. Even if you'd told me, I still would have come."

"Fiona's right about your making a graceful exit, you know. You can claim a family emergency and nobody would be the wiser."

"No, I don't think I will. Firstly, I don't plan to give up on Miss Fiona quite so easily. And secondly, I've nothing important to do back in London."

"Nobody wishes to see her wed to Sir Harry, but she seems determined."

"I'm equally determined to fight for her. At any rate, I'd genuinely like to make myself useful, and working for charitable organizations gives me pleasure."

"In that case, I'll take you to meet the vicar, Mr. Hamish, at St. James tomorrow and you can survey the damage. In the meantime, I'll send word to Lara, Angelica, and William that all is well here. I know they won't rest until they know we've set things right."

A maid stepped into the doorway to let them know their rooms were ready, so Rory and Miles followed her into the entrance hall and up the stairs. Rory found Blythe Manor to be a very gracious home and was looking forward to seeing more of it. Perhaps he could convince Fiona to give him a tour tomorrow and they'd have the opportunity to converse. He certainly preferred getting better acquainted with her in this sort of setting, rather than the whirlwind atmosphere of the London Season. There, every look and gesture was scrutinized, commented upon, and criticized, and few people could truly be themselves. The artificiality of the Season often worked to the benefit of shallow idiots like Lord Moordale, but made it difficult for most people to gauge true compatibility. No, as awkward as his arrival at Blythe Manor had been, he would try to turn it to his advantage. Whether or not Fiona was receptive, however, remained to be seen.

Hot, sudsy bathwater comforted Fiona and helped soothe her nerves. Her emotions had been tossed around the last few days like the brightly painted wooden diabolo she used to play with as a child. She was grateful and impressed Miles and Rory had come all the way from London to set things right. Furthermore, she was terribly relieved she was still part of the family after all. Measured against those blessings, she couldn't even find it in her heart to despise Iris Braithwaite. In fact, much to her surprise, she felt almost sad for a woman who was so obviously filled with anger. Of course, the notion she would be living on the other side of the Atlantic Ocean before long likely had something to do with Fiona's compassion.

She allowed herself to giggle just a little bit.

Tonight's dinner would prove interesting. The presence of Rory Braithwaite would lend the gathering a certain spark, but she had to be guarded in her manner toward him. He'd been solicitous and kind that afternoon, however, his attentiveness was motivated by obligation so as to make up for his sister's malevolent actions. Fiona had to be careful not to neglect Sir Harry, since *he* was the man who'd proposed to her. No doubt Rory and Miles would return to London tomorrow and she'd be left to consider her future once more.

"Lady Wren," she murmured out loud, to see how the words rolled off her tongue. "Mrs. Rory Braithwaite."

Her maid called from the next room. "Is everything all right, Miss Fiona?"

"Yes, Moira."

Fiona scrubbed her skin with a washcloth and marveled at her change of mood. Several hours ago she'd meant to accept Sir Harry as soon as possible. At present, however, she wasn't quite so eager to rush into an engagement. If Miles didn't intend to propose to Lara until his graduation, Fiona wouldn't be on the shelf quite *yet*. And as far as her public humiliation regarding Lord Moordale, perhaps she ought to just laugh it off. Now that she wasn't surrounded by gaggles of other silly girls desperate to catch the viscount, he didn't seem like such a prize. If it was true the man had accepted money to stay away from Iris, he was most certainly unappealing in the extreme.

Fiona dressed for dinner in a peacock-blue silk concoction featuring a saucy bustle and a fitted bodice. The lace edging around the deep V-cut neckline was both elegant and flirtatious.

"Thank you for bringing this dress, Moira. I wasn't really in the proper frame of mind to help you with the packing this morning, and I'm glad I could rely on your good judgment."

"Well, I didn't have time to pack much, but I tried to pick those gowns which suited you most. This one in particular has always been my favorite."

Fiona smiled. "It's perfect."

"I'm glad you're feeling so much better. It seems as if being back at Blythe Manor has perked you up."

"I believe it has." She reached for her gloves. "I'm going down a little early. I'd like time to speak with Papa before everyone else arrives."

Her father usually enjoyed a little solitude in the library before heading into the drawing room, so Fiona hastened to join him. When she entered the library, he was examining the globe in the corner.

"Hello, Papa. I thought I could find you here."

"Hello, Fiona. You look spectacular this evening."

"Thank you, Papa."

He pointed at the globe. "I was just contemplating how small the world has become with all the steamships crossing the oceans, willy-nilly. For example, it used to take months to cross the Atlantic, but now you can be transported from Liverpool to New York City in a matter of weeks."

"It's rather remarkable, I grant you. Papa, I just wanted to say that I still haven't made up my mind regarding Sir Harry. If you give him your permission to marry me, it doesn't mean we're engaged. You might want to make that clear to him."

"I'll be happy to refuse my permission, if you like. Have you had second thoughts?"

"No, but I just don't see the need to rush into anything."

He peered at her. "I can't argue with good sense, but does this reemergence of caution have anything to do with the arrival of Mr. Braithwaite?"

She felt her face warm. "Not at all! Mr. Braithwaite and I are barely acquainted."

"I'm not a fool, Fiona. When we were in the garden this afternoon, your blood turned to ice water as soon as you heard his name. At present, however, you're quite animated and cheerful. I won't pry, but I suspect you and Mr. Braithwaite had some unfinished business which he has now ably managed."

"Only that his sister behaved toward me like the worst sort of tormenter all Season, and he came to apologize on her behalf! Don't mistake his gentlemanly manners for interest, because I don't."

"Quite so. Yes, it makes perfect sense for a young, handsome gentleman to deliver in person an apology that could more easily be posted in the mail. Especially with the additional and, may I add, somewhat silly pretext of rescuing a church with which he has no connection. No, I don't think I could mistake his manners at all."

"You're quite wrong, Papa, and I don't wish to discuss it further."

To her annoyance, her father chuckled.

Rory and Miles entered the drawing room promptly at six thirty, where a footman was waiting to offer them a glass of sherry. No sooner had they taken a sip when Fiona arrived. Rory felt as if his eyes were riveted to her, and he had no wish to look away. The blue color of her gown was stunning, particularly in contrast to her vibrant hair.

"Good evening, gentlemen," she said.

Miles nodded. "Good evening."

"Good evening," Rory echoed. "Would you care for a glass of sherry?"

He gestured with his glass and splashed a bit of wine onto his hand in the process. As she crossed toward the drink cart, he was obliged to put his glass down on a table and mop the spill with a napkin before Fiona noticed.

She accepted a glass of sherry from the footman. "Mama and Papa will be along directly, and I'm certain Sir Harry won't be far behind."

"Blythe Manor is a lovely house," Rory said. "I'd love to see more."

"Miles can give you a tour. He's quite familiar with every nook and cranny by now, I'm sure."

Fortunately, Miles had Rory's best interests at heart. "But I can't possibly do justice to the place like someone who has grown up here. I'm sure you've many stories to tell."

"That's true. Well, I'll be happy to show you around if you have time before you leave."

Miles gave Fiona a sidelong glance. "You'll have Rory thinking you're inhospitable by trying to rush him out the door."

A slight flush stained her cheekbones. "I didn't mean it that way. Although I enjoy your company, Mr. Braithwaite, I assumed you'd be eager to return to town."

"Nothing could be further from the truth. My sister is in a mood, as you might well imagine. Until she departs for America, I intend to avoid our London residence as much as possible."

"You can always take refuge at Greystoke townhouse when you're in London," Miles said. "You're welcome at any time."

"That's very kind of you. I might—"

Rory broke off as the butler announced Sir Harry. When Fiona put down her glass and went to greet the new arrival, Rory leaned toward Miles.

"She's not making this easy."

"Slow and steady, Rory. I expect it'll take some time for Fiona to trust you. Don't forget, Moordale's ill treatment of her is still a fresh wound."

"Blast that fellow! I hope I never have to hear his name again."

Fiona returned with Sir Harry by her side. "Sir Harry, you

already know Mr. Greystoke, and I believe you've met Mr. Braithwaite."

"Yes, Mr. Braithwaite and I met at the Quarterbury ball." Sir Harry gave Rory an appraising glance and shook his hand with an unusually firm grip. "What brings you lads so far from the pleasures of town?"

"We heard St. James is damaged due to the rains," Miles replied. "Rory came to offer his services as an engineer."

Sir Harry's eyebrows rose. "A benevolent gesture, to be sure. I imagine, however, we have sufficient talent in the neighborhood to overcome any challenge."

"Mr. Braithwaite spent time in India, helping the missionaries drill wells," Fiona said. "I expect he'll have much to add."

"Yes, if St. James needs a well." Sir Harry smirked. "Blythe Village may be in the country, but we're hardly bumpkins, Mr. Braithwaite. I'm certain we can manage without you."

Inwardly, Rory bristled, but he kept his composure. "Sometimes young blood and new ideas are necessary to spot problems older eyes cannot."

"Ha! I believe I've been put in my place."

Although Sir Harry laughed, Rory didn't believe he was truly amused. Truth be told, the man was radiating an immediate and intractable hostility. Mr. and Mrs. Robinson entered the drawing room at that moment, and Sir Harry excused himself to greet them.

Fiona touched his arm. "I'm sorry, Mr. Braithwaite. I'm sure Sir Harry didn't mean to be insulting. Excuse me." She left to join Sir Harry and her parents on the far side of the room.

Rory cocked an eyebrow at Miles. "He jolly well *did* mean to insult me. In fact, the old fellow sent a shot across my bow!"

"He's a retired army commander and I expect he's used to getting his way. Clearly, he senses he has some competition for Fiona's affections."

"She's not a military campaign to be waged!" Rory made a sound of frustration. "I suppose age and maturity in a man don't necessarily go hand in hand where women are concerned."

At dinner, Rory was glad when Fiona was seated between him and Sir Harry, relieving him of the obligation to address the older man directly during the meal. Mrs. Robinson was across the table from Rory, and they conversed about his time in India. Although Sir Harry was largely engaged in speaking with Fiona, Miles, and Mr. Robinson, he apparently overheard and proceeded to talk about India unceasingly. Sir Harry's military command had commenced during the Indian Rebellion of '57, as it happened, and his adventures in that country were inevitably more extensive, harrowing, or exciting than anything Rory had to offer. Inwardly, he rolled his eyes at Sir Harry's gamesmanship, but he let him have the floor.

Despite a rising sense of frustration, Rory managed to exchange a few whispers with Fiona when Sir Harry's attention was diverted by his meal.

"I noticed a rather beautiful oil painting of Blythe Manor in the entryway. That wouldn't be yours, would it?" he asked.

She looked at him with astonishment. "How did you guess?"

"It wasn't hard. I admired it when I first came into the house, and read the signature on the bottom. You possess a marvelous sense of perspective and a skilled use of brush strokes."

"Why...thank you."

"I should like to see more of your work while I'm here."

Her hazel eyes studied him a moment, as if trying to gauge his sincerity.

"I'm perfectly serious," he said. "Art is one of my passions."

"If you promise not to judge me too harshly, I'll show you a few of my paintings and sketches after dinner."

"I'd enjoy that very much."

To Fiona's dismay, she could scarcely eat anything with Rory sitting so near. His presence couldn't be ignored, much like the innervating sound of a church bell ringing out at midnight. How could one man command her attention so fully? She dared not sneak more than a few glances in his direction, lest her expression reveal her innermost thoughts. When finally he spoke to her, his voice sent delicious shivers down her spine, but fortunately she managed to reply without humiliating herself. Success emboldened her to ask Rory a few questions of her own, but since Sir Harry had come to dinner at her particular invitation, she couldn't neglect him.

She tried to imagine how it would be when they were married. Would their dinnertime conversation be as lively as it was at present, or would they fail to have anything in common? Until children arrived, what topics would they have to discuss?

Fiona dipped a spoon into her serving of raspberry and brandy trifle. "Sir Harry, what is your opinion of art?"

"Art?" He seemed taken aback. "Why...I've nothing against it."

Rory leaned forward slightly, as if to catch Sir Harry's eye. "Fiona happens to be a very talented artist."

A ray of warmth formed at her core. "You're too kind, Mr. Braithwaite."

Sir Harry shrugged. "Many ladies amuse themselves with embroidery and watercolors and the like. I think art is a fine pastime."

"Lara tells me Fiona has won several judged competitions," Miles said. "I quite agree with Rory about her ability."

"Fiona's always had a knack for the creative." The note of pride in Mrs. Robinson's voice was evident. "Nobody in Blythe Village draws as well as she."

With a chuckle, Sir Harry nodded. "I'm glad to hear it. Every woman should exhibit many talents."

His disinterested reaction was somewhat disappointing, but perhaps Fiona was expecting too much. Nowadays, men and women often lived vastly different and separate lives. As Sir Harry's wife, she would reside close enough to her parents to visit them frequently. And, as a married woman, she could even travel by herself to London and beyond. Freedom was an undeniable benefit of marriage that appealed to her very much, even if certain aspects of marriage to Sir Harry didn't.

Her mother startled her from her reverie. "Fiona, shall we go through?"

"Oh. Yes, of course."

The gentlemen stood as the ladies departed. Fiona cast one final glance over her shoulder as she left. Sir Harry was preoccupied with selecting a cigar to go with his brandy, but Rory was gazing at her with a sweet smile.

Chapter 13

Games

While Rory savored a snifter of brandy, Sir Harry blew a waft of cigar smoke in his direction. "Mr. Braithwaite, might I inquire after your sister?"

"She's well, thank you. I didn't realize you were acquainted with Iris."

"We've not been formally introduced, but I overheard her mention her engagement at the Quarterbury ball."

"She's had a change of heart. In fact, she's looking forward to visiting relatives in America at the end of the summer."

"America?" Sir Harry chuckled. "How dreadful."

Miles gave the man a level glance. "I'd like to visit America someday myself."

"I have relatives in Chicago. They claim it's actually quite civilized." Mr. Robinson drained his brandy and poured himself another.

Another puff of smoke. "Nevertheless, if you send Miss Braithwaite off to America so soon after a failed *affaire de coeur*, tongues will wag. Society may presume her to be ruined."

Mr. Robinson shifted in his chair. "Come now, Harry."

Rory gritted his teeth. Whatever disagreements he might have with Iris, he'd never countenance anyone besmirching her reputation. "My sister's virtue is beyond reproach, I can assure you."

The older man waved his hand, dismissively. "Of course it is, and I didn't mean to suggest otherwise. It's just that many a girl has been whisked off to the country to hush up a scandal involving a bas—"

"Sir, I must protest!" Miles had gone rigid.

"So must I," Mr. Robinson said. "Harry, that's entirely inappropriate."

"I demand your apology, sir." Rory's tone was even. "No gentleman would ever suggest such a thing about a lady!"

"Tut, tut. Naturally, I apologize if you think I was casting aspersions. Let's change the conversation to something else."

Had he been in any other social setting, Rory would have taken his leave and retired for the night. He was looking forward to spending time with Fiona, however, and refused to allow Sir Harry to spoil the evening. The man might be rich and powerful, but how could she contemplate marriage to him?

For the remainder of the time at the table, Rory was forced to listen to Sir Harry query Mr. Robinson about his investments. Rory found the conversation boring in the extreme, and from the somewhat glazed look on Miles's face, he probably did as well. Nevertheless, Rory feigned polite interest and counted the minutes until it was time to rejoin the ladies.

* * *

While the gentlemen stayed behind in the dining room to indulge in male conversation, drinks, and cigars, Fiona and her mother returned to the drawing room. Although Mrs. Robinson picked up her embroidery hoop, she ignored it in favor of gossip.

"You've made a conquest, I wager."

"Well...Sir Harry has already declared himself."

"No, silly girl. Mr. Braithwaite seems taken with you. He sang your praises quite loudly at the dinner table."

"I caution you not to read too much into his compliments." Fiona was unsure if she spoke for her mother's benefit or for her own. Since overestimating Lord Moordale's affection for her, she wasn't eager to make the same mistake again. "As I informed Papa earlier, Mr. Braithwaite's sister was unforgivably rude to me and I'm sure he feels obliged to make up for it."

Her mother laughed. "Sir Harry felt the need to talk himself up over dinner, so he obviously sees Mr. Braithwaite as a rival." She paused. "Do you like him?"

"I don't know him very well." Fiona tried and failed to keep a smile from her lips. "I confess, however, I find him exceedingly attractive."

"Just as I thought. Well, we'll have to play this carefully. It wouldn't be wise to turn down Sir Harry's proposal until Mr. Braithwaite makes you an offer of marriage."

"You're getting too far ahead of yourself, Mama. Mr. Braithwaite has no such intentions, I'm sure. And at any rate, I can't keep Sir Harry waiting forever!"

"Mark my words, it won't take forever for Mr. Braithwaite to declare himself."

Fiona was relieved when Mrs. Robinson changed the subject to the Season. If she'd had to discuss Rory any longer, she might run the risk of embarrassing herself. As she told her mother about the many soirées, dinners, galas, and musical assemblies she'd attended with Lara, however, she wondered if she should allow herself a tiny amount of hope where Rory was concerned. No, it was foolhardy to set herself up for disappointment again...unless he gave her some clear reason to expect otherwise.

When Miles and Rory entered the drawing room, Mrs. Robinson glanced toward the door.

"Where are Mr. Robinson and Sir Harry?"

"Sir Harry had something he wished to discuss with Mr. Robinson," Miles said.

"I see." Fiona's mother gave her an innocent smile. "Fiona, dear, I've not had a moment alone with Miles since Christmas. Why don't you show Mr. Braithwaite your artwork in the gallery?"

"I'm looking forward to it with great anticipation," Rory said.

"All right." She rose and nodded toward the archway at the far end of the room. "The gallery is in the music room, just through there."

He accompanied her into the next room, where a white, shiny baby grand piano angled out from one corner. Several chairs and sofas were arranged around a fireplace tall enough for Fiona to stand inside without stooping, and numerous paintings and framed sketches graced the twenty-foot-high paneled walls.

Rory had a look of admiration on his face. "This is a lovely room and a beautiful piano."

"It's Mama's piano. She and Angelica play quite well—certainly far better than I do. Do you play?"

"A little."

"Perhaps you'll play for us while you're here."

"If you wish." He glanced at the walls. "Is all this artwork yours?"

"No, not all, but a fair portion." She laughed. "Growing up in the country, sometimes there isn't much for me to do but draw and paint."

He was attentive as she pointed out which paintings and sketches were hers, including the ones awarded ribbons in various competitions.

"I'm impressed. Not only are you beautiful, but you're talented."

"And you possess charm in abundance."

"I'm very sincere in my praise, I assure you."

She gestured to a nearby sketch of Lara in repose, which captured the essence of her sister's comeliness. "My sister's the beautiful one, I freely admit it."

Rory shook his head. "I wish you could see yourself like I do. You're earthy, vibrant, and untamed, like an exquisite wild tiger. Your supposed imperfections are perfection itself. Admire your sister if you like, but trust me when I tell you I could watch the flames in your eyes all night long."

Her mouth went dry and her heart hammered against her chest. "You shouldn't speak that way, Mr. Braithwaite. It isn't proper."

He studied her lips a moment before capturing her gaze once more. "That's true. I haven't earned the right. Not yet."

Sir Harry strode into the room. "I understand you're giving a tour of your artwork, Miss Fiona. I'd love to tag along."

His arrival broke the invisible force gripping Fiona, and she suddenly realized she'd almost forgotten to breathe.

"I'm so glad you're here, Sir Harry," she lied. "Let me begin the tour again."

Although Harry made a tremendous effort to pay Fiona every compliment, as the evening progressed he could almost feel her slipping through his fingers. Several days ago, she'd been emotionally vulnerable, grateful for his assistance, and willing to consider his suit. The arrival of Rory Braithwaite, however, had obviously changed the equation. Ordinarily, there would be no way for him to compete with the young, handsome, and brash lad for Fiona's affections. Nevertheless, Harry was a strong believer in the proverb that said, "old age and treachery will overcome youth and skill." With the right strategy, Fiona would become his wife—but he would have to act decisively. The more time she spent with Braithwaite, the more she would fancy herself in love with him. Just like with Lord Moordale, a little emotional attachment would ultimately accrue to Harry's benefit—if he played his cards right. A simple grasp of human nature and strategy had always served him well in the past.

When Fiona had finished giving her tour of the music room, Sir Harry made his first move. "I'd no idea regarding the depth of your talent, Miss Fiona. I stand corrected if I seemed in any way dismissive at dinner."

She seemed pleased. "Thank you, Sir Harry. It's wonderful to have people take an interest in my work."

To Harry's annoyance, Rory spoke up. "I consider myself fortunate you've chosen to share it with me."

"I feel the same way." Harry flicked him a level glance. "If you'll excuse us, Braithwaite, I'd like to speak with Miss Fiona for a moment."

"By all means." Rory bowed and returned to the drawing room.

When Harry was alone with Fiona, he took her hand in both of his. "Your father has given me permission to marry you. All that remains is for you to accept my proposal."

"But I—"

"I'm planning a European tour for our honeymoon. We'll visit Rome, Florence, Venice, Paris, Vienna, Dresden, Zürich, and Madrid, and stay at the finest hotels. In fact, we can travel anywhere you want to go. I intend to treat you like a princess."

He kissed her hand.

"You're uncommonly generous, Sir Harry, but please understand I haven't yet decided whether or not to accept. There is a great deal for me to consider."

He studied her. "Miss Fiona, I must start a family as soon as possible. If you don't wish to marry me, let me go. Although my heart will be broken, I would at least be able to return to the Season to seek another bride."

Her eyes widened, and a slight look of panic ensued. "I understand."

His smile was, he hoped, kind. "I'm going to London first thing tomorrow, and I'll be back in a few days. Might I expect an answer then?"

She gulped. "Yes. You'll have my answer when I see you again."

A nod. "Now, I've said good night to your parents, so I'll take my leave." He paused. "I can make you happy, my dear. I promise."

"Thank you, and good night."

In the carriage on the way home, Harry devised a strategy to deal with Rory Braithwaite. In cases such as this, knowing one's enemy was of inestimable value. The young man had unwittingly revealed so much about himself tonight that Harry's battle plan was relatively easy to formulate. There would be the possibility of failure, of course, but the risk made the whole thing much more amusing.

Twenty minutes later, Harry entered the drawing room of Sheepfold Abbey and found his elderly mother dozing in a chair. He patted her hand, and she awoke with a start.

"Oh, you're back?" Mrs. Wren blinked up at him. "How was dinner at the Robinsons? Did you manage to acquire a fiancée?"

"Not yet, but I'll have Miss Fiona's answer soon. I'm

heading to London tomorrow morning. While I'm gone, I'd like you to invite her to a formal luncheon two days from now. Pull out all the stops and spend whatever you like."

"May I invite Mrs. Robinson as well? I enjoy her company very much."

"Have them both to lunch, if you desire, but I want the event to take up most of the afternoon."

"Why?"

He paused long enough to invent an excuse. "To impress Miss Fiona, of course. I wish her to understand what her life could be like if she becomes my wife."

Mrs. Wren clasped her hands together in delight. "What fun! You know how much I love to entertain."

"Good." Harry leaned over to kiss her cheek. "I'm going to turn in now, and I'll be gone at first light. Just remember, the luncheon must be for the day after tomorrow."

"Yes, Harry. Leave it to me."

As he left the drawing room, he could hear his mother humming. Her happiness removed any small guilt he might have otherwise felt for involving her in his plot. It was often best to utilize the innocent in these sorts of schemes because their earnestness helped to allay suspicion. Besides which, his mother had reached an age where she needed to feel useful. In this particular case, she would prove to be very useful indeed.

Slightly shaken, Fiona perched on the piano bench for a few moments to consider Sir Harry's ultimatum; she must accept his proposal within days or lose him forever. Oh, this was a dreadful pickle! She'd thought she would have several weeks to decide, if not the rest of the summer. With no other prospects, what else could she do but accept? Yes, Rory had flirted with her earlier, but flirting was not a serious declaration of love. To think he might propose to her before Sir Harry returned was the height of foolishness. What if she turned Sir Harry down only to have Rory depart for London with a wink and a smile? Prudence dictated she decide in Sir Harry's favor.

Furthermore, she couldn't deny the prospect of a Grand Tour was seductive. Her father was not adventuresome and had never seen the need to take his family beyond the borders of England. As Sir Harry's bride, she would visit the Louvre, shop for clothes at the House of Worth, and marvel at all the artistic treasures of Rome! It would be as if her dreams had come true...even if the man at her side didn't quicken her pulse or make her mouth go dry. Yes, she ought to accept Sir Harry and put an end to her prevaricating, once and for all. She would be the toast of Europe, with many wonderful stories to tell her friends and family after her honeymoon. The envy of all her friends, she'd be accepted socially in the highest levels of society. Wasn't that the life she'd always wanted for herself?

When Fiona returned to the drawing room, Miles and Rory were playing jackstraws at the table in the corner, her father was reading, and her mother was embroidering a colorful floral pattern on black linen. Fiona sank down on the chair directly opposite her.

"Your embroidery is coming along well, Mama."

Mrs. Robinson glanced up. "Oh, thank you dear. Sir Harry has gone, then?"

"Yes, it seems he's off to London tomorrow."

"So he said." She lowered her voice. "Have you settled anything?"

"Only that he expects an answer when he returns."

Her mother gave her a sympathetic glance. "A difficult dilemma, I'm afraid."

"Not really. I'd be a fool to refuse him, wouldn't I?"

Rory's voice rang out. "Please join us for a game of jackstraws, Miss Fiona."

She stood. "Thank you, I shall."

Rory smiled as she drew near, and Fiona suddenly felt bathed in warmth...as if she'd just stepped out from the shadows into the morning light. She tried to ignore her feelings and gave him and Miles a stern look instead.

"I warn you, as far as jackstraws is concerned, I've a frightfully steady hand."

Rory chuckled. "More skillful players make for a more challenging game."

Miles looked at him, askance. "Come now, Rory. You don't mind being beaten by a lady?"

"Not if she wins fair and square. Besides which, hasn't anyone ever told you the truth of the matter? Sometimes you must lose to win, particularly when the fairer sex is involved." Rory winked.

"Hear, hear." Mr. Robinson didn't even glance up from his book as he spoke. "You're wise for your years, Mr. Braithwaite."

Miles gathered up the slender carved ivory straws and let them fall into a pile on the table. "Who goes first?"

Rory gestured toward Fiona. "Why, the lady, of course."

She flexed her fingers. "Gentlemen, prepare yourselves for defeat."

Chapter 14

Effervescence

Sunlight was streaming through the windows when the butler showed Moordale into the library of Sir Harry's Belgrave Square townhouse. The viscount scowled and blinked at the light.

"It's too bloody bright in here."

Harry gestured toward the tea service on the table in front of him. "Would you care for tea?"

"No! What the devil do you mean by summoning me at the crack of dawn?"

"It's eleven o'clock in the morning, lad."

"I rarely rise before noon."

"A result of perpetual late-night debauchery, no doubt. Since I was up early to catch a train, spare me your complaints."

Albeit grudgingly, the viscount sat down. "What do you want?"

"That's hardly a gracious attitude for your generous benefactor." Harry sipped his tea. "I need you to perform a service for me regarding Miss Iris Braithwaite."

"Again?"

"Yes. This time, you're to elope with her."

"You must be joking! I've no interest in marrying her at all, as you're well aware. Her father did me an inestimable service by paying me off."

"It won't get as far as marriage. My sources tell me the girl has canceled her social engagements and has been confined to the house for some reason. I can't think why, unless it's to prevent her from slipping out to meet you. She's besotted."

"If she only knew the facts, she'd realize her mistake immediately."

"Be that as it may, you're to write a letter begging her to meet you at midnight tonight, ostensibly to elope."

"How on earth am I to get this lurid communication past her father? I doubt if he'll let me speak with her, and he most certainly would intercept any letter."

"You'll use a Trojan Horse." Harry nudged a slender tome which lay on the table next to the tea tray. "Call on Lady Quarterbury this afternoon with a romantic tale of woe. Tell her you've written Miss Braithwaite a *billet doux* secreted in this book of poetry, and ask her to deliver it for you."

"What makes you think she'll do it?"

"She's always been quite fond of you for some reason, and she's a hopeless romantic."

"Assuming she agrees, then what?"

"Before midnight, you'll be waiting in a carriage outside Miss Braithwaite's residence. After she joins you, you'll travel to Liverpool."

"Why?"

"Her brother, Rory Braithwaite, will strike out in pursuit. I need you to lead him a merry chase until I've wed Miss Fiona."

"Iris Braithwaite's reputation will be ruined. I suppose you don't care about that?"

"It doesn't matter. Her father is taking her to live in America."

"And what of *my* reputation? Viewed as the worst sort of libertine, I'll not be fit to move in society afterward!"

"Since the Braithwaite family will be eager to hush up the scandal, no one will ever know the slightest detail of what has occurred. I'll pay your travel expenses, of course, with something left over to line your pockets." He dropped an envelope full of cash on the table.

After a short pause, Moordale picked it up. "I suppose I've no choice." His expression was sour. "Fiona Robinson is a delightful girl, and far too good for you." He averted his eyes. "She's far too good for me as well, if it comes to that."

Harry felt an inexplicable flash of pity. "She would never have married you, lad. Once her father found out about your debts, he would have put an end to it like all the others. You did the proper thing by breaking it off."

"Perhaps so, but I don't have to be happy about it...no matter how much you pay me."

"Do you imagine yourself to be the only man unable to marry where his heart leads him? Lady Wren was not my first choice for a bride, and yet we were perfectly happy in our own way."

"Who was your first choice?"

"That's unimportant. The fact remains, I need an heir. So I do what I must."

* * *

Lady Quarterbury's butler showed Moordale into the countess's cozy sitting room. She rose as he entered and kissed his cheek.

"I'm so glad to see you! Have you set a date for *le mariage*, dear boy?"

Moordale gave her a sad smile. "Unfortunately, Miss Braithwaite's father has refused his permission for us to marry."

"Oh, no! That's simply too cruel."

"What's worse, he's forbidden us from writing to one another. I'm really quite distraught."

"I hate to see young *amour* thwarted! If I put in a word on your behalf, do you suppose it would do any good?"

A shake of the head. "I doubt it. The irony is that after my estate is sold, I'll have plenty of money to settle all my debts. Iris understands, of course, but her father doesn't."

"Can I do anything?"

The woman's desire to help was so sincere, Moordale hated himself even more for what he doing—if that was at all possible.

"Actually, there *is* something you can do." He retrieved a volume of poetry from his pocket and opened it to reveal an envelope. "This letter is a plea to Iris, begging her to elope with me at midnight. If you could deliver this book into her hands this afternoon without alerting her father as to the contents, I'd be terribly grateful."

She beamed as she took the book. "Consider it done." A sigh. "An elopement is so awfully romantic of you, Iggy. Where will you take Miss Braithwaite tonight?"

"I haven't decided." He shrugged. "A hotel, I suppose. We'll need to catch the train to Liverpool first thing tomorrow morning. Mr. Braithwaite won't think to look for us there."

"Use my carriage for the elopement tonight, and bring her here for the night. Miss Braithwaite will be quite comfortable, I'm certain of it."

Here, at least, Moordale could be completely truthful. "Countess, you've always been so kind to me. I can't thank you enough."

* * *

For days, Iris had felt like a prisoner in her own home, unable to go out anywhere or do anything. If only she could get word of her plight to Aunt Naomi, surely the woman would convince Papa to let her go to Paris! Unfortunately, Iris wasn't permitted to send or receive correspondence unless her father read it beforehand. She could entertain callers, but only so long as her father was present. When pressed for an explanation regarding her absence from the social whirl, however, she was only permitted to say she was busy preparing for her upcoming journey. Truth be told, she'd no desire to mention the actual reason, since it reflected poorly on her character. How she wished she hadn't been found out!

When her father summoned her to his study, Iris arranged her features into a pleasant expression before entering the room. Perhaps he'd had a change of heart, and if he detected any sullenness, it would be the worse for her. She found him sitting at his desk with a letter on the blotter in front of him. She peered down at the missive with suspicion; was she to be blamed for something else?

Peyton glanced up. "I've just received a rather odd message from Sir Harry Wren, and I wondered if you happened to know him?"

A shrug. "I know who he is, but I don't think we've ever been introduced. Why?"

"It seems the chap had dinner with Rory last night at the Robinson's country house, and says he was very impressed."

"Apparently, the man is easily impressed."

"Can't you keep a civil tongue in your head? Sir Harry wants to pop by tomorrow morning to meet the both of us before he heads north again."

Iris's snort of derision wasn't especially ladylike, but she didn't care. "If you imagine the man intends to look me over as a marriage prospect, I doubt it very much. Rory can't have had anything good to say about me."

"You sell your brother short. Despite your differences with him, Rory would never do anything to damage your prospects. Nevertheless—"

The butler appeared in the doorway. "Excuse me, Mr. Braithwaite, but Lady Quarterbury has come to call on Miss Iris."

Peyton's eyebrows rose. "Thank you, Glade. Please tell the countess that Iris and I will be there momentarily."

"Very good, sir." The butler left.

"I wonder what Lady Quarterbury wishes to see you about?"

Although Iris was no less surprised, she didn't let on. "I'm not good enough to receive a visit from a countess?"

"Not every remark is meant as an insult, dearest." He rose. "Let's not keep her waiting."

Lady Quarterbury was standing near the piano when Iris and Peyton entered the drawing room.

"How lovely of you to come, Lady Quarterbury." Iris curtsied.

The countess crossed over. "Thank you, Miss Braithwaite. I'm so happy to have found you at home."

"Please allow me to introduce my father, Mr. Peyton Braithwaite."

He bowed. "What a pleasure to meet you."

The countess giggled. "*Enchanté.*" She lowered herself onto a sofa. "Miss Braithwaite, come sit next to me." She gave Iris a surreptitious wink.

Mystified, Iris complied. Although she didn't know the woman well enough to interpret the gesture, she realized a winking countess must have some hidden agenda.

"I won't stay long, but I wished to return the book of poetry you lent me." Lady Quarterbury reached into her bag and produced a small, leather-bound volume which Iris had never seen before.

"Er...you must have me confused with someone else, Lady Quarterbury. I don't recall lending you a book of poetry."

"Yes, you did. You wanted me to read this poem in particular."

The woman turned toward Iris, opening the book in such a way as to shield it from Mr. Braithwaite's view. An envelope was wedged between the pages—obviously some sort of message.

Iris nodded and accepted the volume. "Oh, I remember it now. Forgive me, but it's been many weeks."

"That's my fault." The countess pouted. "I'm sorry it took me so long to return the book, but the beautiful phrases quite drew me in. Perhaps we'll discuss it when we meet next."

"I don't know when that might be." Iris's gaze flickered toward her father. "I'm off to America at the end of the summer, I'm afraid, and my stay there might be of some duration."

Lady Quarterbury's eyes widened. "On purpose?"

Peyton cleared his throat. "We have relatives there."

"How adventuresome." She rose. "Well, I must be going."

Peyton got to his feet. "It was a pleasure to meet you, Lady Quarterbury. Er...might I ask if you're acquainted with Sir Harry Wren?"

A momentary change of expression rippled across her face. "Why, yes. He's *très distingué* and quite wealthy. A savvy businessman, from what I understand, and a good catch for the right young lady. Why do you ask?"

"He's asked to call upon us tomorrow morning. It seems he dined with my son recently."

"You can never have too many friends. Well, *au revoir!*"

The butler showed the woman out.

Peyton wore a bewildered expression as he turned toward Iris. "Lady Quarterbury is quite handsome, I suppose, but a bit...eccentric." He held out his hand for the book. "May I?"

Oh, no! Fear struck Iris as she gave it to him, but he merely glanced at the title, shrugged, and handed it back without opening the pages. "How strange you should share a love of poetry with a countess."

A sigh of relief. "Yes."

* * *

Clad in an old riding habit, Fiona entered Blythe Manor. As she was removing her gloves and hat, her mother's voice rang out from the drawing room. "Fiona, is that you?"

"Yes, Mama. I'll be there in a moment."

A few moments later, she hastened into the drawing room and perched on the edge of a red velvet-upholstered chair.

"I'm home only long enough to arrange a picnic lunch for Miles and Mr. Braithwaite at the church. They're working with the vicar on plans for new drainage ditches and the like, and will be there all afternoon."

"So Mr. Braithwaite feels something can be done?"

"Oh, yes! He's ever so clever. He had a look around, took a few measurements, and immediately began to sketch out a solution to the flooding problem. Mr. Hamish was very impressed."

"I'm so glad." Her mother peered at her worn clothes. "Didn't we buy you several new riding habits before the Season?"

"Yes, but they remained in London when I left. It's not important; this one will do until Angelica sends the rest of my things."

"I hope you have something suitable to wear to a formal luncheon? You and I have received an invitation from Mrs. Wren for tomorrow."

"I'm sure Moira can find me a gown. I wonder why Mrs. Wren is having us over to lunch?" Fiona laughed. "Perhaps she intends to register her objections to me as a possible daughter-in-law?"

"I certainly doubt that. More than likely, she wishes to know you better. Have you absolutely made up your mind to accept Sir Harry's proposal?"

"No." Fiona bit her lip. "Every time I make up my mind, something unmakes it again."

"Something or some*one?*"

"Mama, Sir Harry has promised me a European tour! You know how much I've always longed to travel."

"But why must he be in such a rush?"

"He wishes to start a family as soon as possible."

"I suppose at his age that's a reasonable justification, but it doesn't give you much time to decide." Mrs. Robinson sighed. "It's a dilemma for you, no two ways about it."

"It's a choice between a solid offer and a will-o-the-wisp." Fiona shrugged. "If nothing else, Sir Harry's ultimatum forces me to be practical."

"Dearest, if you're really torn, I advise you to tell the gentleman to wait until you're sure. If you lose him, so be it."

Fiona's heart gave a great leap. "Do you really think so?"

"I do."

"And you won't blame me if he withdraws his offer?"

"Not at all." Mrs. Robinson smiled. "I have a feeling you won't have to wait long for another proposal—one you'll accept without hesitation."

Fiona jumped up to deposit an ecstatic kiss on her mother's

cheek. "Thank you, Mama! Excuse me while I have a word with the cook about the picnic."

* * *

After Lady Quarterbury left, Iris scurried to her room, extracted the envelope from the pages of the book, and slit it open. As she read the message inside, she gasped with pleasure. Lord Moordale wanted to elope with her? What a wonderful and serendipitous development, and the answer to her prayers! She danced around the room in happiness...until she realized time was running short to prepare. What should she take away with her? A small carpet bag would be all she could carry, so she'd have to pack carefully. None of her gowns could possibly fit in such a small space, but she should be able to manage a few undergarments, a nightdress, petticoat, stockings, a pair of shoes, and a chemise or two. More importantly, since she didn't know for sure how long she would be gone, she'd need to take a great deal of portable property to sell if necessary. Sadly, she possessed very little in the way of pocket money, and her most important pieces of jewelry were locked up in her father's safe. How she wished she could take the heirloom diamond necklace she'd worn to Lady Quarterbury's ball! Still, she had quite a few rings, lesser necklaces, earbobs, and brooches which could be sold for cash, as well as several jeweled hatpins.

Of course, there were also small objects of value waiting to be liberated from the house. The servants were too canny not to notice if she nicked the antique pill box collection in the drawing room, but the silver candle snuffer in the library wouldn't be missed for several days. A slow delighted smile spread across Iris's face when she remembered neither Rory nor his valet were in residence. His bedroom would likely yield a myriad of cufflinks, gold shirt studs, watch chains, and possibly even money. She'd take everything of value and not even feel the least bit of guilt in the process. After all, he'd caused her a great deal of mortification and deserved a portion of grief in return.

When the servants were having their tea, Iris brought a knitting bag into Rory's room and set about stripping it of valuables...even down to the silver shoe horn in the closet and the silver letter opener on his desk. A few coins rested in a small silver dish on the dresser, so she took the coins and the dish too. The embroidered handkerchiefs were too much bother, although she was tempted. The linen squares weren't especially valuable, really, but their absence would cause her brother a great deal of trouble. Of special interest, however, was the pretty Nicholas Noël Boutet pocket pistol in Rory's nightstand—a gift from Aunt Naomi on the occasion of his graduation from Cambridge. Rory had shown Iris how to fire it before and had allowed her to practice with it when they were in the country. The pistol was one of Rory's favorite possessions, and he'd be particularly vexed to find it gone. The pistol and its case went into her knitting bag.

She giggled as she crept from the room. "Burgling is rather fun."

Two footmen brought the picnic to the church in a gig, while Fiona accompanied them on horseback. When the small convoy reached St. James, laborers were already setting down wooden stakes where the ditches were to be constructed. After the picnic was laid out under a shady tree across the street, Fiona sent one of the footmen to tell Miles and Rory lunch was ready. She smiled when the gentlemen hastened over right away.

"So how are things coming along?" she asked.

"The project was less of a problem than I'd imagined," Rory said. "Fortunately, we've hired a local construction foreman who'll help supervise digging the ditches. All told, I doubt the work will take longer than a week."

Miles chuckled. "Rory underestimates his role in the situation. If I had any doubts about his engineering abilities, they've been swept away."

"Don't I know it! I told Mama how impressed we all were when he sketched out his plans with such authority."

Rory shook his head. "Thank you, but the flooding issue should've been dealt with long ago. Despite what Sir Harry may think, nobody local has volunteered to help before now."

"As you said last night, sometimes a pair of young eyes is exactly what's needed, and here you are." Fiona sank down onto the blanket. "Come eat! The cook has very generously provided several different kinds of sandwiches, roast chicken, pickles, bread and butter, fruit, and gingerbread. Oh, and the footmen have pots of hot tea or cool, sweet lemonade."

"What a treat," Miles said. "I confess, I'm starving."

"It was lovely of you to suggest a picnic, Miss Fiona," Rory added.

"I'm just trying to do my part."

Fiona was pleased when the gentlemen heaped their plates full. A steady breeze kept the insects at bay, and the temperature under the tree was pleasant indeed. Although she tried not to look at Rory overmuch, her gaze kept straying to his face.

Unfortunately, as he was preparing to bite into a pickle, he caught her staring at him. Immediately, he reached for a napkin. "Have I crumbs on my chin?"

She hoped he didn't notice her blushing. "No, you're perfectly fine. Actually, I was thinking what a fine subject you'd make for a sketch. Would you sit for me after dinner?"

His mouth quirked up in a crooked grin. "That depends on whether you'd sit for me at the same time."

"What?"

"If you'd be so kind as to furnish me drawing materials, we can make a contest of it. You and I shall sketch one another for a half hour, after which Miles will judge which likeness is better."

Rory's suggestion pleased Fiona no end, but she pretended to be unsure. "What of poor Miles? He'll be dreadfully bored watching us draw."

"Never mind me," Miles said. "I can always play solitaire while nursing a brandy."

"I know...I've an hourglass timer with twenty minutes per turn," Fiona said. "Our contest will last from the first grain of sand until the last."

"And I'll play the role of timekeeper," Miles said. "I've only ever seen Rory draw engineering plans, so this should be fun!"

"Actually, I've never drawn a person before, only wild animals," Rory said. "I suspect in your case, Miss Fiona, it amounts to the same thing."

"Don't tease me. I don't bite."

"I heard a rumor to the contrary."

"I've been defanged."

He regarded her appraisingly. "You do seem tamer than usual today, but I take nothing for granted."

"Good." She winked. "A lady should always keep a gentleman guessing."

Throughout the rest of the picnic, the conversation between Fiona and Rory was light and convivial. She realized she was flirting outrageously, but she had no wish to curb herself. In fact, her mother's advice had buoyed her so much that she felt unfettered and effervescent. If her manners made Rory uncomfortable, let him return to London. In fact, she'd already given him a ready excuse he could use at any time. *If you should happen to receive an urgent message from your father, I think no one would look askance at your departure.* Until then, she'd encourage his interest as much as possible. Perhaps *Mrs. Rory Braithwaite* didn't sound quite as grand as *Lady Wren,* but Fiona suddenly didn't care a jot. Her feelings toward Rory already far outstripped anything she could ever muster toward Sir Harry—despite all the older man's wealth, power, and prestige. If Rory should ever declare his love for her, Fiona suspected she would float away with happiness, joining the glorious white clouds suspended in the sky overhead.

Chapter 15

Urgent Business

As Fiona put pencil to paper in her quest to capture Rory's image after dinner that night, a sense of joy was unleashed. Not only was she engaged in one of her favorite activities, but she could stare at the man all she liked without fear of censure or embarrassment. What a shame the contest would last only twenty minutes! She drank in the shape of his blue eyes, nearly flawless nose, and well-shaped lips that most women would die to possess—or kiss. Once she'd finished sketching his square jaw, she moved onto replicating his fair hair, admiring the way it curled at the nape of his neck and swept back from his brow in a regal fashion reminiscent of a lion's mane.

Miles tapped the hourglass. "Time."

So soon? When Fiona tore her gaze away from her subject, she felt somewhat bereft. After glancing at her sketch, however, a pleasurable sensation ensued. With more time, she would have sketched more fully the top of Rory's broad shoulders, crisp white shirt, black evening jacket and bow tie. Nevertheless, the rest of the sketch reflected his masculine qualities rather well, in her opinion.

Miles gestured. "Can you turn your easels toward me so I can judge?"

"Oh, have our dueling artists finished?" Mrs. Robinson put down her embroidery hoop and rose from her chair. "I'd love to have a look."

Mr. Robinson glanced up from his novel. "I'd like to form an opinion as well."

As the Robinsons hastened over, Fiona came to stand next to Miles so she could better view the sketches. Her jaw dropped slightly at the idealized version of herself gazing out from the paper. Rory had drawn her as a far more beautiful woman than she could ever be in real life. The woman in his sketch was warm, self-possessed, and desirable—nothing whatsoever like the somewhat unremarkable girl she truly was. Her insides melted, and something nudged her into strange, unfamiliar, wondrous territory. A few moments before she was just a girl, and now she was a girl...in love.

Mrs. Robinson made a sound of admiration when she saw Fiona's sketch, but gasped when she glanced at the drawing of her daughter. "Isn't that lovely! Mr. Braithwaite, I had no idea you were so talented."

"By Jove, that's Fiona to a tittle." Mr. Robinson bent to have a closer look. "And that's Mr. Braithwaite, as if he were standing right in front of me."

While Fiona's parents and Miles discussed the two sketches, Fiona joined Rory off to one side. "It's a beautiful drawing of me, Mr. Braithwaite, but not faithful at all."

"I sketched what I saw." He nodded toward her sketch. "I daresay you were far too kind in your depiction of me."

"As you say, I sketched what I saw. However, I do believe you've bested me tonight. I bow to your superior skill."

"No, my skills were enhanced by my subject, Miss Fiona. I was feeling inspired."

"You're quite the gallant." She touched Miles on the shoulder. "You needn't pronounce the winner. I concede to Mr. Braithwaite." Unspoken was the realization she'd also surrendered her heart.

"I was about to say both sketches are extremely praiseworthy. I believe them both to be winners."

Fiona laughed. "Very diplomatic, I must say."

"I don't have a vote, but I agree," Mr. Robinson said.

Mrs. Robinson nodded. "I couldn't decide between them, even if I tried."

As the Robinsons returned to their former fireside activities, Rory gave Fiona a bow. "We are—I believe—well matched, Miss Fiona."

Her eyes widened at his turn of phrase. Was he referring only to their artistic abilities or was there a deeper meaning to his words? Her stomach fluttered, and she became breathless.

"Well...that's settled then. And now, Miles, it's your turn to sit for me."

Miles held up his hands to ward off the suggestion. "Oh no, I couldn't possibly!"

"Nonsense. I daresay Lara would treasure your likeness very much. Perhaps you'll join me in the effort, Mr. Braithwaite. I'd enjoy seeing more of your skill."

"If you wish, but I'm not certain Miles will provide the same inspiration."

"Ha!" Miles settled himself in his chair. "I want you to know I'm only agreeing to sit because of the jolly nice picnic Fiona brought to the church today. Good deeds deserve a reward."

She frowned. "I can't bring you lunch tomorrow, unfortunately, but I will send along servants with a hamper. It seems Mama and I have been invited to dine with Mrs. Wren."

"Never mind me," Mr. Robinson murmured from several yards away. "I'm fine by myself."

Mrs. Robinson clucked her tongue. "Oh, Wilfred, you wouldn't want to have lunch with us anyway. It'll just be ladies."

Fiona and Rory sketched in silence for a little while.

"Mrs. Wren is Sir Harry's mother, I take it?" Rory asked finally.

"Yes, and she's a good friend of Mama's."

"When will we have the pleasure of Sir Harry's company again?"

Fiona shook her head. "He mentioned being gone only a few days."

"Let's hope the man finds something so absorbing in London that he cannot tear himself away for several weeks."

Although she couldn't say so aloud, Fiona agreed with the sentiment wholeheartedly. Now that she'd decided to refuse Sir Harry, she wasn't looking forward to delivering the news. He was a forceful man, and she suspected he wouldn't accept her decision gracefully. As long as Rory was nearby, however, her courage would rise to the task. In addition, when she announced her refusal, she fervently hoped Rory would be encouraged enough to make a proposal of his own.

Miles's eyes slid toward the timer. "How much longer?"

"No talking!" Fiona admonished.

Miles resumed his pose. "I was just going to suggest Rory play the piano for us after this."

"What a delightful suggestion," Fiona said. "In fact, I'd love it if you would, Mr. Braithwaite."

Rory winced. "I'm rather rusty, but if you promise not to

judge, I'll be glad to play. Actually, ever since I saw that piano in the music room, I've wanted to hear how it sounds."

Fiona smiled. "Your fingertips will coax only the loveliest of music from its keys, I'm certain."

* * *

"Good night, Colleen." Iris sat on her bed, clad in nightdress and wrapper. "I'll see you tomorrow."

"Very good, Miss Braithwaite. Sleep well."

As soon as the maid left, Iris sprang into action. First came the farewell letter she'd leave for her father. She'd been composing it all afternoon in her head, but hadn't dared commit the words to paper lest the letter be discovered too early. After she'd written it, she was surprised at its short length...but what else was there to say? The letter ended with her promising to write once she and Moordale had married, with the expectation her father would invite them to return to London. Once confronted with the reality of the situation, her father couldn't fail to welcome the newlyweds with open arms. In addition, Rory would be forced to be gracious because as the wife of a peer, she'd outrank him!

After sealing the envelope, Iris arranged it on her pillow for Colleen to find the following morning. Next, she stripped off her nightclothes and dressed herself in two pairs of everything wherever possible. Until Moordale took her shopping, she'd have to look presentable in what she could smuggle out of the house. Although she was rather warm bundled up, it couldn't be helped. Her carpetbag was stuffed to bursting with her belongings—purloined and otherwise—and couldn't hold anything else.

At the appointed hour, Iris snuffed out her oil lamp, opened her door, and felt her way down the hall in the dark.

When she was nearly to the stairs, however, she heard a creak on the floorboard overhead. Frozen with fear, she flattened herself against the wall and held her breath. If caught, how could she possibly explain being fully dressed and clutching a carpetbag full of valuables? Her heart hammered against her chest as she waited to see if she'd been found out. Fortunately, whoever was stirring at that time of night didn't come down the staircase.

She sucked air into her lungs and crept down the stairs once more, praying she didn't trip and break her neck. When she reached the entryway, she was glad that the streetlights shining through the glass in the door gave her a little illumination. Wincing at every little noise she made, Iris teased open the hidden drawer in the calling-card table where a spare key to the front door was kept. She was also pleased to discover the butler's purse—a small leather envelope contained cash used to pay messengers, deliverymen, and cabs. Glade would be vexed to find it missing, but her need was greater. She pocketed the money, unlocked the door, and eased out into the night.

Moordale, looking as dashing as ever, was waiting for her next to a grand carriage. Without a word, he whisked her and her bag into the cab and signaled the driver to drive on.

Iris giggled as she threw her arms around his neck. "This is so exciting!"

He patted her back. "Yes, it is."

"Well, kiss me!"

The rushed peck on the cheek wasn't exactly what she'd had in mind, but she supposed a speeding carriage wasn't conducive to amorousness. She sat back, smoothed her skirts, and tried to relax. Eloping was extremely trying on her nerves.

"Er...did you have any trouble getting away?" he asked.

"No, although I was certain I'd be caught any moment. Where are we going?"

"It's too late to catch a train, so I thought we'd spend the night at Lady Quarterbury's house and start our journey tomorrow. You won't be missed until then."

"Oh, Iggy, I do love you so." She rested her head against his shoulder, closed her eyes, and breathed in his cologne. "Have you a special license so we can be wed?"

He cleared his throat. "No worries, my dear. I'm taking care of everything."

* * *

Harry ate breakfast at his London townhouse, and then asked the butler summon a cab to take him to the Braithwaite residence. After asking the driver to wait, he stepped down from the cab, lifted the brass knocker on the shiny red door and gave the plate several sharp raps.

His knock was answered almost immediately by the butler. "Are you Sir Harry Wren?"

"Why, yes."

"We've been expecting you. Please come in. Mr. Braithwaite will see you right away."

The butler took Harry's hat and coat and showed him into a study where a gentleman was pacing. Harry could see the man's resemblance to his son immediately, although Mr. Braithwaite's face was creased with anguish and worry. Harry pretended not to notice.

"Sir Harry Wren at your service." He extended his hand for a handshake.

"Peyton Braithwaite."

"It's a pleasure to meet you. Please forgive the early hour of my visit, but I'm just on my way to catch a train north, and I wanted to meet you before I left town. As I said in my message, I dined recently with your son and found him quite charming."

"I apologize, sir, but you find me exceedingly preoccupied this morning. I must ask you to do me a small favor, if you will." Mr. Braithwaite retrieved a letter from his desk. "Could you take this message to Rory? He must return to London immediately on a matter of extreme urgency."

Harry feigned concern as he took the letter. "Of course I'm happy to oblige, but is there anything I can do?"

"I'm afraid not, but I'll be greatly in your debt if you deliver the message without delay."

"Count on me, Mr. Braithwaite. I hope when next we meet, the circumstances will be far more favorable."

"As do I, Sir Harry. As do I."

Mr. Braithwaite rang for the butler to show Harry out. Moments later, Harry emerged from the house with a broad smile on his face. He tucked Mr. Braithwaite's letter into his coat pocket and gave it a pat. "I love it when a plan unfolds."

* * *

All morning, workers had been busy with spades and shovels, digging shallow trenches to channel rainwater away from the foundations of St. James church and toward a narrow creek downslope. Pleased with the progress so far, Rory was conferring with the construction foreman when Miles appeared.

"Excuse me, Rory, but there seems to be a huge boulder embedded underneath the topsoil across the easternmost trench. Do you want to reroute, or should the workers use pickaxes?"

The foreman grimaced. "Cutting through rock will slow us down something awful, Mr. Braithwaite."

"I expect we'll have to reroute, then," Rory said. "Let's go have a look and see what we're up against."

Just as they'd finished plotting a workaround, a cab stopped in front of the church. When Sir Harry emerged, Rory exchanged a dismayed glance with Miles.

"Rotten luck. I was hoping I'd seen the last of him for a while."

"Why is he *here* of all places?" Miles muttered.

"Probably wants to tell us what we're doing wrong."

As the older man approached, Rory forced a smile. "To what do we owe the honor, Sir Harry? I thought you were in London."

"I've just this moment returned. I stopped by your father's house this morning to introduce myself before I left. He was in a bad way, I'm afraid."

Although it was a warm summer day, Rory suddenly felt cold. "Is he ill?"

"He seemed to be in excellent health, although exceedingly preoccupied." Sir Harry produced an envelope. "He sent a letter along, and asked you to return home immediately."

"Did he mention what this is about?"

He shook his head. "I don't know. I didn't want to pry, of course, but whatever it is, your father requests your assistance."

With bloodless fingers, Rory tore open the letter and read his father's scrawling hand. A muttered imprecation wasn't enough to vent his feelings afterward.

"What is it?" Miles asked. "What has happened?"

Despite his ill feelings toward Iris, Rory was unwilling to blacken her name in front of Sir Harry. "The less said here the better, but indeed I must leave immediately."

"Can I do anything to help?" Sir Harry asked.

"No, but thank you for delivering my father's letter so faithfully." Rory checked his timepiece. "It's just noon. If I hurry, I can probably catch the one o'clock."

Concern creased Miles's brow. "May I come with you?"

"Actually, I was hoping you would. Let me have a quick word with the foreman and we'll be off."

"After the cab drops me at home, I'll send it over to Blythe Manor for you," Sir Harry said. "That way, you won't experience any delay getting to the station."

"Thank you again." Rory shook his hand. "I'm more grateful than I can say."

After Sir Harry climbed into his cab and was out of earshot, Rory gave Miles a grim glance. "Iris has run off with Moordale, and I'm returning to London to track them down."

His friend looked shocked. "I'll help you, of course, but I'm so sorry! Does he mean to marry her?"

"How? By all accounts, he has no money for a special license."

"Perhaps he borrowed money from a friend?"

"Who would lend it to him except someone who didn't wish to be paid back? He could take Iris to Gretna Green, of course, but there's a three-week residency requirement for marriage. Surely he'd know I'd find them by then. No, I suspect he won't marry her until my father pays him a huge sum of money."

"How dastardly!"

"You understand what this means for Iris?"

"I think I comprehend the situation perfectly."

"You can't tell anyone *anything* right now—not even Lara. If society catches wind of this, my sister will be ruined. I doubt she'd be able to escape the scandal, not even across the ocean in America."

"I'm afraid you're right."

"You've no idea what this will do to my father. After my mother died, he wasn't the same." He shook his head. "He'd just begun to show interest in life again, but this will set him back immeasurably. I can't believe Iris could be so bloody selfish!"

"Give the foreman instructions and I'll bring the horses around."

"Thank you, Miles." He frowned. "There's something else. We must be exceedingly casual about our departure from Blythe Manor or awkward questions will arise."

"Mr. Robinson left on business this morning, so the entire family is out for the day. A casual departure shouldn't be difficult."

Rory gritted his teeth. "Blast Iris for causing trouble just when I was starting to make inroads with Miss Fiona! I'll do what I can to recover my sister, but I won't ever forgive her."

* * *

The sumptuous and lengthy luncheon repast at Sheepfold Abbey rivaled anything Fiona had ever seen in London. She lost count of the number of courses, but by the time desert came around she could barely manage to sink a fork into the scrumptious lemon curd and vanilla cream-filled cake. Although her mother and Mrs. Wren talked about all manner of things, Fiona's thoughts were pleasantly occupied with the music Rory had played the night before. He'd begun with a simple lullaby to warm up his fingers, and then segued into Chopin. She could have listened to him play all night long. What would he play for her tonight?

"Mary, have you begun preparations for the Harvest Festival yet? I'm so glad you're the chairwoman this year. Nobody organizes as well as you do," Mrs. Robinson said.

"Actually, I've been working since the beginning of the

year." Mrs. Wren glanced at Fiona. "Young people always lend a wonderful amount of energy to any undertaking. I hope we may count on your participation. "

"Certainly. What sort of participation are you looking for?"

"Perhaps you and Miss Lara might be in charge of soliciting goods for the church bazaar? Your pretty faces will have the donations rolling in."

"Why, thank you for the compliment." Fiona smiled. "When I return home this afternoon, I'll write Lara to ask for her commitment. I've not been as devoted to charitable endeavors as she has been, but I'm trying to improve myself. I welcome the opportunity to help."

Sir Harry sailed into the dining room. "May I join you ladies for dessert?"

Fiona's heart sank. She'd hoped he would be away for several more days at least.

"Harry, I'm surprised you're back so soon," Mrs. Wren said.

He took the seat next to Fiona. "I finished up my business sooner than I'd anticipated and caught an early train."

She forced a smile. "Good afternoon, Sir Harry. We were just talking about the Harvest Festival. Mrs. Wren has asked Lara and me to take charge of bazaar donations."

"I don't know if that will work." Sir Harry rubbed his hands in anticipation as a footman set cake in front of him. "Miss Fiona and I might still be on our European tour by then."

Fiona exchanged an uncomfortable glance with her mother. "I haven't yet given you my answer, Sir Harry."

"I know, but I'm quite hopeful." He paused. "By the way, Mrs. Robinson, your house guests have departed."

"What?" Fiona exclaimed.

"Yes, I ran into them at the train station. Mr. Braithwaite and Mr. Greystoke asked me to convey their sincere thanks for your hospitality, but Mr. Braithwaite was called back to

London. Apparently he'd received a letter from his father this morning, or so he said."

Mrs. Robinson was obviously taken aback. "Did he act as if anything was amiss?"

"Not at all." He winked at Fiona. "I daresay the urgency of his business had something to do with his lack of amusement here in the country. You know how it is with young men and wild oats. They can't stay away from the excitement of town for long."

"What about his work at St. James?" Mrs. Robinson asked.

"I understand it had reached the stage where a foreman could take charge." Sir Harry took a bite of cake. "Mmm. Heavens, but this is delicious!"

The tart lemon curd turned to sawdust on Fiona's tongue. So Rory had departed on a pretext after all, without even bothering to say good-bye. After last night, he'd undoubtedly sensed her growing attraction to him and decided his absence would be the kindest response. Unless, perhaps, he'd left a message for her? She seized upon that slim hope to keep her from falling completely into the depths of despair. Nevertheless, Sir Harry's announcement had sent a shock to her system. Her eyes locked onto her mother, and Fiona sent her a silent plea for help.

Mrs. Robinson folded her napkin and tucked it next to her plate. "Mary, I can't tell you how much we've enjoyed lunch, but I'm afraid we must go. I seem to have developed a little tickle in my throat, and I shouldn't take any chances."

"What a shame." Mrs. Wren pouted. "I was hoping we could enjoy a small glass of sherry after dessert."

"Perhaps next time."

Fiona remembered her manners. "Thank you, Mrs. Wren. Everything was delightful."

"Mother, why don't you have your sherry and I'll have one

with you?" Sir Harry stood. "Pour two glasses and I'll see the Robinsons out."

As they headed toward the door, Sir Harry fell into step with Fiona. "May I call on you tomorrow? I'm looking forward to hearing your decision."

"Yes. I'll give you my answer tomorrow."

Chapter 16

Delly

In the carriage on the way back to Blythe Manor, Fiona stared straight ahead without speaking. Mrs. Robinson seemed to be at a loss for words as well. Finally, she reached over and gave Fiona's hand a comforting squeeze.

"I'm sure Mr. Braithwaite's reason for leaving is a very good one."

Fiona's eyes grew moist. "He didn't even say good-bye."

"If an emergency has called him away, you can't blame him for that."

"You heard Sir Harry's assessment of his demeanor; nothing seemed amiss. No, I believe Mr. Braithwaite has left Blythe Manor on a pretext and won't return. I must have made him uncomfortable by fawning over him last night."

"You weren't fawning that I could tell. And even if you're right, isn't it better to know how he truly feels about you than to have false hope?"

Despite her best efforts to control her emotions, her lower lip began to tremble.

"No. Sometimes false hope is better than none."

Meeting her mother's sympathetic gaze was her undoing. With a strangled sob, she dissolved into tears. "It hurts, Mama! I really care for him."

"I know."

Mrs. Robinson drew her into an embrace and let her cry until the carriage pulled into the driveway. "You must pull yourself together now. You can't let the servants see you upset."

Fiona dried her eyes, took several deep breaths, and clung to the notion that Rory's abrupt departure was not as it appeared. When she entered the house, she immediately descended the stairs to the staff level to seek out the butler.

"Truman, is there a message from Mr. Braithwaite for me?"

"No, Miss Fiona."

She gulped. "Did he receive a letter from anyone this morning?"

"Not that I recall."

"When he left, did he appear to be distressed in any way?"

"No, although he and Mr. Greystoke seemed to be in a rush to depart. I overheard something about a lady, but more than that I can't say."

Her voice was barely above a whisper. "Thank you."

So that was that.

Fiona fled to her room and sank down into the corner rocking chair with a pillow clutched in her arms. Tears pooled in her eyes and spilled out onto her face so freely that the high lace collar around her throat grew moist. Rory Braithwaite wasn't to be the romantic hero of her melodrama after all, no matter how much she wished otherwise. He'd come to Blythe Manor to apologize for his sister, and out of pity or remorse had said a few pleasant things to buoy the flagging confidence of an unexceptional girl. If she'd mistaken his kindness for anything more, it wouldn't be the first time she'd misunderstood a man's intentions. What did she know of true love, really, other than what she'd read about in books? She needed to grow up now and put silly daydreams behind her. Tonight she would cry for what could never be, and tomorrow she'd start a new phase of her life as the future Lady Wren.

* * *

While a grim-faced Peyton stood nearby, Rory read Iris's farewell letter aloud. Afterward, he tossed it onto his father's desk in disgust. "I can't believe it. That's the most selfish and self-centered nonsense I've ever read."

"Moordale should be horsewhipped for his part in this," Miles said.

Peyton gave him a sad glance. "I know we can count on your discretion, lad. Our predicament isn't to leave this room."

"Of course. I've come to help in any way I can."

"And we're grateful to you."

A myriad of questions were running through Rory's mind. "How did Moordale manage to arrange an elopement when you were monitoring all her mail and visitors?"

"I suspect he had a willing accomplice in Lady Quarterbury." Peyton held up a thin volume. "The woman paid Iris a call yesterday, ostensibly to return a book of poetry she'd borrowed. I'm guessing a message from Moordale must have been tucked in between the pages."

Miles shook his head in bewilderment. "But Lady Quarterbury is a countess and quite respectable!"

"Even a countess can be misguided."

Rory made a sound of frustration. "Have you contacted the police?"

"Yes, but there's little they can do. Iris is of age, and all the evidence suggests she left of her own accord."

The volume of poetry caught Rory's eye and he picked it

up for a closer look. The worn binding was soft green leather with gold embossing. Entitled, *Regard—Lovely Poems of Love,* the spine was stamped with a Roman numeral three. Unfortunately no bookplate or inscription inside the cover indicted the name of the owner.

"This doesn't belong to Iris. She loathes poetry." Rory glanced at his father for confirmation. "Don't you agree?"

"Yes, it's not hers. As you see, it's one of a set. I checked, and we have nothing like it in the house."

"Perhaps it belongs to Lady Quarterbury," Miles said.

"Undoubtedly it does. Well, lads, do you have any ideas on how we're to find Iris?"

"If we knew where Moordale lived in town, we could start with his residence," Miles said.

"I believe Moordale and Iris were corresponding several months ago," Rory said. "The writing desk in her room will probably contain his old letters with a return address."

"That's brilliant." A ghost of a smile finally lifted the shadows on Peyton's face, but his smile quickly faded. "Er... there's something else you should know, Rory. The staff went into your room this morning to clean and noticed your possessions were in disarray. Although I didn't mention it to the police, I believe Iris may have stolen some of your valuables."

Rory's thoughts immediately went to his Boutet pistol, but he didn't want to add to his father's worries. "Never mind that now; possessions can always be replaced. Miles, will you help me search my sister's desk for Moordale's address?"

"Yes, and when we find it, we'll pay him a call immediately."

"And if he won't let you in?" Peyton asked.

Rory exchanged a glance with Miles. "We're prepared to force the issue." He slipped the volume of poetry into his jacket pocket.

Before heading to his sister's bedchamber, Rory ducked inside his own room just long enough to confirm the pistol and many of his belongings were missing. "Just as I feared, Iris stole my pocket pistol along with whatever else she could find."

Miles was dumbfounded. "Why would your sister steal your firearm?"

"It's one of my most treasured possessions, and she knows it." He shook his head. "I have the distinct impression Iris wanted to hurt me as much as possible."

"Don't forget, she's under Moordale's influence."

"Perhaps so, but she's cooperated quite willingly. I daresay he didn't tell her to steal my shirt studs."

"I expect not. Come one, let's find those letters."

Fortunately, the writing desk in his sister's room contained Moordale's letters in a bundle tied with a rose-colored grosgrain ribbon.

Rory cocked an eyebrow at the return address. "Moordale's London address is in Pimlico? I would never have guessed that."

"Hardly a fashionable part of town."

"Most decidedly not. I can't imagine he'd bring Iris there, or that she'd willingly stay with him if he did." A shrug. "Well, so long as he doesn't become my brother-in-law, I don't care about his circumstances a jot. Let's go see if he's receiving visitors."

* * *

Rory and Miles arrived at Moordale's shabby boarding house address and climbed to the third floor. Not surprisingly, nobody answered their knock. The landlord heard the noise, however, and emerged from a door down the hall.

"If you're looking for Lord Moordale, I haven't seen him

since early yesterday." He gave them an appraising glance. "Are you two gents creditors?"

Rory cleared his throat. "No, we're friends of his. The thing is, he's gone missing and we're worried about his welfare."

"Perhaps you could let us into his residence?" Miles asked. "We'll check for clues as to his whereabouts."

The landlord's eyes narrowed. "The fellow owes me rent. I'm not sure if I can remember where I put the extra key."

Rory produced a pound note and held it up. "Perhaps this will help?"

The landlord took the money, produced a key ring from his pocket, and unlocked the door. "When you see His Lordship, tell him I'm going to start selling his clothes to pay his back rent."

"Er...we'll mention it to him."

When Rory and Miles entered the room, they discovered the interior was just as shabby as the exterior. The carpets and draperies were threadbare, and the furniture was utilitarian at best. The bed hadn't been slept in and the chamber pot hidden behind a ripped screen was empty.

"Thank heavens for small favors," Miles murmured.

When Rory opened the wardrobe doors, he noticed very few clothes inside, and whatever remained was in disarray. "It looks as if someone packed in a hurry. I'm guessing our quarry has decamped."

Miles dumped the wastebasket on the bedspread and began to sort through bits of assorted refuse. "Overdue bills from tailors, hatters, the jewelers, and a stationery store."

Rory peered at the large pile. "Moordale was living on the edge of financial disaster, apparently, but he always kept himself well-dressed."

"Wait...these bills have all been marked paid quite recently."

"He must have come into a small sum?"

Miles smoothed out a crumpled letter. "Here's correspondence from his lawyer, mentioning taxes due on his country estate, Bramble Hall."

"I wonder if Moordale would've taken Iris there?"

"And risk scandalizing his neighbors and servants? I doubt it."

Frustrated, Rory ran a hand through his hair. "This investigation isn't getting us far."

Miles frowned as he glanced around the room. "Why don't you look through the drawers of the desk, and I'll check that valise on top of the wardrobe?"

Rory craned his neck. "There's a valise on top of the wardrobe?"

"It's easy to miss unless you're standing at a distance."

While Miles retrieved the flat leather bag, Rory searched the desk drawers. Unfortunately, he found nothing of interest except pots of ink and writing instruments. When the bed creaked, he turned to discover Miles perched next to the pile of bills with a yellowed letter in his hand and a peculiar expression on his face.

"What do you have there?"

"Moordale may very well be a blackmailer. It seems Lady Quarterbury has a colorful history."

Rory was dubious. "It's common knowledge she used to be a governess or something."

"She was never a governess." Miles tapped the letter. "According to this, she used to go by the name of Delly Delphinia, back when she was a member of the demimonde some years ago."

"That's awkward. How do you suppose Moordale discovered her secret?"

"This letter is from the late Wallace Rupert Montague,

Moordale's father. It seems Miss Delphinia used to be a great favorite of his in his youth."

"Debauchery runs in the Montague family, apparently."

"Indeed. When their affair ran its course, Wallace introduced Delly to his good friend, the Earl of Quarterbury."

"Which is how Delly became Lady Quarterbury."

"This letter may explain how Moordale persuaded the countess to deliver his message to your sister. I expect she'd do anything to keep this information private."

"I'm amazed Moordale left that letter behind, but I suppose he was in a rush."

Miles gave the missive to Rory. "Well, it's yours now, along with an enormous amount of leverage."

"In that case, let's pay the countess a call without delay."

* * *

Although Rory pressed him, Lady Quarterbury's butler was adamant about refusing his request for admittance. "The countess is not at home. I'll be happy to take your calling cards."

"Please tell Lady Quarterbury that we've an urgent message for her about Miss Delphinia," Rory said.

"Very good, sir."

The door closed. Miles sighed. "What now?"

"We wait."

Very shortly thereafter, the butler returned to whisk them from the doorstep and into the drawing room. When Lady Quarterbury joined them, her demeanor was regally cool, but Rory detected an element of fear behind her aquamarine eyes.

"What's this nonsense about, gentlemen?"

Rory got straight to the point. "I'm looking for my sister, Countess. You conveyed a letter to her from Lord Moordale yesterday. They eloped last night, and I suspect you know where they're hiding."

"I haven't the slightest idea to what you may be referring."

Rory held up the Montague letter. "This missive describes the transformation of Miss Delly Delphinia into Lady Quarterbury."

"Where did you get that?"

"I found it in Moordale's belongings. Was he blackmailing you with it?"

"Of course not! I doubt very much he would ever think of such a thing."

Rory placed the letter on the table between them. As Lady Quarterbury stared at it, her fingers twitched. "Have you come to sell it?"

"No, but I'd like some information in exchange. I must find Iris and take her out of harm's way. I think your help isn't too big a price to pay for a piece of paper."

"Miss Braithwaite isn't in any danger, whatsoever. Yes, Lord Moordale asked me to give a letter to your sister, asking her to elope. I let them spend the night here last night—in separate rooms I might add. They left for the train station just before noon today."

"Where were they going?"

"If I tell you, you must both promise not to touch him."

Rory exchanged a glance with Miles. "You have our word."

"They were bound for Liverpool."

"Why Liverpool?"

She shrugged. "Moordale told me he wished to avoid Miss Braithwaite's family until a special license is granted. Although I offered to conceal them here in the interim, he insisted on leaving London. I recommended the Adelphi Hotel as a place to stay, and I believe you'll find them there."

Miles gave her a level glance. "Did you give him money for the special license or travel expenses?"

"No. I've offered Iggy money upon many occasions, but he's always refused. My assistance to him has always been more in the realm of society contacts and introductions. I'm a member of Almack's—now Willis's Rooms—and I assist him with vouchers every year."

Rory produced the book of poetry. "Is this yours?"

The countess shook her head "Moordale left it with me to employ in his ruse." She reached for the Montague letter "If that's all..."

He held up a quelling hand. "Just one more thing. In your opinion, is he in love with my sister?"

Lady Quarterbury's eyebrows drew together. "I confess, on that point, I'm somewhat puzzled. Naturally, I assumed he was. When I saw the two of them together this morning, however I felt the affection to be rather one-sided on Miss Braithwaite's part. I didn't pry, but if that's the case, I can't understand why he asked her to elope."

"Neither can I. Thank you, Countess." He picked up the Montague letter and gave it to her. "You may be assured of our silence regarding Miss Delphinia."

"I certainly hope so." She crumpled the letter, threw it into the fire, and smiled. "*C'est la fin d'une époque*."

On the way out of Bowerhaven Hall, Miles gave Rory a curious glance. "My French is rather rusty. What did she say?"

"She said 'It's the end of an era.'" Rory frowned. "Her problems are solved, perhaps, but not mine. We must depart for Liverpool as soon as possible."

* * *

Although Iris had contented herself with a light, late night supper of clear soup, a small portion of roast chicken, Yorkshire pudding, and vegetables, Moordale was working his way through a huge rack of lamb and an amazing number of side dishes. As they sat in the dimly lit, nearly empty public dining room of the Adelphi Hotel, she tried to catch his eye.

"You seem to be ravenously hungry, Iggy."

"Being cooped up on trains for seven hours does wonders for my appetite. At any rate, the food is quite good. I must remember to thank Lady Quarterbury for her recommendation when I see her next."

"We arrived at the hotel so late, we're fortunate there were rooms available." She bit her lip. "I'm really not sure why we had to leave Lady Quarterbury's lovely house at all. We could have stayed out of sight and nobody would have been the wiser."

"It would have been rude to impose on the countess. Besides which, if your father connects her visit to the elopement, he'll look for you there. We'll be safe in Liverpool until the special license comes through."

"When do you suppose it will be granted? For propriety's sake, we should wed as soon as possible."

He finally spared her a glance. "These things take time, dearest."

"Well, I only ask because if we're here for more than a few days, I must have more clothes. The countess was kind enough to lend me this gown, but I came away with very little else."

"We'll discuss it when I arise."

"Shall we meet for breakfast at half-past eight?"

He shook his head. "The desk clerk mentioned a gentlemen's card game in the salon, so I may not get to bed until very late. I doubt if I'll rise much before midday."

Iris was taken aback. "What am I to do with myself all morning?"

"Why don't you go shopping? The concierge can suggest some suitable establishments."

She lowered her voice, even though few restaurant patrons remained in the dining room to overhear. "I'm sure he could, but I've very little money."

"Have the shops send the bills to the hotel."

"If the Viscount of Moordale came along to introduce me that might work. Otherwise, no shops will extend credit to a complete stranger."

"I'd like to give you shopping money, but I must conserve my cash for the game. I'll be able to buy you some things out of my winnings tomorrow."

For not the first time since she'd left home, her faith in Moordale wobbled. "The card game involves gambling?"

"Cards are not much of a risk for me." He winked. "I'm really rather clever at it."

"If you say so." She frowned. "It's quite late, so I'll say goodnight."

"If you wait until I finish eating, I'll walk you to your room."

"N-No, that's all right. Enjoy your meal and I'll see you tomorrow."

Before Iris left, she deposited a kiss on his cheek—which he received with little outward sign of pleasure. Although her feelings were wounded, she shook it off. The day had been long and they'd traveled in less than ideal conditions. Undoubtedly his congeniality would reemerge after he'd had a night's sleep.

As she made her way from the dining room and through the hotel's luxurious lobby, she was puzzled at the desk clerk's pointed stare. He nodded to a bellman, who immediately trotted over and fell into step beside her. Confused, she paused.

"Is something wrong?"

"I'm sorry, but the hotel doesn't allow unescorted ladies in the lobby after hours."

Her face flamed so hot with embarrassment, she could hardly respond. No powder dusted her nose, no rouge reddened her cheeks, and her borrowed gown was modesty itself, so how could the staff take her for a lady of dubious repute?

"Heavens! I'm not *unescorted*. Well, I'm unescorted *at present*, but I'm not ordinarily. Your implication is offensive, I must say."

Unbending, the bellman gestured toward the stairs. "Forgive me, miss, but I'll just walk you to your room."

As quickly as her dignity would allow, Iris mounted the steps without deigning to glance at her unwanted escort. After she was alone in her room, however, she collapsed onto a chair and covered her face in shame. She'd considered posing as Moordale's wife when checking into the hotel, but then the desk clerk would have given them adjoining rooms. Although in the eyes of society she was already "fallen," her morals would not let her go that far! Moordale had told the hotel she was his cousin, Miss Montague, but clearly they hadn't believed him. The hotel staff had pronounced judgment and her humiliation was complete.

She sat back, let out a slow breath, and tried to cope with an onslaught of doubt and regret. The realization had come on slowly over the course of the day, but it was finally so plain she couldn't ignore it any longer; running off with Moordale was rapidly losing its luster. Her initial escape from her father's house had been exciting, and she'd been thrilled Moordale had brought her to Lady Quarterbury's abode. Since that morning, however, things had seemed to go downhill quickly. The long journey to Liverpool had been wearing, although she supposed that wasn't Moordale's fault. On the other hand, if he'd managed to rise at a reasonable hour, they could have taken an earlier train and reached the hotel earlier. What was worse, because she wasn't traveling with a lady's maid or some other female companion, she'd been subjected to several hostile stares by fellow travelers, as well as whispered impertinent remarks. She couldn't exactly lay the blame for that at Moordale's doorstep either, but the cumulative effect had eroded her enjoyment of the adventure.

Furthermore, he couldn't give her a definite date for their wedding ceremony. Although she might be slightly besotted, she wasn't stupid. Special licenses to marry were expensive, but not altogether impossible to manage, especially for a peer. If his intent on taking her away was other than matrimony, however, he'd shown little interest in *that* too. Had he been the least bit romantic, she supposed she would have put up with a great deal, but his attitude had been exceedingly reserved. In short, she was forced to conclude she'd made a terrible mistake.

Tomorrow, she would demand to return to London and beg her father for forgiveness and mercy. Hopefully, he would escort her to Philadelphia as planned and she could put this nightmare—and Moordale—behind her.

Chapter 17

Dire Straits

Moordale's stomach was full and his wallet was flush with the cash Sir Harry had given him for his travel expenses. So far, the plan to whisk Iris from London had gone flawlessly, although Moordale was glad he didn't have to marry her. Certainly the woman was handsome enough to have caught his eye at the beginning of the Season, but after he'd met a certain auburn-haired beauty, his interest in Iris had waned. Although Moordale realized he wasn't the right man for Fiona, he hoped she would be happy with Sir Harry. The older man had a tremendous amount of money, at least, and she'd never lack for material possessions.

He ordered a glass of cognac and brought it with him into the smoke-filled salon, where a lively game of pharo was underway. His manners and cash won him ready acceptance, and he was gratified to discover his luck (aided by his expertise with sleight-of-hand) was strong. As the hour grew late, the players dropped off one by one until the game dissolved altogether. The last remaining player, Mr. Carney, gave him an engaging grin.

"I can tell you're a man of good luck and high aspirations." Carney's voice had a distinct American accent. When coupled with the man's somewhat foxlike appearance, Moordale found him amusing. "There's an elite, high-stakes game in a warehouse by the docks. Care to join me?"

Moordale's pocket watch revealed the time as three o'clock. "It's a tempting offer, but I'd best turn in for the night."

"It's up to you, of course, but with your luck and ability, I suspect you could make a fortune. Last night I watched a man win ten thousand pounds, and he had nowhere near your skill."

Moordale bit his lip. Ten thousand pounds would solve a great many of his problems, such as paying the taxes on his country estate and bringing the property back up to snuff.

"You need an introduction, of course, which I'm happy to furnish." Carney stood. "I'm heading there now."

Despite his better judgment, Moordale was nearly persuaded. "Is it safe walking around at this time of night? Liverpool is rife with gangs, I understand."

"The warehouse is less than five minutes from the hotel. Besides which, I carry my own protection." Carney revealed the pistol secreted in his pocket. "I've never actually had to fire it, but the few times I've been accosted by wayward youths, a flash of this sends the villains running for cover."

"I expect so." Moordale chuckled. "All right, I'll join you for a little while."

"Good. If the game isn't to your taste, I'll escort you back to the Adelphi. I suspect, however, you'll be tonight's big winner." Carney gave him a broad smile and a wink. "I must be careful not to bet against you."

* * *

When Iris woke in the morning, she donned the only fresh change of clothing she possessed and tried to do something with her hair. Yesterday, Lady Quarterbury's lady's maid had helped her dress and arranged her golden tresses, but today she was on her own. After a frustrating half hour of failing to achieve a passable style, she finally braided her hair into a pigtail and wound the braid into an unflattering bun at the nape of her neck. How she'd taken her lifestyle before now for granted!

Although she was famished, Iris was reluctant to go downstairs to the dining room for breakfast alone. Last night's episode with the hotel staff had embarrassed her so much she was still feeling the sting of humiliation. Increasingly annoyed at Moordale for putting her in a difficult position, she rang for tea and toast to be brought to her room. While she waited, she counted up her paper money and coins to determine how extensively she could go shopping. After she added the sum, however, she realized she wasn't even sure how much clothes actually cost. It had always been her habit to buy whatever she wanted and have the bills sent directly to her father. There'd never been the need to economize or live within a budget. Indeed, whenever she stayed with Aunt Naomi, the wealthy woman had encouraged her to buy only the most expensive and luxurious items. As Iris stared at her small cache of money, her plan to go out shopping that morning suddenly seemed almost too daunting to manage.

Her breakfast was taking altogether too long to arrive, so Iris decided to ring again for a servant. Just as she was reaching for the bell cord, however, a knock came at her door.

"Thank heavens!"

Iris opened the door, expecting to see a servant with a tray. Instead, a well-dressed man was waiting in the hall.

"Miss Montague? I'm the hotel manager, Mr. Pruning. Will you kindly come with me?"

Nonplussed, Iris blurted out the first thing that came to mind. "I'm sorry, but I'm waiting for breakfast."

"You'll have to wait a little longer, I'm afraid." He stepped back to let her pass. "This way, please."

She gulped. Were they tossing her out of the hotel as a tart, or had they somehow discovered her true identity and sent a message to her father?

"W-What is this about? I'm not leaving the hotel without Lord Moordale."

"We've bad news about your cousin, and the police are here to speak with you." He emphasized the word *cousin* ever so slightly.

"Bad news? What sort of bad news?"

Mr. Pruning refused to say anything more, so Iris was obliged to retrieve her door key, and accompany him downstairs. He escorted her through the busy lobby, past the front desk, and into a suite of offices. A policeman was waiting inside and the trickle of fear down her spine became a flood. Had her father told the police that Moordale had kidnapped her?

The hotel manager shut the door and offered her a chair. The officer, whose name badge was marked O'Hara, peered at her for several long moments before speaking.

"After the nighttime desk clerk got off duty this morning, he discovered a gentleman in the alleyway behind the hotel. He'd been beaten, robbed, and shot once at close range. The clerk remembered him as having registered at our hotel."

Iris squeaked in horror. "Not Lord Moordale?"

"The very same."

"Where is he? Oh, don't tell me he's dead!"

"He's at Liverpool Royal Infirmary."

"I must go to him!"

"Not so hasty, lass. I'm afraid I've some questions for you regarding your relationship. You see, I did some checking in *Burke's Peerage*, and it seems the Viscount of Moordale, doesn't have any female cousins."

For her family's sake, Iris was determined to keep her real name to herself. "What does that matter?"

O'Hara leaned forward. "We believe Lord Moordale was lured from the hotel in order to rob him, and we think you had something to do with it."

"What? You're mad!"

"It's been my experience when somebody lies about their identity, they've a great deal to hide. I want you to give me your real name, identify your accomplice, and tell me where to find him. If you don't feel like answering my questions, you can accompany me to the bridewell and sit in a cell until you do."

The manager cleared his throat. "I don't mean to be indelicate, but before anyone goes anywhere, the hotel charges must be settled." He brandished the bill.

Iris gripped the armrests of her chair with shaking hands, praying to awaken from the nightmare. Perhaps she could retrieve her things and slip out of the hotel without anyone noticing. "I have a little money. Let me go to my room to fetch it."

O'Hara shook his head. "No need. I'm having your luggage brought down now."

A second policeman came into the office just then, carrying Iris's carpetbag and reticule.

"What did you find, Sergeant Callahan?" O'Hara asked.

The sergeant chuckled. "She's a right thief, this one. Her bag is full of all sorts of items purloined from some chappy with the initials R.A.B. She even stole his Frog pistol!"

O'Hara raised one eyebrow. "A pistol, eh?"

"Yeah, I'm thinking maybe we just found the murder weapon."

Iris felt the blood leave her face. "*Murder?* You didn't say anything about Iggy being dead!"

Callahan scoffed. "He ain't dead yet, you stupid strumpet, but if he dies, you'll swing for it."

It was all too much. Iris finally lost consciousness and slumped over in her chair.

Fiona went through her day with an air of resignation. She'd lain awake most of the night trying to come up with a legitimate reason to refuse Sir Harry but couldn't think of a single one. She'd tried to convince herself her feelings for him would grow over time. If not, she'd be in good company, since few girls married for love.

In the drawing room, the sketching materials and easels were still in view from her contest with Rory. He hadn't bothered to collect the one he'd done of her, and she couldn't bear to look at it—or at the one she'd done of him. Miles hadn't even taken the ones she and Rory had drawn of him. She asked one of the maids to pack the sketches away and to return the easels to the room where they were usually stored. It might be a very long time until she had the stomach to draw another portrait again—if ever. Landscapes, still life tableaux, and animals would have to suffice.

She wandered into the music room and sat on the piano bench a moment, remembering how enthralling Rory's playing had been the previous evening. Although Rory wasn't quite as skilled a pianist as Angelica, she'd loved his interpretations all the same. After running her fingers lightly over the ivory keys, she lowered the fall and turned away. It was time to focus on a future that didn't include him. Certainly, she had much to look forward to, including travel and children, and it would be a relief to put the messy business of courtship behind her forevermore.

When Sir Harry finally came to call that afternoon, she didn't shrink from giving him the answer he wanted to hear. She couldn't feign giddy pleasure at their official engagement, but he didn't seem to mind. Her parents greeted the news with reluctant acceptance, but Sir Harry didn't seem to mind their lack of enthusiasm either. In fact, he didn't act surprised in the least.

"Now that that's settled, we should set a date." He practically bristled with energy. "While I was in London, I took the liberty of applying for a special license so we can marry as soon as possible. How about next Wednesday morning?"

Mr. and Mrs. Robinson exchanged a bewildered glance, and Fiona snapped out of her lethargy. "What?"

"I see no reason to wait."

Fiona looked to see if he was joking, but he seemed perfectly serious. "Sir Harry, we can't get married that soon. My sister won't be home until the end of the Season!"

"I think you may call me Harry now that we're affianced." He shrugged. "We can wed in London, if you prefer. That way, your extended family may attend the wedding without any trouble at all."

"But your mother is chairing the Harvest Festival. How can she take time away from her duties to travel to London?"

"All the more reason to have the wedding quickly so Mother can get back to her duties. Our honeymoon tour will most assuredly be concluded by Michaelmas, so we might even be able to attend the festival, if you desire."

Mrs. Robinson finally found her tongue. "Sir Harry, a proper trousseau can't be assembled in a week's time."

"Fiona may buy whatever she likes in Paris. I'm prepared to be very generous."

"You're generosity itself, I'm sure, Harry." The familiar moniker felt awkward on Fiona's lips. "But you must consider how strange it will seem for us to marry in such a hurried manner. Such haste is usually considered unseemly."

"Nonsense. Licentiousness would never be attributed to a man my age."

Mr. Robinson coughed. "I wouldn't say *never*."

"I share my daughter's concerns." A rosy flush stained Mrs. Robinson's face. "Society may think a hasty marriage is somehow *necessary*, if you catch my meaning."

Sir Harry smiled. "Such speculation will last only for a few months. Even the least clever people can count to nine, Mrs. Robinson."

Fiona realized to delay the inevitable was probably pointless. "You're very persuasive, Harry, and I can understand why you've been so successful in business. Let's set the date two weeks from Wednesday at the earliest. That should give Papa enough time to put the announcement in the paper and for us to send out handwritten invitations."

"Excellent."

"But I want Mr. Hamish to marry us at St. James, where I was baptized. If Lara and the Greystokes cannot attend, I'm sure they'll send their best wishes."

Even though Fiona knew she was doing the proper thing, she felt as if a dark cloud had filled the room and was pressing down on her. Sir Harry exchanged a few more pleasantries with her parents, and she allowed him to kiss her cheek before he left the house. As soon as the door closed, however, the tears began to fall. Mr. Robinson hastened to enfold her in his arms.

"What's wrong, Fiona?"

"Nothing, Papa. I'm just...happy."

* * *

Rory and Miles entered the private train compartment and heaved their bags onto the overhead luggage rack. After they settled themselves into their seats, they exchanged a weary glance.

"Last leg to Liverpool. We'll arrive just before dark." Rory shook his head. "I've traveled to the city once before, but I'd forgotten what a long journey it is from London."

"I'm actually quite glad we're traveling without valets or heavy trunks. It's made the transfers a little easier." Miles laughed. "I must say, my family was shocked to see me at breakfast this morning. They'd all gone to bed when I arrived home last night."

"I daresay they hadn't expected you for another week at least."

"Yes, and I'm not sure they believed my explanation. Lara was particularly unhappy I was leaving again so soon, but I told her I was accompanying you on a matter of business that couldn't be delayed. Fortunately, she didn't press for more details."

"I'm sorry to take you away from Miss Lara, and I wish you could have told her the truth. If this situation with Iris can be sorted out, I hope you can eventually tell your entire family what has transpired. I shouldn't like to be responsible for driving a wedge between you and them."

"I have every confidence we'll find your sister and that everything will turn out well."

"I hope you're right, but I can't help but think there's more to this story than we know. I mean to press Moordale for answers when we're face to face."

"I quite agree. I've tried to take Moordale's measure, but there are so many contradictions as to make it impossible.

Considering his financial woes, I find it curious he never pressed Lady Quarterbury for money, especially since he possessed the key to her downfall with his father's letter. That speaks well to his character."

"It *is* curious, but he's still a villain in my view. Whatever his problems, he'd no business leading Iris astray the way he has."

"When we recover her, perhaps she'll have seen the error of her ways."

"If not, she'll have plenty of time to think it over while during her voyage to America."

The female jailer's firm push sent Iris stumbling into the cellar holding cell, and the clang of the closing iron lock echoed in her ears. As her eyes strained to adjust to the dim lighting, a strident, coarse female voice made her jump.

"Welcome to paradise, dearie!"

A chorus of cackles rang out from the depths of the large dungeon-like room, but Iris made no reply. She found a seat on the bench closest to the door and pressed her back into the bricks as if she could somehow dissolve into the mortar. The horrible place made her skin crawl, and it was too dark to make out the horrors lurking in the corners. For all she knew, rats were eyeing her ankles even now. Perhaps spiders dangled overhead, destined to entangle themselves in her hair. More than likely, her human companions posed bigger dangers. She'd been thrown in with depraved criminals of the worst sort, who certainly despised her kind. Would they strip her of her finery and laugh at her nakedness?

In short order, the stench of stale drink, mold, and the contents of a ripe chamber pot reached her nostrils. Not even pressing a perfumed handkerchief underneath her nose could blunt the smell.

"Eh, look, it's the Queen of Sheba. She's too good for the likes of us."

More cackles.

"Oh, leave off. Can't ye see she's scared?" A heavily painted older woman approached and sat down nearby. "Hello, dearie. Never mind this lot. They just like to hear themselves talk. I haven't seen ye in here before."

"No."

"My name's Lizzie.

"Iris."

"That's a pretty name. Have ye got a bully yet, Iris?"

"Excuse me?"

"A man who procures for ye."

"No. I-I'm not a prostitute, or any sort of criminal at all. I'm in here by mistake."

General laughter followed her remark, followed by exclamations of "Me, too!" and "That's what they all say!" Lizzie shushed them as best she could, and turned her attention back to Iris.

"Of course yer not a common prostitute." She looked Iris up and down. "I can see yer more of a high-class girl, ain't ye? Well, when ye get out of here, come see old Lizzie at the Foggy Notion Tavern, dockside. I'll introduce ye to Mrs. Pompadore, the madam of the Liverpool Venus Club. She only takes the freshest high-society girls, and ye can earn a smart living under her wing."

Horrified, Iris could only squeak out her whispered thanks before lapsing into silence. Although she'd lived a sheltered existence, she knew what a madam was and what Lizzie meant. Merciful heavens, what if Moordale died before he could clear her name? Even if she convinced the police of her innocence in the robbery, they'd never believe she hadn't stolen the property in her carpetbag. If she asked them to contact her father, would he help her out of this predicament? If not, she'd be convicted of theft and go to jail for a long time. Truth be told, she really *was* a thief and deserved to be locked away, didn't she? After her incarceration, what could she possibly do but seek employment as a working girl or a maid...even though she'd had no experience with either profession. Iris glanced around, wondering how many of the women in the miserable cell had been forced into unsavory occupations by bad luck or dire circumstances. She prayed she wouldn't be one of them.

* * *

Bags in hand, Rory and Miles approached the front desk of the Adelphi Hotel, where the clerk gave them a bright smile. "Do you gentlemen have reservations?"

Rory shook his head. "No, we need two rooms, but we're also looking for someone. Is Lord Moordale staying with you?"

The man's eyes widened. "Er...might you be friends of his?"

"Not exactly, but we must speak with him. Could you tell us what room he's in?"

"Let me get the manager, Mr. Pruning."

As the clerk disappeared into an inner office, Miles caught Rory's eye. "He knows something about Moordale. That's a positive sign."

Rory was dubious. "Did you see the man's expression? It's what he knows that worries me."

Moments later, they were ushered into Mr. Pruning's office, where Rory introduced himself and Miles to the manager.

"Our business is with Lord Moordale. Could you take us to him?"

Mr. Pruning shook his head. "I'm afraid the poor fellow has

been taken to the Liverpool Royal Infirmary in dire condition with a gunshot wound."

Miles gasped. "What?"

A shock went through Rory, but he forced himself to remain calm. "He was traveling with a woman. Is she safe?"

"Miss Montague, as she called herself, has been taken to the Hotham Street Bridewell as an accessory to the robbery."

Rory was stunned. "That's completely absurd!"

Mr. Pruning shrugged. "If you know the woman, perhaps you can vouch for her. The police believe her to be in possession of stolen property."

Inwardly, Rory groaned. How had Iris gotten herself into such a horrible mess?

"Mr. Pruning, can you tell us everything you know about the robbery?"

"I really don't know very much. Last night, Lord Moordale spent several hours in our salon, playing cards. The night clerk saw him leave the hotel with another gentleman around three o'clock. Thereafter, that same clerk found His Lordship in the alley, beaten and shot. Unfortunately for Miss Montague, she happened to have a pistol in her possession."

Rory shook his head. "Sheer coincidence. There's been a dreadful misunderstanding."

"Mr. Braithwaite and I will need rooms for the night while we sort this all out," Miles said.

The manager nodded. "Certainly. Forgive me for asking, but if you're friends with Lord Moordale, perhaps you could settle his bill and take it up with him later?" He slid an invoice across the desk.

"Of course." Rory glanced at the bill and reached for his wallet. "Just one thing, Mr. Pruning. I'm certain you would never want the security of the hotel brought into question?"

The man stiffened. "Why, no! We pride ourselves on protecting the safety of our guests!"

Rory laid cash on the manager's desk. "I don't want to see anything about these events in the paper or the subject of casual gossip by the staff. Otherwise, I might find it necessary to bring up to the press the lapse of security that led to Lord Moordale's robbery. Do we understand each other?"

A tight smile lifted the corners of Mr. Pruning's lips as he collected the cash. "Perfectly."

"Good. Please have our luggage put in our rooms." Rory and Miles stood. "We'll need a cab to take us to the bridewell."

Chapter 18

Loose Ends

Freeing Iris from the lock-up house was taking a Herculean effort due to Sergeant O'Hara's uncompromising attitude. Even as Rory laid out the facts, the policeman's expression remained obdurate. Only Miles's level-headed presence prevented him from exploding in frustration and making everything worse.

"Everything in Miss Montague's bag has either my initials or my family crest on it, as evidenced by my ring." Rory removed the signet ring from his finger and placed it on the sergeant's desk. "The Boutet pistol case is engraved with my full name, which appears on my calling card as well as my initiation card from White's of London."

Rory produced both cards and placed them on the sergeant's desk next to the ring.

"I can swear to you that Miss Montague had all those items with my permission, and if you've examined the pistol, you already know it hasn't been fired. You simply don't have any reason to hold her any longer."

O'Hara still seemed unconvinced. "Maybe she isn't a thief

exactly, but there's still the matter of her involvement in the robbery itself."

Even Miles was losing patience. "Come now, Sergeant. Miss Montague had no motive whatsoever to cause Moordale any harm. In fact, she was under his protection."

"You'd do better to search for the man who was in Moordale's company when he left the Adelphi Hotel early this morning," Rory said. "You must have a description of him from the night clerk."

"Hmm." O'Hara's eyes narrowed. "You're hiding something about the girl. If her name's Miss Montague, I'm Sir Robert Peel."

Rory gritted his teeth. "Surely you can't fault us for shielding a lady's reputation?"

"Sergeant, have you managed to speak to Moordale about what happened?" Miles asked. "He could clear things up immediately."

"He hasn't regained consciousness, as far as I know. The surgeon said the bullet didn't hit any vital organs, but Lord Moordale was beaten badly and might not ever wake up."

Despite Rory's distaste for the viscount, he winced. Whatever Moordale's motive in running off with Iris, he'd never wanted him beaten to death.

O'Hara studied him a moment. "All right, I'll release the girl into your custody. I must say, Mr. Braithwaite, you're a good brother. If my sister had run off with His Lordship, I'd be tempted to let her spend the night in jail."

Rory was startled. "How did you know?"

"I'm a detective, Mr. Braithwaite. Besides which, you and your sister look like two peas in a pod. Sorry for putting you through your paces, but I had to be sure."

* * *

When the cell door opened and her name was called, Iris's blood ran cold. Was she about to learn Moordale had died of his injuries and she was to be charged with his murder?

Lizzie gave her a nod. "Good luck, dearie. Just remember to come see old Lizzie at the Foggy Notion Tavern. I'll get you set up with the right people."

"Thank you. You've been very kind."

Her gratitude was sincere. Lizzie had kept the other women at bay and had been an ally of sorts. Although the air in the corridor was only slightly fresher than that of the cell, Iris took a deep breath when she emerged. However grim her stay had been, Iris knew the neighborhood lockup was probably luxurious when compared to a real prison. As she waited for the female attendant to lock the door behind her, she knew she'd do almost anything to avoid being put back behind bars.

"Come on, lass." The woman motioned for Iris to follow her down the hall and up the stairs to the street level.

"Where are you taking me?"

"Upstairs. Sergeant O'Hara says you're to be released."

Relief made her head swim. Moordale must have cleared her name!

"Lord Moordale has vouched for me then?"

"No. A couple of gents have come to collect you."

Her pace slowed. None of her acquaintances knew where she was, so Iris was mystified. Could the gentlemen possibly be procurers—bullies, Lizzie had called them—looking to take her on? If so, she would refuse to leave the bridewell! At the top of the stairs, she caught sight of Rory and Miles, and she'd never seen anything more beautiful. She threw her arms around her brother and clutched him tight.

"Thank you." Her face was pressed into his coat lapels so her voice was muffled. "Thank you."

After she finished hugging him, she embraced and thanked

a startled Miles, too. Finally she stepped back and managed a wobbly, tearful smile.

"I don't understand how you came to be here, but I'm terribly grateful."

Sergeant O'Hara tipped his hat. "Stay out of trouble, Miss Montague...or perhaps I should call you Miss Braithwaite?"

"Er...yes, sir. Is there any word about Lord Moordale?"

"I couldn't say."

"We're going to the hospital to visit him right now." Rory pressed her reticule into her hands and picked up her carpetbag.

"I'll hail a cab." Miles strode toward the exit.

Iris turned to the sergeant. "There was a woman I met in the lock-up named Lizzie. She works at the Foggy Notion Tavern. Why is she in custody?"

"She won't be much longer. Once she's been brought in front of a judge, she'll be sent to the workhouse. Lizzie got behind in her rent, you see."

"She's a debtor?" Iris opened her reticule. "I want to pay what she owes."

O'Hara looked at her askance. "Why, if I may ask?"

"The woman was kind to me when I was in the cell. Considering my providential rescue, I think it's the least I can do."

After Iris paid the relatively small sum, she joined Rory at the door.

"What was that all about?" he asked.

"Nothing, really. Let's just say I've learned to appreciate my good fortune and thought I should do a good deed for once."

From the set of her brother's jaw, Iris could tell it would be long time until he forgave her—if ever.

"Rory, I want you to know I'd already decided to come home last night. That was before I'd heard about the robbery, of course." She gulped. "I was quite mistaken about Iggy's regard for me."

He gave her a level look. "I hear no regret about what pain you inflicted upon Father, not to mention the trouble and inconvenience you've caused me and Miles."

"I feel nothing but regret for my actions! If you want me to say I'm selfish and pig-headed, then I freely admit it." She bit her lip. "I stole from you as well, and I'm thoroughly ashamed of myself. Truly, I have no excuse."

Her brother stared straight ahead, seemingly unmoved. "I daresay Miles has secured a cab for us. We should go."

As Iris accompanied him from the bridewell, she wasn't sure what more she could do to express her contrition. For now, she decided it was best to leave it alone and let her brother's anger burn itself out. She waited until she, Rory, and Miles were inside the cab before she said anything further.

"How did you find me?"

Her brother's response was terse. "Moordale didn't cover his tracks especially well."

She dropped her gaze to her lap. "Everyone must know that I ran off with him."

"Only Lady Quarterbury, and she's unlikely to say anything."

"The countess is a good woman." Iris's shoulders began to relax for the first time that long, hideous day. If her reputation survived this misadventure, she knew it would be nothing less than a miracle.

Miles spoke. "Miss Braithwaite, do you have any idea how Moordale came to be robbed?"

"I have my suspicions. At dinner last night, Iggy mentioned joining a card game in the salon. He seemed unusually confident in his ability to win. Much more confident than the ordinary player, I think."

As he caught her insinuation, Rory lifted an eyebrow. "If Moordale gained an edge by cheating, he might have set himself up as a target. The only way to know is to ask him."

Miles frowned. "If he can speak."

* * *

Although it was well past dark out, Rory slipped a few coins into the ward nurse's hand to overlook the lateness of the hour. She brought them into a large open room populated by male patients with every sort of ailment or calamitous injury. The smell was nauseating, and the sights were unappetizing. Even worse was the howling noise from somewhere in the bowels of the institution. Rory wanted to believe it was an animal, but he knew better.

Iris's eyebrows drew together. "Is someone screaming?"

"Oh, yes. We have a ward devoted to the insane." The nurse noticed her blanch. "Don't worry, we're perfectly safe here. Those patients are behind locked doors, and escapes are almost unheard of."

Almost unheard of? Rory exchanged an unsettled glance with Miles.

The nurse stopped in front of a rolling screen. "His Lordship is in the next bed. Poor fellow hasn't been conscious since he arrived, which is a mercy."

"Why?" Iris asked.

"The surgeon who operated on him said the bullet was lodged quite deep. I doubt if His Lordship could have withstood the pain of its removal, had he been conscious."

The woman ushered them past the screen, and Moordale's form became visible. In the glow of the gaslight lamps, the viscount was barely recognizable. Both his eyes were rimmed with dark bruises and his nose was swollen twice its normal size. A sheet and blanket were pulled up to his armpits, and a heavy bandage appeared several inches underneath his collarbone. Iris gasped and began to cry. The extent of Moordale's injuries took Rory aback as well.

"I knew he'd been shot, but I hadn't realized he'd been beaten quite so severely."

"Nor I," Miles said. "His nose has been badly broken."

Rory glanced at the viscount's hands. "There are no abrasions on his knuckles, so he didn't try to defend himself against his assailant."

Miles frowned. "It was a surprise attack, I imagine. Quite cowardly in the extreme."

Rory turned toward the nurse. "Is there any way to get Lord Moordale into a private room with his own nurse?"

She shrugged. "Private rooms cost money, and His Lordship didn't have so much as a penny in his pockets."

"I'll pay in advance."

"In that case, I can arrange it." The nurse bustled off.

Iris clutched Rory's arm. "Thank you."

Miles gave him a crooked smile. "Uncommonly generous, I must say."

"Not really. Although I *do* feel sorry for Moordale, I'm not being completely altruistic. If he doesn't recover, we'll never learn who attacked him. More particularly, I want to know who put him up to this business with Iris."

His sister peered at him. "What do you mean?"

"We believe someone paid Moordale to whisk you away."

"That can't be true...can it?" Her expression shifted from disbelief to shock and then confusion. "If you're right, I feel like an utter fool!" She shook her head. "I can't imagine who would want to do such a malicious thing to me."

"The villain was rather bold to involve a countess and a

viscount in his scheme," Miles said. "Miss Braithwaite, have you any enemies who would like to do you harm?"

"A great many people dislike me, I suspect, but I can't think whom it would benefit to see my reputation in tatters."

"We won't unravel the mystery without more information," Rory said. "Let's return to the hotel for the night. I'll come back tomorrow to see if Moordale's awake. If he can reveal the culprit, we'll have our answers."

"And if he's not awake?" Miles asked.

"We escort Iris back to London like we'd planned. I'll send a telegram to Father tonight to let him know we've recovered her."

"But we can't leave Iggy here by himself!" she exclaimed.

"Iris, he might never wake up."

She moaned. "Don't say that."

Her handkerchief was so moist by then, Miles gave her one of his. "Rory has a point, Miss Braithwaite. We can't stay here forever, and your father is expecting you home."

"I'll leave instructions with his nurse on how to reach me," Rory said. "It's the best I can do."

* * *

Feeling listless and out-of-sorts, Fiona picked at her breakfast while her mother chatted about the upcoming wedding and festivities. Her father did his best to ignore the conversation by ducking behind his newspaper.

"We haven't a lot of time, so I've made a list of what must be done." Mrs. Robinson tapped a piece of paper on the table next to her plate. "Your presentation gown will make a lovely wedding dress."

"Yes."

"And even though Sir Harry insists on buying your

trousseau in Paris, we must still drive into York to purchase a going-away suit."

The idea of shopping for clothes had never before seemed so unappealing. "I'll write to Angelica this morning, urging her to send my trunks along. I've plenty of traveling suits already."

Mrs. Robinson was undeterred. "Even so, you must have a few pretty garments for the wedding night."

Fiona anticipated her wedding night would be nothing but perfunctory. "I don't see why we should spend money on garments that will get little use."

Her mother's face fell, and from behind his newspaper, Mr. Robinson made a sound of disgust. "Must you two discuss this in my presence?"

"Sorry, dear."

"Sorry, Papa."

As she glanced at her mother's crestfallen expression, Fiona relented. "We'll go shopping if you like, Mama. Just tell me when."

"Let's go Friday, shall we?"

Her lips curved into a forced smile. "That sounds perfect."

The butler entered the dining room and presented Fiona with an envelope. "This just arrived for you."

"Thank you, Truman." She glanced at the brief message. "Mrs. Wren would like me to stop by this morning. I'm to collect her donations for the church bazaar."

Her father lowered his paper to reveal an expression of incredulity. "Is the woman mad? Why is she insisting you work on the bazaar when you've a wedding to prepare?"

"Actually, I don't mind. Since Lara is to volunteer as well, if I can do my part now, even if it's just for a little while, less work will fall on her shoulders later on. Besides which, I should get to know my future mother-in-law better."

After breakfast, Fiona wrote a letter to Angelica. She

wished to make sure Lara and all the Greystokes knew they were welcome at the ceremony, but that it was very short notice and she would understand if they couldn't attend. The letter was cheerful, but she bit back tears as she wrote it. A wedding without her entire family was definitely not what she'd always dreamed of...but then neither was Harry. In closing, she asked for her things to be sent along as expeditiously as possible, since she would need some of her clothes for the honeymoon trip.

After leaving the letter with Truman to post, Fiona drove the gig over to Sheepfold Abbey to meet Mrs. Wren. The elegant older woman emerged from the drawing room as the butler admitted her into the house.

"Good morning, dear. I saw you arrive just now. You handle a gig quite smartly, I must say."

"Thank you. I enjoy driving in an open carriage, especially in the summer. The breeze is rather refreshing."

"Indeed, it is, but it's difficult on my coiffeur! Before you ask about him, Harry's not home. He's off on business again for the next few days."

Fiona was taken aback. "He seems to be away a lot on business."

"Yes, but this was unexpected, even for Harry. He told me not to say anything to anyone, but I'm sure he didn't mean *you*." She lowered her voice. "He's off buying a financial interest in a Newcastle glassworks factory."

"Oh? I think Papa has an interest in a Newcastle glassworks factory. I wonder if it could be the same one?"

"I haven't a clue. I try never to interfere in Harry's investments." She smiled. "I hope you didn't mind the short notice this morning, but I couldn't resist the opportunity for us to chat a little. Also, I'd like to give you a tour of Sheepfold Abbey. Since this is to be your home, you should know how it runs."

The older woman took Fiona through the lower level,

where various workrooms, the kitchen, and the laundry were located. In the staff dining room, one of the servants was stacking logs and kindling in the fireplace. The young man jumped to his feet when they appeared.

"Good morning, Mrs. Wren." He nodded to Fiona.

"Good morning, Jack. Why are you building a fire? It's already hot as blazes in here."

"Before he left this morning, Sir Harry asked me to burn some old books."

Fiona's puzzled gaze dropped to the small stack of books on the heavy dining room table. Although they were slightly worn around the edges, the seven volumes were attractively bound with green leather and embossed in gold.

"I don't understand." Fiona wrinkled her nose. "Why anyone would want to burn such beautiful books?"

"Aye, but it's a set, and Sir Harry told me one of the volumes has gone missing."

"What a shame!" Fiona scanned the bindings. "I see now... the missing book is volume three."

Mrs. Wren laughed. "One thing you should know about my son, Fiona, is that he likes things neat and tidy, with no loose ends."

"Would you mind awfully if I take the books with me as a donation for the bazaar? Someone will buy the set as it is and enjoy it very much, I'm sure."

"What a good idea! Jack, carry the books out to Miss Fiona's gig, along with the other donations I've assembled in my sitting room. Look for the wicker basket marked 'bazaar.'"

"Aye, Mrs. Wren."

The servant picked up the stack and carted them out the door. Mrs. Wren gave Fiona a bright smile. "Shall we continue?"

Several minutes later, they reached the drawing room,

where the portrait of a delicate young woman caught Fiona's eye.

"Is that painting of the first Lady Wren?"

"Yes. Gwyneth and Harry adored one another. She was a sweet and pretty little thing, but always somewhat sickly. The only child of their union was stillborn, and after that Gwyneth went into a slow decline. She's been gone almost twenty years now."

"How sad. Why didn't Harry remarry sooner, do you suppose?"

"I don't know, really. After Gwyneth passed, he focused his attention on building up his investments. But now he wants children. In the end, that's what marriage is all about."

As Mrs. Wren continued the tour, Fiona's thoughts drifted to Harry's first marriage. He'd apparently loved Gwyneth so much he hadn't considered taking another wife for two whole decades after her death. It was a romantic and sad tale, but oddly comforting at the same time. If Harry was still in love with Gwyneth, there was no danger he would ever fall in love with *her*. Therefore, she needn't feel any guilt about never loving him in return.

Chapter 19

Want

Rory returned to the hospital the next morning to ensure Moordale had been settled into a private room and to check if his condition had improved. His new nurse had noticed a little more movement in his fingers overnight, which was a good sign, but the physician on duty said there was no way to predict when the viscount would awaken.

"There was a great deal of trauma. It all depends on how fast the swelling in his brain goes down."

"But you think he *will* recover?"

"If his bullet wound heals without ward fever setting in, I see no reason why not."

Rory gave the nurse instructions how he could be contacted if there was any change in Moordale's condition, and left enough money so the viscount would receive the best care. As he rode in a cab back to the Adelphi, Rory wondered why he was going to so much trouble on Moordale's behalf. He *did* want to discover who was behind the plot to remove Iris from the bosom of her family. Now that his sister was safe, however, that knowledge was no longer critical. Perhaps visiting the man's sad London residence and learning more about him had had a greater impact on Rory than he'd realized. The silly, vain fellow now seemed less the villain and more like a hapless pawn in someone else's game.

When he joined Iris and Miles in the hotel lobby, he noticed a definite change in his sister's demeanor. The arrogant attitude he'd come to expect was gone and she seemed eager to get along. She even managed a smile. "How is Iggy?"

"Very little change, but the doctor was optimistic."

A flicker of pain crossed her face. "I feel dreadful abandoning him like this."

"He has the best care money can buy, and I've asked the nurse to send a telegram to London if she has news."

"Thank you." She gave him a kiss on the cheek.

Somewhat nonplussed at her seeming sincerity, he gestured toward the waiting cab. "We've a train to catch."

As the driver helped Iris climb into the carriage, Rory turned to Miles.

"Let's hope my sister's good humor lasts at least until she leaves for America."

Despite having to leave Moordale at the hospital, Iris was glad to have Liverpool at her back. She, Rory, and Miles took a private compartment on the train, but as the countryside slipped by, nobody said much. Since Rory and Miles were usually quite talkative with one another, she realized her presence was putting a damper on the conversation. Although she'd been careful to be on her best behavior, it was clear from Rory's manner the ice had not yet begun to thaw—not that she blamed him overmuch. When she glanced at him, her brother had a far-off look on his face. Undoubtedly, his thoughts were of a certain redhead.

"Rory, how was your visit with Miss Fiona?" she asked.

"Pleasant...while it lasted."

"Will you return to see her after I'm safely home with Papa?"

He exchanged an uncomfortable look with Miles. "My departure was so abrupt, I may have given offense. I'm not certain I'd be welcome."

Iris bit her lip. "Didn't you tell her why you had to leave?"

"Of course not. I was afraid of besmirching your reputation."

Miles cleared his throat. "We kept the reason for our journey to ourselves, Miss Braithwaite. Nobody even knows we went to Liverpool, except for your father and Lady Quarterbury. It was she who told us where to find you."

"Thank you for being so discreet, Mr. Greystoke, but you must tell your family the truth." She glanced at her brother. "I'd rather my elopement wasn't generally known to everyone—for obvious reasons—but I encourage you to tell Miss Fiona and the Robinsons, too. You have my permission, if that's your concern."

Her brother peered at her. "You don't mind?"

"I no longer have the right to mind, do I?" She shrugged. "I believe I forfeited that right several times over. At the moment, I'm more concerned that there's a misunderstanding between you and Miss Fiona. I've already done enough damage as it is."

Rory took a deep breath and let it out slowly. "I confess, being able to relate how dire the situation was may help my case."

"Mine as well." Miles chuckled. "Lara was none too pleased with me when I left."

"If you don't mind, Miles, I'd like to return to Blythe Village to finish what I started," Rory said.

"The project at St. James?"

"Yes, and Miss Fiona especially."

Miles nodded. "Then we'll return tomorrow."

Iris studied Rory a moment. "Although you don't need my approval, I believe you and Miss Fiona suit one another."

"I *don't* need your approval, Iris." He paused. "But it's nice to have it, all the same."

His sudden smile reminded her of a wild stallion running free, and the atmosphere in the compartment seemed to lighten a bit. Iris leaned back against the seat, closed her eyes, and pretended to sleep. As she listened to Miles and Rory joke about things they'd seen in Liverpool, she realized it felt peaceful not to be at cross-purposes with the world for once. Perhaps when she finally left England, the injuries she'd inflicted on her brother might finally begin to heal.

* * *

Yet again, Miles surprised his family by appearing for breakfast the following morning.

"You're popping up so unexpectedly and often these days, we should call you Jack-in-the-Box," his brother observed.

"Rory needed my help on a delicate matter, I'm afraid. We've had rather an adventure."

Since Miles had permission to be forthright, he related Iris and Moordale's entire story from beginning to end. Lara was seemingly transfixed with horror, especially when he got to the part about the vicious assault and robbery on Moordale and Iris's arrest as an accomplice. As he spoke, the entire table hung on his every word.

"If anything positive has come from this debacle, perhaps

it's that Miss Braithwaite appears to have changed for the better," he concluded. "She was far more tolerable on the journey back to London than she ever was before."

Angelica scoffed. "I hope she was scared witless and will never be the same! What could she have been thinking to put everyone to so much grief and aggravation?"

"I daresay she wasn't thinking about anyone other than herself," William said. "I imagine her short stay in the bridewell taught her a valuable lesson."

"I don't approve of her actions, of course, but I'm glad she's safe and uninjured." Lara shuddered. "Poor Lord Moordale!"

William shook his head. "I doubt the Liverpool police will ever apprehend the robber. Even if Moordale could give them a description, I suspect the fellow is probably long gone. If the rogue was intelligent enough, it's possible he was wearing a disguise the entire time."

The butler brought the morning post, with a letter for Angelica.

"Oh, thank heavens! It's from Fiona." She tore open the letter and began to read.

Miles, who'd been enjoying sausages with fried bread, paused when he realized his sister-in-law had gone pale. "Is anything wrong?"

When Angelica didn't answer right away, Lara's eyes grew wide. "Do tell us what's in the letter!"

"I'm sorry to give you bad news." Angelica glanced around the table, stricken. "Fiona's to be married to Sir Harry in less than a fortnight."

Even William gasped in dismay.

"Fiona must be teasing!" Lara was incredulous. "It's not like her to be so impetuous. Besides which, she doesn't like Sir Harry at all!"

"She goes on to write that she'll understand if we can't

attend with such little notice, and begs me to send along the remainder of her trunks without delay," Angelica said.

"I can't imagine why Fiona would agree to such a hasty union," William said, aghast. "It makes absolutely no sense."

"Miles, did Mr. Braithwaite and Fiona quarrel before you left?" Lara asked.

"No, they seemed to be growing closer. I wonder..." He trailed off.

"What?"

"Well, I wonder if perhaps our departure made Fiona assume Rory didn't care for her. He expressed his worries to me about that very possibility when we came away without a good explanation. We were trying to protect Miss Braithwaite's reputation, you see."

"I suspect you're right." Angelica sighed. "Fiona has been at a very low point lately and may have taken his departure as a rejection."

"Nothing could be further from the truth! In fact, Rory was quite angry at the interruption to his courtship. We'd planned to return to Blythe Village this morning so he could resume it." Miles made a sound of frustration. "He's going to be heartbroken to learn he's too late."

"Until the vows are exchanged, it's not too late." Lara folded her napkin and tucked it next to her plate. "I'm going to Blythe Village with you. As William Congreve wrote, *married in haste, we may repent at leisure.* I'll do everything I can to ensure my sister doesn't repent a hasty marriage for the rest of her life."

"I'll have Fiona's trunks brought down." Angelica gave Lara a pleading glance. "Please dissuade her by any means necessary."

"Believe me, I'll try my best."

William caught Miles's eye. "While Lara is getting ready,

perhaps you should dash over to the Braithwaite's residence to give your friend the news. It's best if he hears it from you."

"I'll go, of course, but I doubt if hearing it from me will make it any less painful."

* * *

After breakfast, Rory returned to his room and finished preparations for his journey north. He'd recovered his purloined belongings from Iris and tucked his pistol back in its drawer, but his valet had his hands full sorting out the remainder. The butler knocked on his door.

"Sir, Mr. Greystoke has come to call."

"Oh...I'll be right down."

Bewildered, Rory hurried down the stairs and met his friend in the drawing room.

"I thought we were to meet at the station, Miles. I'm sorry, but I'm not quite ready to go."

"Forgive me, but I had to speak with you before we leave."

"Can't it wait? If we tarry, we'll miss the ten o'clock train."

"There's another one at eleven. An hour won't make any difference now."

Rory peered at him. "You're beginning to alarm me."

Miles told him about a letter Angelica had just received from Fiona with news of her engagement.

"If this is a joke, it's in bad taste," Rory managed.

"I'm perfectly serious. Lara is traveling with us to Blythe Village this morning to see if she can't talk sense into her sister."

Fiona's engagement felt like a stinging rebuke. "It seems to me there's nothing to be done about the matter. She's made her preference plain!"

"Don't talk nonsense."

"The night before I left, I felt as if she and I were on the brink of an understanding. Obviously, I was wrong."

"No, I expect she's convinced herself of your indifference and made a rash decision without knowing all the facts. The way events unfolded, it was almost as if someone planned to pull you and Fiona apart."

Something seemed to click in Rory's mind. "What did you say?"

"It's just terribly ironic that Iris chose to run away just as you and Fiona were beginning to form an attachment."

A dawning suspicion. "It wasn't irony. It was intentional."

"Sorry, I'm not understanding you?"

"I don't know why I didn't see it before, but Iris had me so worried I couldn't think straight. We thought someone paid Moordale to ruin her reputation, but that wasn't it at all."

"What other motivation could there be?"

"Who benefited the most from my absence? In hindsight, it's so obvious."

Miles looked startled. "You can't possibly mean Sir Harry!"

"It all fits. The night of the Quarterbury ball, I noticed Sir Harry arguing with Moordale in the bar. Afterward, Moordale rebuffed Miss Fiona and unexpectedly proposed to my sister. Sir Harry must have convinced a reluctant Moordale to throw Fiona over so he could swoop in and take his place."

"You never mentioned witnessing an argument."

"No, because it didn't seem particularly important at the time. Don't you think it was an odd coincidence Sir Harry should happen to stop by here on the morning Iris disappears? Thereafter, he delivered my father's letter directly into my hands, knowing I'd leave for London immediately and without explanation. I believe he set this whole thing up to drive Miss Fiona into his arms!"

"If you're right, it's a dastardly plot. But without Moordale's corroboration, how can you prove it?"

"I don't know." The sudden elation Rory had felt at solving the mystery slumped. "Without evidence, I'm just a spurned suitor casting slanderous assertions against a respectable man."

Miles scratched his head. "I wonder...could it be as simple as connecting that book of poetry to Sir Harry?"

"Even if I could, it would hardly be compelling evidence."

"No, but you might be able to convince Fiona to postpone the wedding at least until you can confirm your theory with Moordale."

"I suppose that's the best I can hope for at this point."

"You already sound defeated." Miles studied him. "Not too long ago, you vowed to win Fiona over. What ever happened to facing down a challenge?"

"It was more of a game to me then. Now the stakes are higher and I have far more to lose."

"The Robinson and Greystoke families are pulling for you."

"I appreciate the support, truly. In the end, however, the only opinion that matters is Fiona's. I'm afraid I've lost her forever."

"She wants you to fight for her, Rory."

Iris's voice rang out from the doorway. "Forgive me, but I couldn't help but overhear. Mr. Greystoke has put his finger on the point exactly."

His sister entered the drawing room without waiting for an invitation. "I understand Miss Fiona better than you might think, Rory. She possesses a passionate nature and wants to love and be loved in return. Prove you truly love her, and she'll break off her engagement. If anyone can win her back, you can."

Rory's doubts suddenly disappeared and a new resolve took their place. "All right, then. I will."

* * *

During the shopping trip in York, Fiona let her mother pick out a nightdress and wrapper for the wedding night, and made all the proper responses about how pretty they were. Thereafter, they picked out a bridal hat and veil together, and a pair of slippers to wear down the aisle. The little pleasure Fiona managed to glean that day was from watching her mother select a lovely blue gown for herself made of fine silk.

"Nobody will be able to keep their eyes off you at the wedding breakfast, Mama!"

"Don't be silly!"

"No, the pleats on your skirt are so clever, and the trim is so delightful, I doubt if any Worth creation could be more fetching."

"We'll see about that! I daresay you'll bring back trunks and trunks of fantastic gowns from Paris," Mrs. Robinson said. "I envy you. I've asked your father several times if we could travel, but he's always been reluctant to spend the money."

"I'm quite looking forward to traveling."

In fact, the anticipation of a European tour was the only thing sustaining Fiona's resolve. She almost regretted asking Harry to push the wedding back a week. Although the delay gave her and her family extra time to prepare, it also allowed a sense of dread to fester. It would have been better to get the nuptials over with quickly and move on to something more enjoyable. When she thought about visiting Paris and Rome, she could almost be happy.

On the road home, their carriage passed by St. James church. Fiona glanced out the window to see workers putting the final touches on the new drainage system. A familiar figure caught her eye and she sat up straight in shock. "What's *he* doing here?"

"Who do you mean?" Mrs. Robinson followed her gaze. "Why, Mr. Braithwaite has returned...and Miles, too! They must have managed their business."

Something twisted in Fiona's chest. "I don't want to see Mr. Braithwaite."

"You can scarcely avoid it, I'm afraid. When we return home, I expect to discover they've both moved back into their former rooms."

Fiona fell silent. Her emotional reaction to Mr. Braithwaite's presence surprised her. When he left before, she'd been forced to accept his indifference. Although she'd cried her eyes out with disappointment, she hadn't laid any blame at his feet. Now, however, the sight of him made her angry. He'd done nothing to deserve her censure, really, other than failing to return her affection. Was it human nature to be angry at the object of one's unrequited love? Perhaps so, but she must marshal her emotions before they met face-to-face. She vowed to be polite, but cool, and endeavor to avoid his company whenever possible. Collecting donations for the bazaar would be the perfect way to avoid him. Surely, the project at St. James was nearly finished and couldn't keep Mr. Braithwaite in Blythe Village for very much longer. How ghastly if he should insist on staying for her wedding!

Fortunately, when Fiona returned home, she was delighted to discover Lara had come as well. All other unpleasant thoughts were pushed aside as she hugged her twin. After Mrs. Robinson greeted Lara, she hastened off to make sure the cook was prepared to handle three extra guests.

Lara took Fiona by the hand and coaxed her into the drawing room. "Let's have a lovely chat, shall we?"

She beamed with pleasure. "I can't believe you're here!"

"Did you think I could stay away after hearing the news of your wedding?"

"But what of the Season? You're missing all the fun."

Lara shrugged. "That depends on your point of view, I suppose. If marriage is the goal of the Season, I've already made my choice."

Fiona averted her eyes. "I saw Miles and Mr. Braithwaite at the church when we drove past."

"Yes, we traveled together from London this morning and brought all your trunks. When he heard you'd gone to York for the day, Mr. Braithwaite decided to ride over to St. James. I expect he and Miles will be back for tea." Lara smiled. "Did you and Mama buy some wonderful things for your trousseau?"

"Actually, Harry and I are—"

Miles's voice rang out. "Hello, there!" He and Rory entered the drawing room. "After Rory and I saw the carriage drive by, we decided to return to Blythe Manor right away."

Fiona was ill-prepared for the dull ache of want accompanying Rory's sudden appearance. It was as if she were a little girl again, gazing at an impossibly wonderful toy, far out of reach in a display window.

"Welcome back to Blythe Manor," she managed.

"Thank you." The timber of Rory's voice sounded like music. "I can't tell you how happy I am to be here with you again."

"You're all politeness, I'm sure."

"Miss Fiona, my departure from here was due to circumstances beyond my control." He sat in the chair next to hers. "Please allow me to explain."

"You owe me no explanation whatsoever, sir. If you'll excuse me, I've just returned from York and I'd like to freshen up."

Before Fiona could rise, her sister touched her arm. "Stay and listen, I implore you."

"If you insist."

"I do." Lara's tone was firm.

Thereafter, Rory related a shocking story involving Miss Braithwaite's elopement with Lord Moordale. Although some of the details seemed difficult to believe, Miles was there to vouch for every word. Afterward, she was uncertain how to respond.

"Is Lord Moordale expected to recover?"

"That's unclear at the moment, but his physician seemed hopeful," Rory replied.

"I don't understand why you would tell me all this, especially when it casts your sister in a bad light."

"Iris insisted I give you a full and complete account of my absence so you'd comprehend more fully why I left here without saying good-bye."

"Forgive me, but I find her sudden altruism out of character."

Rory laughed. "Quite so, but she's trying to make amends."

"Well, I absolve you from any offense I may have taken due to your abrupt departure. No one could fault you for rushing to your sister's aid. In fact, you and Miles are both heroes, I think."

"I hope we're still friends?" Rory's blue eyes seemed to shimmer with emotion.

"Of course." She paused. "I presume you've heard about my engagement to Sir Harry?"

"Yes. I-I wish you every happiness."

"Thank you." As Fiona stood, the gentlemen rose. "Now if you'll excuse me, I really must change."

"I'll go too," her sister said. "We'll see you both at tea."

Lara waited to speak again until she and Fiona were halfway up the stairs. "I'm so glad Mr. Braithwaite told you the story personally. Miles told William, Angelica, and me what had happened this morning, but I don't think I could have given you the details in the same way."

"I'm also glad Mr. Braithwaite came to tell me what happened with his sister. It shows strength of character, I think."

When Fiona entered her room, she closed the door and leaned against it. Now that Rory had shown himself to be so very noble and gentlemanly in his rescue of his sister, she didn't even have her resentment to hold against him. What exquisite torture it was to be in the same room with the one man who could lift her emotions to the heavens! She prayed his residence at Blythe Manor would be of blessedly short duration so her heart could fall asleep once more.

After Lara and Fiona were out of earshot, Rory blew out a slow breath. "I think Miss Fiona has forgiven me. I hope so, at least."

"Why didn't you tell her your suspicions about Sir Harry?"

"One step at a time. If I expect her to believe my accusations against her scheming fiancé, I have to first earn back her trust."

"All right, but don't wait until after the wedding to say something."

"Very funny."

Chapter 20

Pretty Words

When Moordale finally awakened, he wished he hadn't. His head ached, his face felt numb, and he couldn't move without searing pain lancing his shoulder. Although his eyelids seemed glued shut, he forced them apart by sheer willpower. The vision of a plain white ceiling rewarded his efforts, but did nothing to inform him where he was or how he'd come to be there. He was definitely not at the Adelphi Hotel, where the decor had been far more pleasing to the eye. What had transpired to being him to this place and in such a pitiable condition?

Then he recalled the calamitous events that had come before. His amiable new friend, Mr. Carney, had accompanied him out of the hotel. When they reached the dark alley, the man had punched him full in the face without so much as a word beforehand. After he fell to the ground in pain, Carney pulled out his pistol and fired. The next thing he remembered was the hotel clerk kneeling by his side just around dawn.

By all rights, he should be dead. The tremendous amount of writhing he'd done after the blow to his face had probably prevented his assailant from getting off a clear shot. The murderous scoundrel deserved to be drawn and quartered, but he'd been an utter imbecile for trusting the man! Lured by the promise of easy, big money, he'd exercised the poorest judgment imaginable. How could he have been so gullible?

In a burst of panic, Moordale suddenly remembered Iris. The young woman was alone and defenseless in a strange city and probably didn't even know what had happened to him! Despite his pain, he had to find her and make sure she was safe—if only he could move. His legs seemed uninjured, but his torso seemed to be stuck to the sheets and he couldn't even lift his head. He'd seen a snapping turtle on its back with more mobility than he had at present.

His call for help sounded more like a croak. With some effort, he managed to produce a load moan. A woman came into the room—a nurse, by the look of her uniform.

"You're awake, milord? You ought not move about or you'll start bleeding again."

She helped him take a sip of water, after which he found his tongue.

"I must find Miss Braithwaite."

The sentence sounded as if he had a tremendous head cold. What was wrong with his nose? Despite his mumbling, the nurse seemed to understand him.

"Don't you fret. She's gone back to London." The woman patted his arm. "You've very good friends, Your Lordship. Mr. Rory Braithwaite has paid for everything."

"What? Where am I?"

"You're in the Liverpool Royal Infirmary."

The information came as a surprise. How had Rory found him so quickly, and why would he have paid his bills? Iris may have convinced her brother to cover his medical treatment, but considering the somewhat offhanded way Moordale had treated her, that explanation seemed farfetched. Perhaps Rory Braithwaite was just a decent chap. Moordale felt humbled.

The nurse checked underneath the bandage on his shoulder. "I'll summon the surgeon to have a look at you, but I don't see any sign of ward fever so far. You're lucky, milord."

"Am I?" He reached up a hand to his face, and was shocked to discover it was a swollen, painful mess. "What's wrong with my nose?"

The nurse gave him a sympathetic smile. "It was broken during the robbery, I'm afraid, and you won't look the same once it heals." She straightened his blankets and fluffed his pillow. "Best thing you can do is sleep and try not to touch your face."

As if the woman had commanded his eyelids to close, they slid shut.

* * *

After Lady Quarterbury's gown had been sponged and pressed, Iris sent it back to the countess with a note of thanks. To her surprise, the woman paid her a visit within the hour. Her father would have been justified in taking Lady Quarterbury to task for her part in facilitating the elopement, but he merely greeted her politely and allowed Iris to speak with her alone in the drawing room. Although Iris had repeatedly expressed her sincere and heartfelt remorse since she arrived home, her father's forbearance earned her additional gratitude.

Lady Quarterbury's aquamarine eyes peered at her. "Now please tell me why you've returned to London? I've not heard from Lord Moordale at all."

Iris began to confide the details of her journey, but when she reached the part about Moordale's gunshot wound, the countess went so pale that Iris was obliged to ring for smelling salts. After the woman was set to rights, Iris directed a maid to bring her a cup of strong tea. Lady Quarterbury gulped down the hot beverage and thereafter seemed somewhat restored.

"*Merci, mon cher*." She closed her eyes, as if bracing herself for horrible news. "Tell me quickly, does Lord Moordale live?"

"Yes."

The countess opened her eyes and sighed with relief. "Forgive me, but his mother and I were great friends and I've grown very fond of Iggy over the years. Please continue."

Iris finished her story, although she had the impression the countess was distracted.

"Obviously, my engagement to Lord Moordale is off." Iris frowned. "But I'm very puzzled why he asked me to come away with him when it was clear he had no real affection for me."

"I do hope your feelings aren't injured too much?"

"A little, but it's no more than I deserve. It's because of my selfishness that my brother may lose the woman he loves."

"Really?"

"Miss Fiona accepted Sir Harry Wren's proposal right after Rory came to my rescue. He feels it wouldn't have happened if he'd stayed."

The countess stared. "Sir Harry is getting married?"

"Rory has gone to Blythe Village to see if there is anything to be done, but the wedding is only days away."

"I sympathize with your brother completely, particularly if he's heartbroken. I myself have always been a fool for *amour*." The woman stood. "I'm off to Liverpool tomorrow morning to offer my assistance to Lord Moordale."

"Godspeed." Iris paused. "I hope he makes a full recovery, for his sake as well as mine. I *would* like to know the reason behind his actions, if I could. Rory thinks somebody paid him to elope with me, but we don't know who."

Lady Quarterbury's eyes narrowed. "I'll get to the bottom

of it, forthwith." She paused. "Before I leave, will you summon your father? I wish to speak with him a moment."

"Certainly. Excuse me."

Iris found Peyton in his study, and persuaded him to accompany her to the drawing room, where Lady Quarterbury was waiting near the door. She gave him a gracious smile when he appeared.

"I owe you my most sincere apology, Mr. Braithwaite, for the part I played in facilitating the elopement. Now that your daughter has related her harrowing adventure, I realize how close to disaster it came. Although I'd believed at the time my heart was in the right place, I shouldn't have interfered. I hope someday you'll forgive me."

His eyebrows rose. "Why, I..."

Instead of waiting for his response, however, the countess sailed from the drawing room and out the front door.

Peyton gave Iris a pained glance. "I'm glad she apologized, but she really is the most peculiar woman."

"Yes, but you'll notice her apology didn't contain a word of French."

"That's something, I suppose."

Glade entered the drawing room. "Excuse me, sir, but a telegram has come for Master Rory."

"I'll take it." Peyton examined the envelope. "It's from the Liverpool Royal Infirmary."

"Open it, Papa,"

"It's addressed to Rory."

"Yes, but if it's bad news about Iggy, Rory would want me to know. I still care about him, even if we aren't to marry."

"You're right." Peyton opened the telegram and scanned the message. "Lord Moordale is awake and expected to recover."

"Oh, thank heavens. The countess is going to Liverpool.

Perhaps she can bring him back to London when he can be moved."

"I'll write a letter to Rory with the news." Peyton hastened toward his study. "If I hurry, I can get it into the last post tonight."

* * *

His nurse propped Moordale up on pillows so he could speak with the police detective without straining his neck.

"While you're sitting up, milord, I'm going to get you a nice, hot bowl of soup for your supper." The nurse beamed. "I'll be back soon."

The woman bustled out, and Moordale gave O'Hara a bleak smile. "I'd rather have roast beef and brandy, but I suppose beggars mustn't be choosers."

"Indeed, you're lucky to be alive, milord. Another few inches to the left, and the bullet would have pierced your heart or lungs."

The policeman cocked a thumb toward a small trunk against the wall. "I brought your belongings to you. We'd been holding your bag at the bridewell since your attack, but there's no reason you can't have it back."

"I'm relieved to have it, actually. Otherwise, I'd have to walk out of here in a hospital gown."

O'Hara flipped open a notebook. "Can you give me a description of your assailant?"

"He was an American who said his name was Carney. He was about your height, of slender build, and wore his clothes well. He had a full ginger beard, ginger hair, and brown eyes."

"Anything else?"

Moordale furrowed his brow. "He wore a Freemason ring,

and spoke in an educated manner. He was so amiable, I was truly caught off guard when he hit me."

O'Hara closed his notebook. "Many cardsharps lurk in Liverpool while waiting for steamers to and from America. I suspect you fell victim to what the Americans call a 'confidence' man. His name probably isn't Carney, and the Freemason ring was undoubtedly stolen from one of his marks."

"Bloody scoundrel! We've enough criminals here in England without importing them from other countries."

"True enough. I'd lay odds the fellow is on his way to New York by now. Should you ever happen to see him again, contact the authorities."

O'Hara dropped his card on the bedside table and left, taking Moordale's optimism along with him. Despite his initial burst of blessed relief at emerging from the attack alive, reality had begun to sink in. Carney would never be brought to justice, and all the cash Moordale possessed had been stolen. In addition, although he hadn't yet had the chance to look in a mirror, his fingertips seemed to suggest his formerly well-shaped nose was now a lump. With no estate, no money, and no looks, he'd never be able to attract an heiress bride. A deep sense of sadness and regret settled onto his shoulders like a mantle. Yes, he was alive, but what was he going to do now?

To his dismay, Rory seemed unable to catch Fiona alone. At tea, conversation revolved around the latest social functions in London. At dinner, much of the discussion was of the upcoming Harvest Festival and church bazaar. After the meal, he and Miles enjoyed a brandy with Mr. Robinson while the ladies went through to the drawing room. When the time came to join them, Rory was disappointed to discover Fiona had turned in early with a headache. Since she'd been in perfect health twenty minutes earlier, he could only conclude she was avoiding his company. Although she'd seemingly forgiven him, he suspected there was some lingering resentment on her part. How could he reestablish their relationship if she refused to cooperate?

Lara noticed Rory's frown. "My sister is planning to ride before breakfast tomorrow morning. Should you happen to show up at the stables, it would be unpardonably rude if she didn't accept your request to ride along with her."

A spark of hope flamed within Rory's chest. "An early morning ride will suit me very well. You have my undying gratitude, Miss Lara."

"Just don't mention you heard it from me."

"I wouldn't dream of it."

Miles cocked a thumb toward the chess set nearby. "Are you up for a challenge?"

Rory laughed. "Why not?"

The following morning, Rory rose early, donned his riding clothes, and headed for the stables. When Fiona arrived a few minutes later, she was clad in a form-fitting riding habit which made the most of her curvaceous figure.

Her eyes widened when she noticed him. "Good morning, Mr. Braithwaite."

"Good morning. I see I'm not the only one who likes to ride early. Perhaps we can ride together?"

She gave him a dismissive wave. "Oh, I planned a sedate ride. I'm sure it would bore you."

"Nonsense. A sedate ride suits me just fine. Your company is exciting enough."

A flicker of some emotion crossed Fiona's countenance. "In that case, I accept."

The stable hands saddled their horses, and shortly thereafter Rory and Fiona were riding across the countryside. True to her plan, Fiona kept her horse to a fast walk.

"I've been meaning to ask you about the portrait I drew of you when I was here last," Rory said. "I came away so quickly, I left it in the drawing room."

"Er...yes. I had a maid put it away."

"I'm very relieved you didn't toss it out. You wouldn't mind awfully if I took it with me, do you?"

The briefest of smiles lit her face. "It's yours to do with what you please."

"Excellent. I wouldn't mind sketching you again. I find your features endlessly fascinating."

She gave him a sharp look. "Mr. Braithwaite, I'm soon to be married. I doubt if my fiancé would approve of your conversation."

"I'm not especially interested in pleasing your fiancé, Miss Fiona. In fact, I have reason to believe he was responsible for my sister's elopement."

Fiona was clearly incredulous. "Come now, Mr. Braithwaite, Harry can't have had anything to do with it! That was all Lord Moordale's doing."

"I believe Sir Harry paid Moordale to take my sister away so I'd be forced to leave Blythe Manor and go after her."

She reined in her horse. "To what purpose?"

Now that the moment had come to confess his feelings, Rory felt his mouth go dry.

"Because Sir Harry saw how much I admired you and wished to clear the field for himself."

A blush spread across her cheekbones. "Your accusation is a very serious one, sir. Have you any proof?"

"Until Moordale confirms my suspicions, I can't give you absolute proof. However, I do have the book Moordale used to pass a letter to my sister. I'm certain the book belongs to Sir Harry."

Her expression reflected disbelief. "You wish me to believe a respectable man is capable of machinations based on a book that may or may not belong to him? Do you realize how ridiculous that sounds?"

His palms were damp from nerves. "I'm not explaining myself very well, but all the facts fit my theory."

She looked at him askance. "If you've some secret resentment toward Sir Harry, I'm not sure *any* explanation of yours will suffice. What do you expect me to do, break off my engagement based on your outrageous allegation?"

"Yes, exactly. Or at least postpone it until Moordale can corroborate what I'm telling you."

Her eyes flashed with anger. "Sir Harry has made me a legitimate offer of marriage, and all I've ever had from you are a few pretty words. You've said you admire me, Mr. Braithwaite, but I'm not certain your admiration extends to my intelligence."

Fiona urged her horse forward. Discouraged, Rory watched her increase the distance between them. Admittedly, his argument hadn't been completely convincing, but he'd expected her to take him more seriously. Just as he decided to return to the stables, he remembered his sister's advice: *Prove you truly love her and she'll break off her engagement.* Obviously, Fiona needed more than a few pretty words from him.

In his pursuit of Fiona, Rory urged his horse into a flat-out gallop. As he pulled level with her, she reined in her mount.

"What now? Do you intend to warn me against Mrs. Wren too?"

"No, I intend to say more than a few pretty words. Miss Fiona Robinson, I'm in love with you and I want you to marry me."

* * *

Stunned, Fiona couldn't believe her ears. She stared at Rory's earnest, handsome face, wondering what sort of universe would play such a horrible joke. Why couldn't he have said something to her before he left, or at least sent a note filled with tender sentiments? As it was, she was already engaged. "You're too late."

"No, I'm not. You're not married yet."

"Don't you understand I've given my word? Respectable ladies don't break engagements with no provocation."

"Just put Sir Harry off until I can prove he's not as admirable as you believe!"

"I can't do that."

Rory's lips tightened. "Do you care for him?"

"No, but my feelings aren't relevant! He has no great affection for me, either, but he needs an heir, and I've agreed to marry him."

A flicker of revulsion crossed his face. "So essentially, he's acquiring a brood mare?"

She gasped. "There's no need to be vulgar!"

"I beg to differ. You and I could be happy together, and yet you insist on throwing your life away on that despicable man. Is it because he's richer than I am?"

"Don't be absurd. His money only makes marriage to him more palatable." She picked up her reins. "Please move from the path so I may continue my ride."

"Certainly." His manner was cold as he reached into an inside pocket, produced a small leather bound volume, and gave it to her. "This is the book to which I was referring. Perhaps when you're next in Sir Harry's library, you can see if he has anything like it. I wish you every happiness, Miss Fiona."

He touched his hat and rode off. Gulping back tears of frustration, Fiona would have liked to hurl the book at his retreating back, but she was afraid she might hit the horse. How could Rory speak to her so, especially when *he* was the one who'd made her an offer too late for her to accept? Furthermore, what was she to do with the stupid book he'd pressed into her hand? Her riding habit was too tight to permit her to slip it into her jacket, but perhaps the book would slide into her boot. When she bent down to lift her hem, the attractive gold lettering on the green leather caught her attention—as well as the Roman numeral three on the book's spine. Shocked, she recalled a set of similar books rescued from Sir Harry's servant, just before they could be burned. In that set, volume three had been missing. The implication made her mind reel.

"Wait!"

Rory was too far away to hear, especially over the pounding of his horse's hooves. Fiona wedged the book into the top of her boot and rode after him, but he'd dismounted and was halfway to the house by the time she arrived at the stables.

"Mr. Braithwaite!"

He paused. She had to wait for the stable hand to bring the mounting block, but as soon as her feet hit solid ground, she retrieved the book from her boot and hastened toward Rory.

"I've seen something like this before. Come with me."

Fiona brought Rory into the house and down a set of stairs leading to the storeroom where she'd begun accumulating donations for the church bazaar. On a table was the set of books which matched the one in her hand. When she slid it into the third spot, it matched perfectly with the others.

Rory shook his head in confusion. "I don't understand. These books are yours?"

"No, they were Sir Harry's. He ordered a servant to burn them, supposedly because one of the books was missing. I didn't want to see them destroyed, so Mrs. Wren allowed me to take the books as a donation."

"So he doesn't know they weren't burned?"

"I don't think so."

His eyes searched hers. "You're beginning to believe me."

"Rory—Mr. Braithwaite—I want to believe you...but this is still not enough evidence of wrongdoing for me to break my engagement."

He stepped closer. "Do you care for me...even a little?"

"You know I do."

"Put off the wedding." His voice was soft as he reached up to caress her face. "Give me a chance to prove my case...and to show you how I feel about you."

His fingertips traced a path from her cheekbone down to her lips. A moment later, his mouth claimed hers in a sweet, tender kiss which left her aching for more.

"He won't ever love you as much as I do, Fiona."

She closed her eyes and melted into his arms, unwilling to interrupt the pleasurable shivers dancing throughout her body. Rory nuzzled her hair with his lips and then began to trail kisses down her neck until he coaxed a moan from deep within her throat.

He pulled back until he could gaze into her eyes. "Marry me."

Reality suddenly brought her to her senses, and she stepped away. "I'll press Harry to push the wedding back a few weeks."

"Fiona—"

"If I simply jilt him for no reason, I'll bring disgrace to my family."

He nodded. "Don't worry, you won't have to jilt him. I'll get him to admit what he did."

"How?"

He grabbed her around the waist, spun her around, and gave her another kiss. "I don't know yet, but I'll find a way."

Chapter 21

Sword of Damocles

At breakfast, Rory couldn't keep the smile from his lips. Although he didn't want to embarrass Fiona by revealing his feelings in front of her family, every so often he would catch her eye and be rewarded with a mischievous smile. Despite his efforts at discretion, he doubted anyone could fail to notice his ebullient mood—or hers. Lara exchanged a knowing look with Miles, and even Mr. and Mrs. Robinson seemed secretly amused.

Finally, Mr. Robinson cleared his throat. "It's a beautiful day. Have you young people made plans?"

"I thought Fiona and I could get started on soliciting donations from the businesses in Blythe Village," Lara said.

"Miles and I must spend a few hours at St. James this morning to ensure the work is completed," Rory said. "Afterward, we'll help you."

Miles nodded. "A capital idea if I ever heard one."

"What fun!" Fiona glanced at her mother. "Mama, have you sent out the wedding invitations yet?"

"Not yet. Perhaps we can write them out tonight after dinner? With Lara's help, I think we can manage."

"Let's wait. I-I plan to ask Harry to delay the ceremony for another two weeks."

Everyone at the table made a noise of surprise—except for Rory.

"I won't be able to tell him until he returns from his business trip, but I can't imagine he'll object," Fiona said.

Mr. Robinson cocked an eyebrow. "You're not having second thoughts, are you?" His glance slid toward Rory.

Fiona blushed. "Well, I...the thing is..."

"It's my fault." Rory grinned. "I've asked Fiona to marry me, but she's not sure if breaking off her engagement is the right thing to do."

The dining room was filled with excitement, but Mr. Robinson raised his hands for quiet. "I must confess, I'm relieved to hear of this development."

Mrs. Robinson beamed. "Oh, I couldn't be happier!"

"I only wish it had come sooner!" Lara exclaimed. "We've all been tied up in knots!"

"Sir Harry will be put out when he hears you wish to break the engagement, of course, but he must realize the age difference between the two of you is insurmountable." Mr. Robinson peered at Fiona. "Why are you hesitating?"

Her eyebrows drew together. "Jilting a man like Sir Harry without cause has consequences. The respectability of our family may be called into question."

"I mean to furnish the cause," Rory said. "For that, however, I need Lord Moordale's testimony."

He described his case against Sir Harry, leaving out only those details which related to Lady Quarterbury's colorful past. After he'd finished, a shocked silence ensued.

"I hadn't thought Sir Harry could be so wicked!" Mrs. Robinson said finally.

"The thing is, I don't think he *is* wicked." Fiona gave Rory an apologetic glance. "I think he's desperate."

Rory stared. "You can't possibly justify what he's done!"

"Please don't misunderstand me. Harry's behavior is inexcusable, but I don't believe for a moment he meant for Lord Moordale to be injured, or for Miss Braithwaite to be arrested. I think Harry wants an heir and simply hasn't considered the consequences of his actions."

"Forgive me if I fail to see the distinction." Rory couldn't keep the frost from his voice.

"Let's not quarrel. I mean to put off the wedding until you can prove his wrongdoing, but I can't help but feel a little sorry for him."

"Proof or not, I stand behind Fiona's decision to break her engagement with Sir Harry—come what may." Mr. Robinson glanced around the table. "Since this may impact the family, has anyone any objections?"

"Quite the contrary," Lara said. "I'm very enthusiastic about the decision, and I expect that goes double for Angelica and William, too."

"I've no objections at all." Mrs. Robinson reached over to squeeze Fiona's hand.

Miles laughed. "I think you can guess my thoughts on the matter."

"All right, then the engagement is off." Fiona smiled. "I'll tell Harry as soon as he returns."

Rory caught Mr. Robinson's eye. "And have I your blessing to marry your daughter?"

"You have it, sir, and I couldn't be happier."

The butler entered the dining room with the morning mail,

which included a letter for Rory from his father. After skimming the contents, he smiled with relief.

"More good news. The hospital sent word that Moordale is on the mend. As it happens, Lady Quarterbury is traveling to Liverpool to see him."

Miles nodded. "Perhaps when Moordale is fully recovered, he can tell us what we want to know."

Fiona couldn't remember ever being more blissfully happy. After Miles and Rory returned from St. James, the two gentlemen accompanied her and Lara into the village. They spent the rest of the morning canvassing local businesses for donations, and then ate a light luncheon at Mrs. Smalley's tea shop. On the way back to Blythe Manor, Miles challenged Rory to a stone-skipping contest at a nearby pond. As the two men raced one another to the water's edge, Lara giggled.

"It seems grown men can be persuaded to act like little boys at the slightest provocation."

"Indeed."

The twins perched on a log to watch.

"I wrote Angelica to let her know the wedding has been canceled," Fiona said.

Lara nodded. "Good. She and William were both very concerned for you."

"I'm sorry for causing so much trouble. Now that everything has worked out for the best, will you return to London for the rest of the Season?"

"Will you?"

"I don't know. I haven't really thought that far ahead."

"To tell the truth, I'm enjoying spending time with you,

Miles, and Mr. Braithwaite. I can't imagine any society party or ball could be more wonderful."

"Nor can I." Fiona's gaze rested on Rory as he skipped a small flat rock across the water. "I finally realize what it means to be in love. I feel so fortunate!"

Lara's lips curved into a knowing smile. "From the moment you first met Mr. Braithwaite, I knew he was the one for you."

Fiona looked at her askance. "How?"

"It was the awe-struck expression on your face that gave it away."

A blush heated Fiona's cheeks. "You're embarrassing me."

"You needn't be embarrassed. In fact, your reaction reminded me of the way I felt when I saw Miles again last Christmas. He'd grown up a great deal since we were fourteen, and I didn't recognize him at first. Nevertheless, I thought him the most handsome man alive."

Fiona hung her head. "I still feel wretched about keeping you apart for those four years."

"I'd hoped we'd settled all that."

"Yes, but after Miss Braithwaite stole my letter of apology to Rory and forged his reply, I realized once again how despicable it is to interfere with other people's personal correspondence."

"Miss Braithwaite's actions were far worse than anything you ever did. When Angelica read that forged letter aloud, I couldn't believe how vicious it was!"

"It was a struggle to cope. I don't like to think about it." She shuddered. "Anyway, Rory says his sister is quite remorseful for what she did, but I'm glad she's bound for America." A wink. "I suspect she and I are too much alike to ever get along."

* * *

After ten minutes of failing to best Miles at skipping stones, Rory reluctantly admitted defeat.

"I hate to admit it, Miles, but you're a champion stone-skipper."

"My skill comes from competing with my older brother," Miles said. "He and I were always trying to outdo one another growing up."

"Well, I consider myself properly...defeated."

"The word sits uneasily on your lips."

Rory laughed. "Quite so. I've won the hand of a fair maiden, and I'm in too good a mood to feel truly defeated about anything today."

"We've yet to finish our chess game. Perhaps a second trouncing will convince you."

"Ha! We'll see about that." He paused. "Thank you for your help with Fiona. I couldn't have succeeded without you."

"I'm glad to have been of some small assistance. Sir Harry's a formidable opponent."

"Indeed he is, but I'm not altogether certain he'll bow out gracefully."

"If he's a gentleman, he will. I'm not really sure how he could do otherwise. "

"On that score, I have my doubts. Fiona may feel sorry for him, but I don't."

"What do you anticipate?"

"I don't know, but the man is not beyond some sort of retaliation, I wager."

"Surely not." Miles clapped him on the back. "You're worried for nothing."

With Fiona's beautiful face smiling at him from ten yards away, Rory could almost believe it. "You're probably right."

The two friends rejoined the ladies, and continued on to

Blythe Manor. When they entered the house, the butler appeared.

"There's a visitor waiting for you in the drawing room, Miss Fiona. Sir Harry Wren has come to call."

Fiona's smile faded. "Oh...thank you, Truman. Er, where are my parents?"

"Mr. Robinson has gone to London for the day, and I believe Mrs. Robinson went to see the vicar, Mr. Hamish."

The butler left. As Fiona glanced at the drawing room doors, Rory noticed a flicker of fear cross her face.

"You don't have to see him," he murmured.

"I agree with Mr. Braithwaite," Lara said. "I can visit with Sir Harry for a few minutes and make your excuses. You can send him a letter, or have Papa speak to him for you when he returns."

Fiona shook her head. "I'm dreading this, I admit, but it's only right that I break things off personally."

Rory held up his hand. "No, *I'll* speak with Sir Harry. He and I have some matters to discuss."

"Do you want me to be present?" Miles asked.

"I think it would be best for me to see him alone, so the two of us can speak freely. If you'll excuse me."

Rory strode into the drawing room, where Sir Harry was eyeing the chess set near the window. The game was in progress from when Rory and Miles had left off the night before.

"Good afternoon, Sir Harry," Rory said. "Are you interested in chess?"

The older man looked up. "A little. Perhaps we can play a game sometime?"

"I rather thought we already have been. I believe it's your move."

Sir Harry gave him an appraising glance. "I'm surprised to

see you back at Blythe Manor so soon. I trust your crisis has been managed?"

"Indeed, the crisis resulted in Lord Moordale being admitted to Liverpool Royal Infirmary."

"What?"

"Oh, don't worry. You'll be happy to know he's doing much better."

"Am I to assume you're responsible for his condition?"

Rory shrugged. "You may assume what you like. Did you really think I wouldn't find out you paid him to elope with my sister?"

Sir Harry's eyebrows rose. "I don't know what you're talking about. If your sister has eloped, however, I feel very sorry for you." He smirked. "When society learns about her licentiousness, the Braithwaite family name will be ruined."

"The couple was caught before any damage could be done, but should you feel the need to spread gossip to the contrary, I would be forced to retaliate."

"In what way?"

"By revealing your part of the scandal."

"We're back to that again? You can't prove I had anything to do with it."

Rory lifted an eyebrow. "Moordale passed a letter to my sister by mean of a certain book of poetry. That book belongs to you."

"I own nothing of the sort."

Rory noted a smug gleam of triumph in Sir Harry's eyes. "Oh, yes, you do. It was volume three in a set of eight. You might recall the set of books you instructed your servant to burn? Fortunately, the set was recovered before the deed could be carried out."

Sir Harry blanched. "You must think yourself very clever, but such evidence is insufficient to prove anything."

"I also have the testimony of Lord Moordale."

"He won't say a word against me publicly, particularly when *you* put him in the hospital."

"Moordale was the victim of a robbery, if you must know, and he suffered a gunshot wound in the process. I didn't put him in the hospital, but I *am* the one paying his bills. I'm sure he'll be very grateful—and cooperative—when I ask him to corroborate your involvement. At any rate, since the Robinsons believe me, your wedding to Miss Fiona has been canceled."

Sir Harry's nostrils flared. "If that's the case, the cancellation will prove rather expensive to the Robinsons. You see, I've just purchased a controlling interest in the same Newcastle glassworks factory which provides Mr. Robinson with his main source of income. I'd think nothing of shutting the factory down for the foreseeable future."

Rory was aghast. "You're more contemptible than I thought!"

Sir Harry laughed. "Nevertheless, I believe that's checkmate, Mr. Braithwaite." He picked up his hat. "If you'll excuse me, I'll show myself out."

After the man left, Rory sank onto a chair. He may have won Fiona's heart, but at the horrendous cost of her family's fortune! How would he ever make it up to her? Movement in the archway to the adjacent music room caught his eye, and he discovered Fiona, Miles, and Lara peeking around the corner.

"Are you alone?" Miles asked.

"Yes." Rory stood and moved over to the window to watch as Sir Harry mounted his horse in the driveway. "He's riding off as we speak."

The three eavesdroppers entered the room.

"You heard our conversation?" Rory asked.

Miles and Lara nodded, and Fiona averted her eyes. "I hadn't thought Harry could be so cold and calculating."

Rory gritted his teeth. "Your erstwhile fiancé is truly loathsome. I hope you feel less sorry for him now."

"I can feel nothing but apprehension. What's Papa going to do?"

* * *

When Mrs. Robinson returned from her meeting with the vicar, Rory recounted his conversation with Sir Harry. Although he tried to impress her with the seriousness of the situation, she seemed to brush aside his concerns.

"We'll just have to wait for Mr. Robinson to return. Surely he'll know how to act. Let me ring for tea. Let's have it in the drawing room, shall we?"

Although the cook provided a tray of thinly sliced cake as well as scones and jam, the general mood was dour. Even Mrs. Robinson's ebullience faded after a short while, and the conversation flagged.

Fiona stared at her cake without eating it. "Mama, was Mr. Hamish awfully cross about our canceling the wedding ceremony?"

"Actually, he was relieved. He, too, had concerns about the match."

A long period of silence ensued, broken only by the rattle of a teacup in a saucer and the clink of a knife against a plate.

Finally, Lara cleared her throat. "I've been thinking, perhaps Papa doesn't derive the majority of his income from the glassworks factory. Despite what Sir Harry said, he couldn't possibly know about *all* Papa's investments."

Miles and Rory exchanged an apprehensive glance.

"The night when Sir Harry came to dinner, he showed a keen interest in Mr. Robinson's business affairs," Miles said.

Mrs. Robinson was puzzled. "I don't remember any such conversation."

"It took place after the ladies had gone through to the drawing room," Miles replied. "Mr. Robinson's investments were discussed rather thoroughly."

"And in excruciating detail," Rory added. "At the time, I put Sir Harry's interest down to nosiness, but now I realize he was planning to hedge his bet where Fiona was concerned."

Lara's smile was half-hearted. "Perhaps Sir Harry is only bluffing. Surely Mrs. Wren wouldn't allow her son to do anything unneighborly."

"That's assuming she knows what he's up to," Fiona said. "She stays awfully busy with her own activities."

Toward the end of tea, Mr. Robinson arrived. Everyone in the dining room jumped up and talked over one another as they tried to tell him what had happened. After a few moments, he held up his hands for silence.

"All is well, I assure you."

Fiona's countenance was a study in worry. "How can you say that, Papa? Everything's a mess!"

"I received a letter from my attorney this morning, informing me that Sir Harry had acquired a controlling interest in the glassworks factory. So I went to the attorney's office in London and directed him to sell my shares in the factory as expeditiously as possible."

Mrs. Robinson beamed. "I *knew* you would handle it!"

"Oh, Papa, that's splendid!" Lara exclaimed.

"I'm so relieved, but how did your attorney know to contact you about Sir Harry's purchase?" Fiona asked. "It doesn't seem like the usual course of action."

"I may rattle on after I've had several glasses of brandy, as Miles and Mr. Braithwaite will attest, but I'm not a complete fool. It occurred to me the morning after our dinner with Sir

Harry that he'd asked too many probing questions about my finances. I then instructed my attorney to keep an eye on the glassworks factory and to alert me about any unusual activity in its shares. It seems I was right to do so."

Fiona's eyes welled up with tears. "So this means Sir Harry holds no Sword of Damocles over our heads, and I'm really and truly free?"

Mr. Robinson's smile was warm. "Yes, my dear. You're free to marry whomever you please."

She gave her father a hug, and then threw herself into Rory's arms. As Mr. Robinson sat down to tea, he chuckled.

"What is it, dearest?" Mrs. Robinson asked.

"Well, because of Sir Harry's reputation as an astute businessman, his investment in the factory increased its worth immensely. My shares fetched a far higher price than they would have otherwise. I doubt that was his aim, but there you have it." A broad smile wreathed his face. "Thanks to him, I'm now an incredibly wealthy fellow."

Chapter 22

Past is Prologue

When Harry returned to Sheepfold Abbey, he summoned Jack. After the man confirmed Fiona had taken the set of books he'd been instructed to burn, Harry fired him summarily. Thereafter, he sought out his mother, who was in her sitting room.

"I've discharged Jack, and I don't want to hear another word about it. Tomorrow, I'll be away on business, and I don't know how long I'll be gone."

Mrs. Wren blinked. "You're going away again? But your wedding is just around the corner!"

"There isn't going to be a wedding."

"What?" His mother wilted. "Oh, Harry, I'd begun to care for Fiona a great deal. What happened?"

He scowled. "I should have known better than to cultivate a silly young girl like her. She doesn't know what's best for her or her family, I'm afraid."

"Harry, I urge you to look for a woman closer to your own age!"

"Unfortunately, a woman my age can't produce an heir."

His mother was blotting tears from her eyes as he turned to leave, but there was little he could say to console her—or himself. He strode into his study to write the letter which would close the glassworks factory, ostensibly for re-tooling. Before he put pen to paper, however, he decided his revenge should wait until he had a clearer head. He was furious at losing Fiona, but there was a more pressing matter—Moordale's potential betrayal. Harry could always procure another wife, but it would be impossible to repair his standing in society if he should be unmasked as a scoundrel. Although Moordale was a somewhat frivolous gentleman, he *was* a peer, and his title carried weight. Rory might be overstating the viscount's shift of loyalties, but Harry couldn't be completely certain. The only way to ensure Moordale's silence would be to buy him off.

He would depart for Liverpool first thing in the morning.

As the hansom cab drove up the long, curving driveway, Lady Quarterbury was afforded a view of the house. Grand and stately it was, in the neoclassical style of architecture prominent in the prior century. It was not so magnificent as her own country estate, but the three-story edifice was indeed very handsome. Harry had done well for himself over the years.

The driver brought the cab to a halt and helped her step down. Long afternoon shadows sharpened the corners of the building and cast the carriage into darkness.

"What's the house called?" she asked the driver.

"Sheepfold Abbey, milady."

Lady Quarterbury glanced at her maid, who sat in the facing seat. "Wait in the carriage, Margaret. I'll be back shortly and then we can resume our journey."

"Yes, milady."

A few minutes later, the butler showed the countess into the drawing room. When Harry appeared, he had a somewhat bewildered expression on his face.

"Forgive me, but I never expected to see you here. I could scarcely believe my ears when my butler told me Lady Quarterbury had come to call."

She nodded toward a portrait hanging over the fireplace. "That's a wonderful likeness of Gwyneth. She was a pretty girl, but I never saw her as your type."

He frowned. "Don't taunt me, Delly."

"Miss Fiona is more your type, isn't she? I understand you paid Iggy to lure your competition away."

Harry sat down. "Did he tell you that?"

"Call it intuition, but I figured it out for myself."

"Ah, your famous intuition. I should have known I couldn't fool you."

She cocked her head. "What do you mean by involving me in your little intrigue?"

"I apologize. Would you have helped me if I'd asked you directly?"

"You already know the answer to that."

He averted his gaze. "I suppose I do."

"I wish you hadn't involved Iggy, either. The lad has enough troubles on his plate what with losing Bramble Hall."

"I needed him to perform a service and I paid him handsomely for it." He gave her a pleading glance. "Come now, Delly. Being married to the Earl of Quarterbury all those years should have taught you a thing or two about fair exchanges."

"You've a point. Because of your scheme, however, Iggy's lying in a hospital suffering from a bullet wound."

"I had nothing to do with that. As a matter of fact, it grieved me to hear he was injured. I'm planning to visit him tomorrow."

"How will you explain that to Miss Fiona?"

"I don't have to." A muscle in his jaw quivered. "She's thrown me over for Rory Braithwaite."

Lady Quarterbury bit her lip to keep from laughing. "I'm not surprised. She's too young for you."

"Yes, but I must have an heir." He gave her an intense look. "Otherwise this would be a different conversation entirely."

Her smile slipped. "We had that conversation once before, remember?"

"You were married then."

"True. If only you'd asked me earlier."

"I was a penniless soldier."

She fixed him with her gaze. "We could have been happy, even so."

"You say that now, but I suspect financial deprivation would have soon killed any feeling you had for me."

"We'll never know." She shrugged. "At any rate, it's all worked out for the best. My husband and Iggy's father could conduct themselves publicly as friends and privately as lovers without a hint of scandal, and in return I was elevated to the nobility."

"Yes, but Moordale's mother at least managed to have one child. You, on the other hand, sacrificed the chance to have any."

"Iggy is my godson. After his mother died, he was as good as my son." She laughed. "Did you know his father wrote him a letter full of the most outrageous falsehoods? He said I'd been his mistress as well as Frederick's."

"I suppose he never wanted Moordale to know the truth."

"He'll never hear it from me, nor you either. You owe me that much."

"Of course. Frederick and Wallace were the best friends I ever had, and you...well, some things are best left unsaid."

"Indeed."

When she rose, Harry stood. "You're not going so soon?"

"I'm afraid I must. I'm on my way to the Liverpool Royal Infirmary, and my maid is waiting for me in the cab. For some reason, I feel a pressing need to see Iggy as soon as possible."

"I hope your intuition isn't telling you something's wrong?"

Her shoulders moved up and down in a slight shrug. "I'm probably being foolish." She reached up to stroke his cheek. "*Au revoir.*"

Despite Lady Quarterbury's attempt to downplay her intuition, a creeping sense of dread accompanied her on her journey north. She reached her destination very late and slept only a few hours before rising for an early breakfast. Thereafter, she took a cab to the hospital and asked to see the viscount. As she followed a nurse to his room, she tried to brush off her premonitions as silliness.

Moordale was sleeping when she arrived. Lady Quarterbury was grateful he didn't see her recoil from the extent of the injuries to his formerly handsome face. Tears stung her eyes at the sight of the butterfly-shaped bruising spreading out from his swollen nose. Where his skin wasn't discolored, however, she noticed it was unusually pale. After reining in her emotions, she removed her gloves and rested the palm of her hand on his forehead.

She gave the attending nurse a sharp glance. "How long has His Lordship's temperature been elevated?"

"It hasn't been." When the nurse checked for herself, her eyebrows drew together. She unfastened the bandage over his shoulder, and clucked her tongue at the festering wound underneath. "Oh, dear. Ward fever may be setting in."

Fear clutched Lady Quarterbury by the throat. "Please get me a washcloth and a basin of cool water."

She removed her hat and jacket. When the nurse brought her the basin, she moistened a washcloth and draped it over Moordale's forehead. His eyelids fluttered open.

"Countess, what are you doing here?" His voice was weak.

"I've come to take care of you, dear boy."

"I got myself in a spot of trouble, I'm afraid."

"Trouble finds all of us, sooner or later." Lady Quarterbury forced a smile to her lips. "Rest now."

Although she kept calm for his benefit, she was horribly worried. If Moordale's body couldn't fight off the fever, her help would be limited to cool compresses and prayers for a miracle.

* * *

Harry embarked on his journey to Liverpool early the next morning in an ambivalent mood. He was unused to being thwarted and was beginning to nurse quite a grudge against Rory Braithwaite for interfering with his plans. On the other hand, Delly's visit had stirred some thoughts and feelings he hadn't allowed himself to reexamine in a long time. Even though the countess was firmly in middle age, she was still *ravissant*, as she would say. Perhaps he should have married her years ago after her husband had died, but he'd chosen to build his fortune instead. As he stared out the train window, he shook off the unwanted memories. No good ever came from lingering over regrets.

Once he arrived in Liverpool, he checked into the Adelphi Hotel and ate lunch in the dining room. After he signed for his bill, he noticed Lady Quarterbury's maid sitting by herself at a corner table and crossed over to speak with her.

"Forgive me for the intrusion, but is the countess in her room?"

Margaret was surprised to see him. "Oh, good afternoon, Sir Harry. You just missed her. Her ladyship came back here about an hour ago for lunch, but she returned to the hospital directly afterward. Lord Moordale is in a bad way, she said."

Harry was unnerved. "I was given to understand he was improving."

"Ward fever has set in, I'm afraid." The maid shook her head. "Lady Quarterbury is beside herself."

"Quite understandable. Thank you."

As Harry hailed a cab in front of the hotel, he was filled with consternation. He knew the viscount fairly well, and even though they'd argued upon occasion, Harry was fond of him. Furthermore, he couldn't help feel responsible for the young man's injuries. Moordale had placed himself in harm's way during the commission of Harry's nefarious plan, after all. Should he ultimately perish, his death would be on Harry's conscience as surely as if he'd pulled the trigger himself. For the first time in his life, he felt helpless and didn't know what to do.

When he finally entered Moordale's hospital room, Lady Quarterbury was arranging a compress on the viscount's forehead. When she glanced up, her eyes were rimmed with red and her face was etched with worry.

"Harry! I'm so glad you've come."

As she straightened, Harry was afforded his first view of Moordale's swollen, bruised face. He swallowed, convulsively. "What the devil happened to him?"

"His robber hit him in the face, but a broken nose is the least of his problems. The bullet wound has become infected, and the doctors here are useless." She lifted the bandage over Moordale's shoulder, revealing a red, puffy, and oozing wound.

"The poor lad's feverish and he's been in and out of delirium all day."

Instantly, Harry knew how to act. He summoned the nurse and scribbled instructions on a piece of paper. "Send a telegram from Sir Harry Wren to Joseph Lister, the Professor of Surgery at the University of Edinburgh, begging him to come right away. A man's life is at stake and money is no object. Please hurry!"

"Yes, sir." The nurse scurried off.

"Who is Joseph Lister?" Lady Quarterbury asked.

"He's a pioneer in antiseptic surgical practices. His methods are controversial, but sound, I believe. If anyone can help Moordale, it would be him." Harry's gaze came to rest on the young man's face. "I pray he'll get here on time."

* * *

As the afternoon turned into night, Harry removed his coat and joined Lady Quarterbury in her efforts to cool Moordale's fever with cold compresses. Although the nurse had brought a return reply from Doctor Lister to say he was starting out immediately, there was no way for Harry to tell how long the journey would take. Whenever Moordale managed to wake, Harry coaxed a sip or two of water down his throat. After faint smiles of gratitude and murmured thanks, Moordale would drift off again.

While they waited for help to arrive, Harry tried to take Lady Quarterbury's mind off the situation by reminiscing about happier times. Despite his best efforts, it seemed her spirits drifted lower and lower with every passing hour. Finally, in the middle of the night, a man with bushy side whiskers entered the room carrying an apothecary case. Harry almost melted with gratitude.

"Bless you for coming, Joseph! Lady Quarterbury, allow me to introduce Doctor Lister."

"Sir Harry. Lady Quarterbury." Doctor Lister gave him a warm smile and bowed to the countess. Thereafter, he immediately turned his attention to Moordale. "What's the p-problem with this young man?" His speech revealed a slight stammer.

The countess blotted her eyes with a handkerchief. "Iggy was shot in the shoulder and now ward fever has set in."

Lister made a sound of frustration as he examined the wound. "I doubt if the surgeons here so much as washed their hands before removing the bullet."

Harry's voice was gravely. "Is there anything you can do?"

"I must cut out the infected tissue if he's to have a chance. Fortunately, I brought surgical instruments with me and the means to sterilize them."

He opened his case and retrieved a bottle marked carbolic acid.

"What can we do to help?" Harry asked.

The physician's glance moved between him and the countess. "You both look as if you're about to drop from exhaustion. Go get some rest and come back tomorrow morning. We'll see where we stand then."

Lady Quarterbury clutched his arm. "Please save his life, Doctor Lister. I beg you."

"I can't make any promises, but the sooner I get to work, the better off he'll be."

Harry took the countess by the hand. "Delly, let me take you back to the hotel. Moordale is in good hands now, I can assure you."

Albeit reluctantly, Lady Quarterbury allowed Harry to escort her to the Adelphi. After they ate a late night supper, he walked her to her room. As she stood in the doorway, she gave him a wan smile. "Iggy looks up to you, did you know?

He told me you're quite informed and a decisive businessman."

"Really? I thought he believed me to be deplorable."

"Well you *are*, quite frequently."

They shared a tired laugh.

"I'll meet you in the dining room at seven o'clock tomorrow morning," Harry said. "After breakfast, we'll return to the hospital to see how Moordale is faring."

The brief moment of merriment faded and Lady Quarterbury's eyes turned bleak. "I don't know what I'm going to do if he dies. He's like a son to me."

He cocked his head. "But he's not your son."

"Not of my body, perhaps, but from my heart. One need not give birth to a child to feel love, Harry."

A frown. "I hadn't ever considered it that way."

Without another word, she nodded and disappeared into her room. Deep in thought, Harry walked to his own room, wishing he could have said something more hopeful to assuage her fears. Unfortunately, he couldn't think of a single thing that wouldn't have been a lie.

Several doctors and nurses were gathered outside Moordale's room when Harry and Lady Quarterbury arrived the following morning. The hospital staff were paying rapt attention as Doctor Lister spoke to them about the proper use of disinfectants. The surgeon excused himself as soon as Harry and the countess appeared, beckoning to them. "Come with me."

Inside the room, Lady Quarterbury immediately went to Moordale's bedside. Harry's nostrils registered a peculiar odor reminiscent of leather or perhaps tar, and he presumed it had something to do with Lister's bottle of carbolic acid.

The viscount was waxy white underneath the bruising, and appeared to be completely unconscious. The countess rested her bare hand on his forehead.

"His temperature is still elevated." She gave Lister a worried glance. "How did the surgery go?"

"He woke up halfway through and we gave him morphine for the pain. I cleaned out as much of the infection as I could, but I've no way to know how far it spread."

Consumed with gratitude, Sir Harry withdrew his billfold and pressed money and his calling card into the man's hands. "This is for your expenses, but I owe you far more. Send me your bill and I'll pay it immediately."

"Actually, perhaps there's something else you could do for me. I've family in London, and a great deal of important work to do there teaching antiseptic surgery. Have you any connections I might call upon?"

"I hold some sway with the board of King's College Hospital, but there will be politics to consider. Your transition there won't be an easy one."

"Undoubtedly, the promise of an endowment—should you be given a professorship—will smooth the way," the countess said. "I'll see to it."

"Thank you, Lady Quarterbury." Lister packed up his case. "I've left instructions with the nurse on how best to change Lord Moordale's dressing, but I'm afraid there's nothing more I can do. He's in God's hands now."

When Moordale came to consciousness, he felt cooler than he had in a long while. He'd been dreaming earlier of wandering in a desert. The heat shimmering up from the white sand enveloped his body, and the sun overhead blistered his skin, yet he kept walking, searching for an oasis. His shoulder was seemingly on fire, and he cried out for relief that never arrived. Suddenly, a red devil had exploded from a dune and stabbed him in the shoulder with a glowing-hot poker.

The memory made Moordale shudder, which brought his attention to the monstrous soreness in his chest. His groan brought someone to his bedside. As he stared up into Lady Quarterbury's exhausted face, he struggled to make sense of her presence.

"Lady Quarterbury...it *is* you after all. I dreamed about you and Sir Harry and thought perhaps I'd been imagining things."

"No, we're both here and have been by your side for two days." The countess felt his forehead and gasped. "Your fever is much better!" She turned her head. "Harry, Iggy's awake!"

The older man awoke with a start, jumped to his feet, and peered at Moordale with such intensity as to give the viscount alarm. "How are you feeling, lad?"

"Dreadful, really, but I suppose I'm a little better." He paused. "I'm afraid I made a frightful mess of the business with Miss Braithwaite. If you've come to get your money back, I'm afraid it's all been stolen."

"No, lad, I'm not here about money. In fact, when you're feeling up to it, we'll talk about your future."

Moordale frowned. "I haven't got one."

"Yes you do, and it's quite bright."

Moisture rimmed Sir Harry's eyes, but Moordale was convinced it must be his imagination again. His stomach gurgled and his throat was parched. "Would someone be kind enough to get me a glass of water...and perhaps something to eat?"

The countess clasped her hands together. "You're hungry?"

Inexplicably, she and Sir Harry began to laugh as if Moordale had told a good joke.

He sighed. "Either everyone's gone daft or I must still be dreaming."

Chapter 23

A Gift for Fiona

Two months later…

The Blythe Village town square had been transformed for the Harvest Festival, with creative displays of bound cornstalks, dried gourds, bales of hay, and a marvelous exhibition of the winners of a scarecrow contest. Booths had popped up like mushrooms, featuring all manner of carnival games, food, and toys. Donated treasures and second-hand goods filled the St. James charity bazaar, which had been set up inside a colorful tent. More games and a hayride drew festival goers into an adjacent field, and giddy children swarmed everywhere like locusts.

People from far and wide had poured into town for the festival, and each passing train brought more attendees. Lara and Fiona had worked at the church bazaar from its opening, but several other members of the congregation showed up to relieve them of their duties mid-morning. As the sisters waded into the crowds, Lara breathed a happy sigh.

"I'm so glad we're finally free to enjoy the festivities. Miles and Rory are supervising the hayride, but they'll be off at eleven."

"Until then, let's have a look around!"

As they crossed though the square, Mrs. Wren hastened over. "My dears, the bazaar is the talk of the festival, and it's all due to your superb efforts!"

Lara smiled. "Thank you, Mrs. Wren. We just hope it raises a lot of money."

"By the way, I purchased the set of poetry books Sir Harry donated," Fiona said. "I felt as if they had sentimental value."

The older woman gave her hand a squeeze. "I'm so glad you'll have something to remember us by."

"Did Sir Harry and Lady Wren embark on their honeymoon trip all right?" Fiona asked.

"Indeed they did. *I've* no wish to see America, of course, but Delly seemed to think it might be a lark." She paused. "I like her well enough, I suppose, but she has a disconcerting habit of sprinkling French into every conversation. It wouldn't be so bad, except that I don't speak French."

Fiona and Lara exchanged an amused glance.

"I'm sorry you're all alone at Sheepfold Abbey," Lara said. "It will be very lonely for you until Sir Harry and Lady Wren return."

"Not at all. After the wedding in London this past week, I brought a very special guest home with me. He's to reside at Sheepfold Abbey as a permanent houseguest. As a matter of fact, I see him now." She waved to someone in the crowd. "Hullo! We're over here!"

When Moordale appeared, Fiona was taken aback. Although his clothes were as dapper as ever, he was a trifle slender and his nose had acquired a distinctive ridge. Instead of detracting from his looks, however, the slightly crooked profile lent him a more masculine appearance. Many a passing lady, young and old, were giving him admiring glances.

He bowed. "Good morning, ladies!"

"I believe you all know one another?" Mrs. Wren beamed. "I'll leave you to it, then. Have fun today, and perhaps I'll see you at the bonfire later on!" She bustled off.

"She has more energy than anyone I've ever met." Lara's perceptive gaze flickered from Fiona to Moordale and back again. "If you'll excuse me, I must step into the Emporium to speak with the clerk about an order."

Without waiting for a response, Lara hastened away. After an awkward pause, Moordale gave Fiona a sad smile. "I heard about your engagement to Mr. Braithwaite. He's a very kind man, and I'm very happy for you." He paused. "I hope you'll be able to forgive me someday for that business with Miss Braithwaite. I understand my actions caused you and Mr. Braithwaite a great deal of difficulty, and I'm very sorry for it."

"Since you nearly paid for your transgression with your life, I think we may put it behind us. I'm just glad you're fit again. Did you know Miss Braithwaite has gone to reside in America?"

"Yes, I'd heard." The lines around his mouth tightened. "I wish her the best, truly. I never meant to hurt her, either."

"Rory assures me she's come through it all a better person."

"No thanks to me, I'm sure." His expression seemed somewhat shy. "I'm quite grateful these days for friends. May I count you among them?"

"Of course you may." She gave him a puzzled glance. "I don't mean to pry, but why are you staying at Sheepfold Abbey?"

"Sir Harry means to take me under his wing, if you can believe it. He'll teach me about business and such, as my mentor." He paused. "My own father was never around much, you know, so it's rather nice to have someone take an interest in me that way."

"I don't mean to be quarrelsome, but I wouldn't trust his motives if I were you."

A crease formed between Moordale's eyebrows. "Considering everything that has transpired, I can well understand why you might feel that way. I don't blame you a bit, but I can only tell you that he seems very changed from before." He shrugged. "Something was responsible for his transformation, and I daresay it has something to do with Lady Wren. They're very well matched."

"Perhaps that's it." The thought of Rory always gave Fiona an inner glow. "True love has a transformative quality, I believe."

A pretty young woman approached. "Good morning, Miss Fiona!"

Although the girl directed her greeting to Fiona, she couldn't keep her sparkling eyes off Moordale. Her interest was so transparent, Fiona bit back a giggle.

"Good morning, Miss Hamish. May I introduce my friend, Lord Moordale?"

Miss Hamish curtsied. "It's an honor to meet you, sir."

Moordale bowed. "The pleasure is mine."

"You must be in town for the festival?"

"Not entirely. I'm actually a new resident."

Miss Hamish beamed. "I'm so happy to hear that."

"As am I. I do believe Blythe Village rivals London for its uncommonly beautiful ladies."

The woman blushed. "You're teasing me."

"Not at all."

"I should tell you, Lord Moordale, that Miss Hamish is the vicar's daughter," Fiona said.

"Is that so? I simply adore vicar's daughters!" He winked.

Miss Hamish giggled, but she was clearly pleased.

"I understand there's a hayride around here somewhere?" he asked.

"Why, yes. It's in the field behind the stables."

"It sounds like great fun." Moordale offered his arm to the young woman. "Perhaps you'd like to show me?"

Her hand slid into the crook of his elbow. "I'd be delighted."

As the couple disappeared into the crowd together, Lara joined Fiona once more. She stared after them, wide-eyed. "Did I just see Lord Moordale arm-in-arm with Miss Hamish?"

"You did." Fiona laughed. "The viscount and the vicar's daughter. It sounds like the title of a romance novel!"

* * *

December 1876

Lara burst into Fiona's room, her face aglow. She had a bit of festive tinsel twisted into her hair and a Christmas angel brooch pinned to her lapel.

"My, but Blythe Manor is full of people! It's a good thing Miles and Rory didn't mind sharing, otherwise Rory's father wouldn't have had a room to himself. He and Papa seem to be getting along famously well, I must say."

"I like him, too. He reminds me a great deal of Rory." Fiona had measured out a length of ribbon and was tying it around a brightly wrapped package. "I'm glad Angelica and William were able to come with the children. Pearl is such a beautiful name for a baby."

"William said she was so perfect and pink when she arrived, she practically named herself." Lara's eyes focused on the window and her lips formed an o. "Look, it's snowing!"

Fiona followed her sister's gaze. "How cozy! That's two years in a row we'll have had a white Christmas."

"How things have changed in a year! We have a beautiful new niece, and—"

"And we're both engaged to the most wonderful men on earth." Fiona jumped up and threw her arms around her sister. "I'm terribly happy."

Lara took her by the hand. "Come on, let's go down. There's a bowl of wassail in the drawing room, and Papa says he has an announcement."

They hastened downstairs and into the drawing room, where the Robinson, Greystoke, and Braithwaite families had already assembled. A tall, fragrant Tannenbaum tree stood in the corner, decorated with colorful satin ribbons, festively wrapped candies, and dazzling blown-glass ornaments. Fiona and Lara went to the sideboard for two cups of hot mulled wine, and then joined the others. Although Fiona longed to nestle into the crook of Rory's arm, she decided to be more circumspect in the presence of his father. She settled for giving her fiancé a tender smile instead.

"How was town?" she asked.

"Not as jolly without you. I'm grateful you invited my father to Blythe Manor, by the way. I would have hated to think of him alone on Christmas. The holidays already seem strange enough without Iris."

She slipped him a sidelong glance. "Strange and yet somehow quite bearable."

Rory chuckled. "I confess, I'm holding up under the separation unusually well. I received a letter from her yesterday, by the way. It seems she's met a banker chap who comes from old money and she's quite hopeful that something will come of it."

"If she marries, will you and your father go to America for the wedding?"

"I expect we will. Father says steamship travel isn't so very bad—except for those people who are prone to seasickness."

"Which is nearly everyone, isn't it?"

Mr. Robinson cleared his throat. "May I have your attention?

Conversation died down.

"In a moment we'll go into dinner, but I have something to say before I change my mind. My investments have done so well this year, I'm inclined toward an act of uncharacteristic generosity. I'd like to invite each and every one of you on a grand tour of Europe next summer at my expense."

Fiona gasped and exchanged a startled glance with Lara. Had their father had too much wassail? Mrs. Robinson was so unnerved by the announcement, she nearly dropped her cup.

"Oh, Wilfred, how perfectly marvelous!"

Mr. Robinson smiled. "Of course, the trip would be much easier to manage if my two youngest daughters were married."

"I've no objection," Rory said. "None whatsoever."

Miles grinned. "Nor I. Shall we set a wedding date for directly after my graduation?"

Lara let out a little squeal. "Fiona and I can have a double ceremony!"

Fiona could scarcely draw breath with happiness. "You wouldn't mind?"

"Not at all! In fact, I couldn't imagine anything more perfect."

Mr. Robinson slipped one arm around his wife and raised his cup for a toast. "Merry Christmas."

Echoes of "Merry Christmas" filled the room, followed by excited hubbub. Rory put down his cup and took Fiona by the hand. "Come with me. We've a few minutes before dinner, and there's something in particular I want to show you."

She put her cup down next to his and accompanied him

toward the music room. Before they entered, however, he asked her to close her eyes. "And no peeking."

Giggling, she complied and let him lead her inside. After he came to a stop, she felt his warm breath near her ear as he whispered, "All right, you can open your eyes now."

She was greeted by the sight of the sketch he'd done of her several months earlier, now surrounded by an elegant frame. The polished wood, set on an easel, complimented the artwork to perfection. "Oh, Rory, how exquisite!"

"One of the reasons I went back to London was to have this framed. When we're married, your portrait will go with us into our house where everyone can see it. Until then, I want you to look at it every day and remember how beautiful you truly are and how much I love you." He wrapped his arms around her waist. "Consider it an early Christmas gift."

"Rory, *you're* my Christmas gift."

She stood on her tiptoes to give him a long, lingering kiss... until Mr. Robinson harrumphed from the doorway.

The End

Sneak Peek at My Fair Guardian

When Bethany is saddled with an unwanted, unrefined, and decidedly common guardian, she must polish him up before he's fit for good society. As for Willoughby Winter, all that stands between him and his inheritance is to marry Bethany off. Can he succeed in his efforts before his past becomes known or will she manage to distract him from his goal—by hook or by crook?

Keep reading for an excerpt...

Excerpt from My Fair Guardian

Bethany paced as she waited with Mr. Ingalls in her study. The solicitor polished his spectacles with a handkerchief and gave her a pained glance.

"You'll not make the situation any more palatable by punishing the carpet in that fashion, Miss Christensen. Your life doesn't necessarily have to change overmuch."

"I beg to differ. I've met—"

"Excuse me, Miss Christensen?" Richmond stood in the doorway. "Mr. Winter has arrived."

Will walked into the room with his cloth cap crushed in one hand. His curly brown hair was so damp with perspiration it looked almost black. Furthermore, his work shirt was nearly transparent with moisture, his boots were dusty, and the smell emanating from his body sent Bethany rushing over to unlatch the window. After she threw it open wide, she turned to address him—more formally this time, considering his change of status.

"Thank you for coming, Mr. Winter. Is it raining?"

He gave her a puzzled glance. “No, but it’s hot and I was sweating like a pig.”

Bethany glanced at the butler. “Richmond, please bring Mr. Winter a glass of water.”

“Very good, miss.” The butler bowed and disappeared down the hallway.

Will drew his sleeve across his face. “Thank you, Miss Christensen. Some water would set me up right nicely.” He glanced down at himself. “Can’t sit, I’m afraid. I’ve been shoveling dirt all day.”

Bethany remained standing by the window, yearning for a breeze. “This is Mr. Ingalls. He was Mr. Leopold’s solicitor and he now advises me.”

The elderly man stood. “It’s a pleasure to meet you, sir.” He nodded instead of attempting to shake Will’s dirty hand.

“Likewise."

Mr. Ingalls cleared his throat. “I have good news to impart to you, sir.”

Will’s eyebrows rose. “Oh?”

Bethany frowned. “The rolled-up paper you discovered in Mr. Leopold’s desk turned out to be a codicil.”

“A coddy-what?” Will shook his head. “I don’t understand.”

“A codicil is a document that modi"es the terms of a pre-existing will,” the solicitor said. “As it so happens, the terms are in your favor.”

Before Mr. Ingalls could continue, Richmond arrived with the glass of water. Will gulped the water down and belched as he returned the glass to the butler’s tray.

“Oh, ’scuse me.”

Bethany’s eyes flickered toward the ceiling. “That will be all, Richmond.”

The butler left, seemingly biting back a smile.

Will gave the solicitor a quizzical glance. “So, my cousin

decided to give me a few quid or some such thing? I'm touched."

"Mr. Leopold was not your cousin, Mr. Winter." Bethany took a deep breath. "He was your father."

Several seconds passed before Will burst into laughter. When neither Bethany nor Mr. Ingalls joined in, however, his merriment faded.

"Wait...you're serious?"

Bethany gestured toward the old journal, which was open on the desk blotter. "Mr. Leopold wrote about his romance twenty-four years ago with a Mrs. Clementine Aldersgate. She was a lady married to a sea captain who was gone for months at a time. When the woman died giving birth to Mr. Leopold's child, he fostered the boy with his cousin, Agnes Leopold Winter and her husband, Edgar."

Will continued to shake his head. "Even if that's true, I don't understand why Frederick wouldn't want to raise me himself."

"Mr. Leopold had your welfare uppermost in mind," Bethany said. "According to his journal, he paid the midwife to tell the captain that the baby was stillborn. Mr. Leopold feared that if Captain Aldersgate discovered you had lived, the man would have tried to kill you." She held up a newspaper obituary, which had been tucked into the journal. "The captain died a few days before the date of the codicil. I expect Mr. Leopold thought it was finally safe to change his will in your favor."

"A change that only came to light because of your serendipitous discovery, Mr. Winter." The solicitor gestured with the codicil. "According to the terms of this document, Frederick Leopold wished for you to be appointed as the new guardian to Miss Bethany Christensen and Miss Jane Christensen until such time as the elder sister marries or attains the age of twenty-five years. For your service, you are to be given a salary and the run of Lansings Lodge."

Will was gripping his cap so firmly, Bethany wondered if he meant to wring out some of the perspiration soaked therein. "What happens to me when the lady marries or turns twenty-five?" His expression was wary.

"At that point, you cease your guardianship and you inherit half the estate. Until then, however, the title of Lansings Lodge will be held in a trust."

Will crossed his arms. "So, all I have to do is to get Miss Christensen paired off as quick as I can?"

Bethany burst out with, "How dare you, sir!"

About the Author

Suzanne G. Rogers is a California native, but she changed coastlines and now lives in romantic Savannah, Georgia, on an island populated by deer, exotic birds, turtles, otters, and gators.

Also by Suzanne G. Rogers

HISTORICAL ROMANCE

Graceling Hall Series

Larken (Book One)*

Lord Apollo & the Colleen (Book Two)

The Vanishing Beauty (Book Three)

The Beaucroft Girls Series

Ruse & Romance (Book One)*

Rake & Romance (Book Two)*

The Mannequin Series

The Mannequin (Book One)*

Grace Unmasked (Book Two)

The Star-Crossed Seamstress (Book Three)

A Chance of Rayne (Book Four)

The Substitute (Book Five)

The Gilded Age Series

Duke of a Gilded Age (Book One)

Lady of a Gilded Age (Book Two)

Standalone Titles

*Spinster**

Lady Fallows' Secrets

*My Fair Guardian**

*Jessamine's Folly**

*The Ice Captain's Daughter**

An American in Paris of the West

Rumer Has It

Courtship on Eaton Square

One Little Kiss

The Glass Heart

The Prettier Sister

**Available in audiobook format*

Also by Suzanne G. Rogers
FANTASY

<u>The Yden Series</u>

The Last Great Wizard of Yden (Book One)

Dragon Clan of Yden (Book Two)

Secrets of Yden (Book Three)

Kira (Prequel to the Yden Trilogy)

<u>Standalone Titles</u>

Dani & the Immortals

*The Dragon Rider's Daughter**

Clash of Wills

Tournament of Chance: Dragon Rebel

Magical Misperception

*Whimsical Tendencies**

Something Wicked in L.A.

Royal Promenade

**Available in audiobook format*

www.ingramcontent.com/pod-product-compliance
Lightning Source LLC
Chambersburg PA
CBHW070549260626
47161CB00002B/549